Foreign Bodies

Colin A. Millar

Foreign Bodies

Colin A. Millar

Colin was born in Cambridge and raised in Dumfries. He attended university in Edinburgh before embarking on a series of what he now describes as 'proper jobs.' He moved to Bedfordshire in the mid 1990's and has lived there ever since.

Having always had a passion for reading and occasionally writing short stories, circumstance and a desire to do something different with his life led to the decision to try writing full time.

He co-wrote three children's books with long time friend Spike Breakwell. Published by Cambridge University Press all three continue to sell around the globe.

Colin decided in 2019 to embark on his first full length novel Foreign Bodies.

He is currently working on his second novel Two Weeks in the Sun.

He has two children and he and his fiancé Roz live with a snake, two cats and a gecko all of which keep him busy and out of mischief.

For Roz, Caitlin and Bryony

Thanks really need to go to too many to mention. Suffice to say that you know who you all are.

Special thanks to Tracy Starreveld for her excellent copy-editing, Rosalind White for the cover art and website, Lyndsey Chivers for her typesetting skills and Scott and Jenna for their input and advice during the writing of this novel.

'00

She sighed as he withdrew for the final time – a juddering, sibilant exhalation of release and relief. She looked beautiful to him then, her features serene and relaxed, a marked contrast to the primal contortions, animal grunts and – finally – screams of the last hour. No longer was her back arched, her neck straining as she writhed, or her head thrown back; legs that a moment ago were constantly moving, sometimes thrown rigidly upwards, other times pulled in, almost foetal, were now still. Her arms were now dropped by her sides, hands open, turned towards the ceiling, no longer clawing at him, pushing and pulling, or pawing his face, chest and back. Sliding his hand down her thigh and under her knee, he gently straightened her leg, which had relaxed into what looked like an uncomfortable position, her knee pointed at the window.

This was when he loved them most, all of 'his' women – at the end, after all the frantic, exhausting, life-affirming and exhilarating action was over. Looking now, as her eyes slowly closed, he compared her to the others, to all those women who had fallen under his spell over the last three or four years. She was one of the best he had ever had, he realised, with a tingle of joy that ran down his spine. He would remember her like this forever.

Their meeting, like many before, had been a chance one. The usual bar room pick-up routine, a long-practised skill he had honed to a fine art over the years. She was Morag or Margaret or was it Marie? It didn't matter, he was extremely adept at maintaining a conversation and ignoring trivial details like names, ages and whatever other inanities women cared to share. As they had talked, he realised there was something different about her. She was erudite, funny and clearly very smart, which he liked – but these were not what he found most alluring. It was her underlying vulnerability, hidden under the layers of confidence, which he had picked up on and was immediately drawn to. There was something almost childlike in her psyche, a need to be led and guided, a desire to feel wanted that sang to his soul, made him want her more than anything, anyone, at any time. Within five minutes of their meeting he knew, he was not letting this one go.

The chat and laughter had continued for some time, she becoming more flirtatious, he more attentive. He began to notice the little signs – the flicks of her long brown hair, the looks through slightly lidded eyes, the touches to his forearm that became longer and more sensuous as the afternoon wore on. Robson and Jerome crooning Unchained Melody coming softly and gently through the bar's speakers seemed to highlight and intensify their burgeoning interest in each other.

Eventually it was she who had suggested they go to her place. He had smiled to himself then, had expected to have to make the running, but this time she had walked straight into his open arms.

Straight into a taxi, along North Bridge and South Bridge, after which the road became Nicolson Street, he'd found himself looking back to his youth and recalling the succession of road names that followed until it became Minto Street. Her house, a fine large Georgian one, typical of that part of Edinburgh, was off a side road on the left. The driver had droned on about that week's news and sport for the entire journey, which accounted for him not seeing the name of the road they had turned into. Who cared whether Steve Redgrave had won his fifth gold medal? It was, he conceded, more important to him to know whether Greece would be granted entry into the Euro, but even this was a small concern right now. There were far more important things on his mind, the beauty beside him being uppermost. Once inside it was straight to business, clothes discarded on the stairs and landing, and into the bedroom. Then the real fun had begun.

Now in the warm, late summer afternoon, a gentle breeze ruffled the curtains through the slightly open window. They lay naked, side by side, her face turned towards him, he on his side, one hand cupping his chin as he propped up his head. He looked intently at her features – beautiful, he thought, her lips slightly parted, eyes closed. This was how he would remember her. Lifting his free hand, he gently stroked her cheek, running it slowly over her chin and then on down her neck, across the smooth curve of her breast until he brought it to rest on her stomach, still damp and sticky from their acts of love. Rubbing thumb and forefinger together, he smiled before licking the salty, sweet taste from his finger. She hadn't moved – a good thing, it would've spoiled a perfect moment. I shall remember you with love always, my dear, he thought as he rose from the bed.

It was time to go – flight to catch in two hours, back to the office tomorrow – but he was finding it hard to tear himself away, to leave such an intoxicating scene. He forced himself to move, staying longer could be trouble. She was married, of course. There had been no need to ask – the photos in the hall, the untanned circle on her left ring finger, oh so obvious in the bar, both testified to that. He didn't know if hubby (poor, hard-working, faithful and trusting idiot) was away on business or due home anytime soon. Whichever it was, the best course of action was to be long gone from there.

He strode across the room into the very luxurious ensuite, showered quickly but thoroughly. Walking onto the landing whilst drying himself, he collected his clothes, tossed seemingly casually on the stairs and landing but very deliberately kept out of the bedroom, and placed them carefully on the floor by the front door, ready to put on before he finally left.

Still naked, he turned and walked back up to the bedroom.

Savouring the sight of her one last time, he inhaled the bittersweet smell that lingered in the warm air. With a final glance at her naked body he stooped to retrieve the eight-inch kitchen knife from the floor. Rising, he nonchalantly wiped it clean on the blood-soaked duvet cover and threw it casually onto the bed, where it gently bounced once, coming to rest near her torn and lifeless body.

He left, then, straightening his tie and whistling quietly to himself.

Chapter One

Anxiety clicked on, as the kettle clicked off, as it had every morning for the last three months. It manifested as a tight, closed feeling in her chest making her feel breathless, joined with the intolerable stomach twisting that was telling her to run and keep running or fight or prowl the rooms of the house. It was this directionless physical reaction of her body to the psychological processes whirring uncontrolledly in her brain that she hated the most. No matter that she knew the cause or the process creating it, it was a wild, untamed gut reaction which left her wanting to scream and tear down the walls with clawed animal hands.

Anxiety soon coupled with the daily stresses of living: getting the kids ready for school, lists upon lists of things to remember, things to do, things to control, and other things to leave to run their course. She could hear Melissa already moving around, heading for the bathroom; she was a good girl and rarely troubled her. Callum, on the other hand, would need waking soon; he was a nightmare to wake and get moving, always grumpy and argumentative in the morning.

A juddering sigh escaped her lips as she lifted the mug of tea to her mouth, reciting her daily mantra: 'You are Charlotte Travers, you are in control and you *will* manage to survive today.' Repeated three times to the kitchen wall, she always felt stupid after saying it but somehow it helped. It calmed and eased the fear and allowed the feeling of lonely, helpless loss and confusion to dissipate into the general background chatter of her mind.

The morning went like many before over the last three months, with the kids quiet and subdued over breakfast,

Melissa looking forlornly around the kitchen for something she knew she wouldn't find, and Callum concentrating on his cereal – trying unsuccessfully to avoid spilling milk on the table. A clunk from the front door made him start and then stare intensely towards the hall, his little body tense, ready to run towards the noise should it prove to be the answer to his recent dreams.

'It's just junk mail, Cally. You know it always comes when you're having breakfast,' Charlotte said gently, stroking the boy's hair softly to calm the growing disappointment and sadness threatening to bring a tear to his eyes. He calmed with her touch and looked at her with a resigned yet hopeful expression on his young face.

'It might've been daddy,' he said sullenly.

'You say that almost every morning Cal and it's really starting to bug me. It's been like months now – when are you gonna put a sock in it!' Melissa, though older, wiser and more cynical than Callum, was still young enough to be affected by his open, unshakable hope. Her eyes welled and her lower lip began to tremble.

'Melissa, please ...' Charlotte's voice remained soft and calm, knowing that her daughter was doing her best to appear able to cope with the events of her recent life while desperately wanting to understand what had happened, was happening, in the way she thought her mother did. To her 10-year-old mind adults had an all-encompassing knowledge of what was happening and why. It was a state of mind she desperately wanted to achieve herself, but as yet it evaded her.

Charlotte wished she could explain everything to her daughter, wished she could give them both the answers they craved, to be able to provide a reasoned explanation for their father's disappearance. She desperately wished

6

for those answers herself, for someone somewhere to explain the unexplainable, to provide clarity or at least a theory as to where her husband had gone, and how and why. Then she wished, as she often did with a guilty, sick feeling since Marcus had disappeared, that she would hear that he was truly gone, found somewhere – cold and lifeless. At least this would be an ending and a chance at a beginning. Instead they were left with nothing, no explanation, no finality or any idea of how to deal with their loss, if it were indeed a loss.

Then the day kicked in: the fifteen requests for teeth to be cleaned, shoes put on, school bags and lunch boxes picked up; the rat race of the school run; the feigned happy chatty of the other parents in the school playground waiting for the kids to be let in; the ritual trip to the supermarket for bits and pieces neither entirely necessary nor particularly wanted; then back home, shopping put away, surfaces cleaned, discarded pyjamas collected and put back in bedrooms, all in time for her to get to work.

Work over and with her mother collecting and feeding the kids today, Charlotte was sitting in her car outside the police station, wondering yet again if it was worth going in. There had been no contact from them for over five days, but then that was nothing new, and as Helen, her family liaison officer, constantly explained – they wouldn't 'bother' her with needless 'nothing to report' updates. It only left families feeling hopeless and depressed, she had said. But Charlotte hated the days with no contact, hated marking time until the by now predictable call came through, telling her that they were no further forward, that there were no new clues to her husband's whereabouts or any new leads to follow, and – was there anything additional she had remembered, that she had perhaps dismissed as trivial but that might just prove to be important? The answer was always no, and the calls always dwindled into the uncomfortable platitudes of 'we are doing all we can.'

But she lived for those calls. They meant that the police were still doing something – even if that was simply remembering to call her once a week – and that there was still hope, a movement towards finding what had happened to Marcus that morning three months ago when, adhering to a routine that had changed little in 10 years, he had kissed them all goodbye, wished her a good day, told Melissa to enjoy school whilst giving her a little hug and ruffled Callum's hair whilst telling him to be good, picked up his briefcase, pulled his tie up and walked out the door to work...

... except he never made it to the office.

They had called around midday, concerned at his absence – he so rarely missed a day of work and never without calling in. She had called his mobile over and over that afternoon to no response, had called hospitals and then their doctor. And finally, at around seven that evening, after bathing the children and getting them ready for bed, when it had reached the time he was always home, every evening for 10 years, regardless of the pressures of work or an impromptu after-work social, she had called the police.

The police had been sympathetic but initially sluggish in their response, although they would consider Marcus missing since it had been reported and they would ask all their officers in and around the town to keep an eye out for him. But people often disappeared for short periods of time, they reasoned, perhaps to think through a personal crisis or just from stress, and it was likely her husband would be home before they could begin to find him. But Marcus hadn't come home. She had continued calling his phone through the night and the next morning until she knew it had either been switched off or the battery had died. She had waited until nearly midday, giving him every chance to come back or contact her, but her phone and the door had remained silent and closed. She contacted the police again and this time they took a more proactive approach.

Three months passed and there was never any news, nothing to tell her or the police where her husband had gone. The story ended more or less where it had begun: he had got ready for work one Tuesday morning, as routinely and unremarkably as any other of the hundreds of previous mornings, said goodbye to his family, walked out the door and simply, completely disappeared. The investigation stalled immediately, descending into a round robin of the same questions met with the same answers.

She changed her mind three times between going into the station or driving home. The need for contact with the investigation and a chance at hope won her over in the end. Exiting the car, she took a deep, calming breath and entered the building. The officer on the desk, who knew her by sight now, simply nodded towards the hard seats against the wall and picked up the phone to call upstairs.

About 10 minutes later DC Tony Handley came through the security door to one side of the front desk. Charlotte was mildly surprised to see him, although he was the investigating officer for her husband's case. She rarely had contact with him and usually saw Helen, the liaison officer. He was a large man with a look that Charlotte could only describe as 'policeman' with no clear idea why that should be. His height and width probably had a lot to do with it.

He was well over six feet, towering over Charlotte's petite stature, his frame was heavy and strong-looking without appearing toned or particularly muscular. With a large head on a bull of a neck, with his hair closely cropped almost to the skin, he had the look of a rugby forward or, well, a policeman.

'Mrs Travers, good afternoon,' he said – his deep, almost monotone, yet surprisingly quiet voice sounding slightly weary and a little exasperated, his words accompanied by a slight exhalation of breath that spoke of overwork and an annoyance at being interrupted. 'I wasn't expecting you. Has Helen not organised when she'll call you again?'

'Hello DC Handley – yes she has but not until next week. I was passing and thought I might get an update? I got the impression from Helen that there was something you were working on, a new development or whatever you call it?' A fiction she had just invented, it sounded weak and pathetic even to her, pleading almost, but there was no helping that now. She wanted contact with the investigation and this was the only way to ensure she got it. If she phoned she would be palmed off with promises of call-backs or updates when they were available.

'Mrs Travers, you know by now we will call you if anything relevant comes along, but,' he stopped there and sighed, rubbing his forehead with a meaty finger then running his hand over the top of his stubbled head, a second sigh escaping as he looked at her. 'Ok, why don't you come up to my office and have a coffee? We can have a chat about the investigation and so on. Let's try and get some things straight for you, eh? Put your mind at rest a little?'

She simply nodded and stood to follow him back through the same door he had entered from. She didn't like the sound of his offer. It sounded like he actually intended to lecture her on interrupting his and his colleagues' work when she knew they would call if they had anything. But again, the need for some hope, some forward movement, forced an optimistic thought into her mind. Maybe he did have something new and had been holding back until he had firmed things up a little? Maybe, just maybe.

His office was in fact a desk to one side of a large open-plan space, full of desks creaking under computers and paperwork. A few officers at their own desks looked up disinterestedly as Handley led her first to his desk to pick up a file and secondly to the coffee machine in the far corner. After selecting and paying for their coffees he led her back past the desks and white boards to a small side office. This looked unused and obviously kept for these sorts of informal 'chats' and for private conversations between officers. It was tiny and cramped with only a desk and two chairs, DC Handley's size seeming to shrink the room further, making the space appear to turn in on itself.

After opening the file and taking a sip of his coffee Handley looked straight at her. He looked hard and uncompromising for a moment and then his expression softened, as though he had just remembered that he was dealing with a victim and not a suspect.

'Mrs Travers,' he began, after holding her gaze for a moment. 'I am sure you realise there is really nothing more I can tell you. I'm not sure why you got the impression from Helen that there was some new development or ...' he broke off, waving his hand vaguely around his head, '...a moment of inspiration or, you know a sudden flash of

11

clarity like on the TV that has moved me any closer to finding your husband. I know this is not what you want to hear but frankly we've no other avenues open to us to investigate. There has been no use of any of his credit or bank cards, his phone hasn't been on since the day he disappeared, and the tracking records for that day are patchy at best – we assume he was using the tube a lot. No one who remotely knows him has heard from or seen him even fleetingly since the day he left. I think you realise where I'm going with this, Mrs Travers, and I can appreciate it's hard to hear, but truthfully there is nothing else I can do. I can't create something from nothing.'

He paused whilst he removed a handkerchief from his trouser pocket and handed it to her. She hadn't even realised she was crying. She felt numb yet angry, helpless yet coiled ready for action.

'It doesn't mean we're closing his file, you understand? Just that active investigation will cease.' This was said quickly, perhaps to quell the tears, perhaps because it was a requirement he say it and had forgotten, she couldn't tell.

'So, what are you going to be doing? If you're not closing the investigation but you say there's nothing else you can do? That's a, a..' She shook her head in frustration at not finding the correct word. 'That has conflicting meanings. There must be something else you can do? He can't just have vanished.' She could feel her voice getting higher as she spoke, becoming more angry with each word and then just as quickly any fight she might have had left now, draining slowly away to dissipate into the gut-twisting tangle in her stomach and the churning, roiling maelstrom of her mind.

'Mrs Travers, there is no easy way to say this but there is a chance your husband has left you and simply does not wish to be found. The letter could have been from a lover or whatever and he's left for a new life with them? Or it had some bad news he couldn't handle and it has sent him off God-knows-where to hide away and deal with it. There is still a chance he will make himself known to us but you must realise that does not mean he wants to be found by you?'

The very idea sent her thoughts reeling – Marcus would not simply leave them. She felt sure he would have told her, regardless of how bad it was, even if he was leaving her for another woman. And why disappear so completely if that was all it was? Why abandon the children? He had, as far as she knew, never lied to her or kept anything of any importance from her. Why would that change so dramatically? No, she could not accept that explanation. It made no sense. But more than that she knew at a visceral, almost animal level that this was wrong – put simply it *felt* wrong and she was sure if there were even a semblance of truth in it, she would have felt it months ago.

They were silent for a few moments, which made her feel inclined to just leave, to run from this pathetic little office screaming her way down the corridor and out into the street, to make the world give up its secret, to wrench the answers she needed from thin air, to beat the solution from the universe itself.

She let the feeling ride over her, calmed herself by force of will alone, as she realised she was still not willing to let this go. As she let her breathing become even and calm, Handley was tidying the file away readying to close the meeting, doubtless to mouth empty sympathies and offers of keeping in touch, and so on and so on. As he looked up from the desktop and file his earlier words sparked something inside her mind.

'The letter,' she said sharply, in complete contrast to her previous defeated tone. 'You haven't mentioned the letter for weeks now. I thought you'd dismissed it as irrelevant? Why bring it up again now?'

Handley shrugged his thick, wide shoulders looking a little lost for a moment. 'I had, more or less, only it's about the last unknown in here,' he said, tapping the file. 'But really, when you think about it, it's the only thing that might just explain your husband's leaving. Is there anything you've remembered about it? A postmark? Is there anything you've realised about the handwriting or the way it was addressed?'

The letter. She hadn't forgotten it exactly – every detail of that morning was etched clear as day in her mind – but the fact it hadn't been mentioned for some weeks had pushed it to the back of her thoughts. The letter. The whole mystery might hinge on the content of that letter or, like everything else, it might be entirely irrelevant.

Marcus had, the day before he left, received a letter in a plain, cream, good quality envelope, address handwritten – it was notable since aside from bills and junk neither of them had received a letter of any kind for years. Marcus had looked only mildly surprised and intrigued when she had handed it to him that evening when he had returned from work. But he had put it to one side when the kids had come tumbling in to welcome their Daddy home and help him lay the table for dinner. It was then forgotten until the following morning and he hadn't opened it until he was standing in the hallway ready to go to work. He had read the contents with no reaction then folded the letter and envelope together and put them in

14

the inside pocket of his jacket as he was walking out the door. He had said nothing about the contents and of course they were now gone with him.

She was straw-clutching, she knew it. The letter could have been anything, a simple missive from work about a pension change or a slightly more subtle form of junk mail, selling insurance or broadband. But. But it could be the answer to everything. It could have been exactly what Handley suspected it was, from a lover giving details of how they would run away together. Only if that was the case then why send it to his home address? Surely, something like that would be sent to his office or done far more discreetly? So, if not that then what? A threat? A promise? She had no more idea than the police and was no nearer to finding the answer surrounding the events of that morning than she had ever been – no nearer to Marcus, no nearer to peace or rest or ever feeling like anything other than an empty husk, an automaton going through the motions of living. She began to cry again, from frustration this time.

A cough made her look up and she realised Handley was waiting for her to reply to his questions. She had none that she hadn't already given. She sniffed, shook her head, couldn't trust herself to speak at that moment. Handley had, it seemed, been expecting just that response. He cleared his throat again and picked up the file.

'Well, Mrs Travers, if anything does occur to you, not just about the letter, anything at all, please do call. As we've said before even if it seems inconsequential or irrelevant, if you remember anything more we will look at it, I promise.'

He continued to talk to her as he led her back out of the station but she didn't hear any of it.

Marcus was gone and there was nothing anyone could do. She knew deep in her soul that he was not coming back, that she would never see him again. He was alive – she was sure she would know if it were otherwise – but the children would grow and slowly his memory, their picture of him in their minds, would fade along with the sound of his voice, the comfort of his touch, the memories of bedtime stories and laughter and games played in the back garden, the love and security and peaceful sleep of a child secure in the knowledge that Daddy was there to care for and protect them.

The tears were still flowing freely when she started the car and headed home.

'01

As DCI Francis Pearson pulled up in the well-heeled London mews, lined with tiny but attractive terraced houses, he could sense this was a normally quiet, professional, 'everyone keeps themselves to themselves' type of place. It was a dead end so at least the forensics boys would have a little less work to do. He pulled his Cavalier over to the side of the road behind one of the two marked cars already on the scene. He also noted the Scene of Crime van as he eased his tall, lean frame out of the car and went to the boot, pulling out a pair of plastic over-shoes and gloves and donning these quickly before heading towards the police tape.

The house was in the middle of the street, so tape had been stretched across the road in two places. You'll have some fun later when the other residents start coming back – Pearson thought, as he approached the uniform guarding this end of the street. He didn't reach for ID … he knew the young officer standing there pale-faced and doing his best not to look back at the house.

'Charlie,' Pearson greeted the young man in his very deep but quiet voice that many found unnerving. 'Are you OK son?'

'Yes sir, more or less,' Charlie responded, his voice a little hoarse and higher-pitched than normal. 'But I'm glad I'm out here – Dan's got the front door, thank Christ.' These last words were delivered with real feeling and a long sigh of relief.

'Can't be your first body Charlie? You've got, what, two, three years now? Reckon I'd had a good couple of dozen by that time when I was uniform.' Pearson smiled but it did little if anything to reassure the PC.

'Yeah, seen plenty sir, but not like this.' Charlie grimaced and twitched his head back to indicate the house, still refusing to turn his head in that direction.

'You'll be fine in a bit son, just do your job here. No one else in the cordon 'til I say so OK?'

Charlie simply nodded and lifted the tape. Pearson patted his shoulder as he passed and walked slowly towards the open door of the house.

At 10 feet from the door Pearson began smelling the tang of drying blood in the air. Jesus, he thought, this is a bad one. A sinking suspicion began to creep across his mind. 'Surely not,' he muttered to himself as he approached the house.

As young Charlie had said PC Daniel Caglieri was at the door looking paler and even sicker than Charlie. Pearson looked carefully at the experienced officer – if he was this affected by what lay inside the house then Pearson had really underestimated what he was about to enter.

Caglieri looked through glazed, withdrawn eyes at the approaching DCI. He had seen many things in his time with the Met, but this? This had to be one of the worst. Now he was going to have to relive the details all over again; Pearson was sure to want to be brought up to speed before entering the house. Caglieri did not want to go in there again. As the DCI drew to a halt in front of him he tried all the tricks he could think of to create a detached, professional part of his mind where he could sort his report and deliver it to the detective without emotion or – even worse – throwing up again, this time all over his superior's nice suit.

'You were first on scene Dan?' Pearson asked. He appeared calm and friendly as he spoke but Caglieri knew he was sizing him up, checking he was up to remaining on scene and giving a detailed enough report.

He drew a deep steadying breath and attempted to speak, realised it would come out as a croak so cleared his throat before attempting it again.

'Yes sir,' he finally managed. 'PC Stance and I received the shout about 1430 – we were nearby so were on scene around 1439. The woman who had called in was outside, hysterical. She took quite a bit of calming down before we could get much sense from her. She's the cleaner and had let herself in when nobody answered the door and assumed there was nobody in. This was around 1415, she says. She realised something was wrong straight away as the baby was screaming upstairs. She went to investigate and that's when she found the, er, the body sir.'

As Caglieri drew breath to continue Pearson interrupted him, 'A baby? That wasn't mentioned when I got the call. Where is it now?'

'WPC Fisher has taken her to hospital sir, to have her checked over.'

'Already? Ambulance must have been quick?'

'Yes sir, St Mary's is just round the corner – they were here within five minutes of us calling. WPC Fisher and PC Cooper were second on scene so they took care of the baby. They've gone with her in the ambulance.'

'Right, of course, sorry Dan, carry on.'

'Yes sir ... so after we spoke to the witness, the, er, cleaning lady that is, PC Stance and I entered the property. There's nothing seems out of the ordinary downstairs, and in fact there was little seemed out of place anywhere, but we discovered the, um, the woman, the, er, victim in the main bedroom.'

Caglieri turned even whiter and looked as though he might be sick. Pearson took an involuntary step back.

'OK Dan, that's fine, thanks. I take it the cleaning lady has also been taken to hospital and that you got all of her details before she left?' Caglieri simply nodded. 'Good, who's in from SOCO?'

'Barrowdale and Michelle, sir.'

'Michelle? Michelle who?'

'She's new sir, that's why she's with Barrowdale – you know the senior officer taking the newbie through their paces, sir?'

'Great,' sighed Pearson, saying no more on the subject. 'OK, well done Dan, you've handled this very well. No one else to enter the house until either I or Barrowdale give the go ahead OK?'

Again, Caglieri simply nodded, not trusting himself to speak further. Pearson gave him an encouraging tight-lipped half smile and walked into the hall.

The smell of blood and early decomposition that greeted him was almost overpowering. With his years of experience, Pearson knew to breathe through his mouth in order to lessen the initial assault on his olfactory senses as he took stock of the layout of the house. Like many other houses of this sort dotted around the capital this one was small, but its location ensured it would be phenomenally expensive. The hallway was well decorated but lacked a great deal of ornamentation or interest. Straight in front of where he stood, stairs led up to the landing which Pearson guessed would mirror the hall. To his right a door, slightly ajar, led to the living room and another door straight in front which he assumed would lead to the kitchen. Putting his head round the living room door he noted that the room was neat and tidy – nothing, as the PC outside had said, was out of place. Steeling himself for what was to come, he gripped the banister and headed upstairs.

As suspected, the landing covered a similar area to the hall, small and square, although now it was dotted with the square metal plates SOCO had placed there to keep contamination from erroneous feet off of the floor. Pearson followed the sound of Barrowdale's slightly squeaky voice into the master bedroom.

Douglas Barrowdale could only be described as a grey man. When seen out of context the automatic reaction to the man was 'accountant'. He was slight and small, with half-moon glasses perched too low on his beak of a nose. His suit was of good quality but a dull grey, his voice high though flat and monotone, and even his skin had a grey tinge to it.

'Number it first girl!' Barrowdale was hollering across the room as Pearson stepped through the door. The until-then unseen Michelle had her back to Pearson but he still caught the faint intake of calming breath. He smiled to himself. No one escaped Barrowdale's blunt, acerbic style of management – new to the job or not. He demanded absolute care and attention to every detail. Pearson liked him. He got the job done and got it done properly.

Barrowdale continued to berate Michelle, 'How can we make sense of spatter patterns if we have no reference to where they are on the wall?' Noticing Pearson in the doorway Barrowdale raised his chin slightly in acknowledgement and continued to bag the pair of knickers he held in his gloved hand.

The mention of spatter patterns drew Pearson's attention to the wall at the head of the bed. Blood was sprayed and smeared in several places, some of which seemed impossibly high up the wall. Following these patterns down to the bed he finally forced himself to look at the body of the woman sprawled naked on top of the blood-soaked duvet.

His earlier suspicion turned to certainty. He had already encountered this particular killer. He had, some months ago, attended an almost identical murder: a young professional woman, with multiple stab and slash wounds, no sign of forced entry and in that case very little useful forensic evidence. They had no leads – the case was still open and being worked on by his team.

The professional in him told him to stop jumping the gun. It was possible that he was looking at an entirely unrelated crime. He wouldn't voice any possible connection between the two to anyone else until all the evidence was collated and gone through. Then, if there were any matches found in the forensics or if he could show a clear correlation in MOs, he would unite the investigations. He was 90 percent certain what the outcome would be but, ever cautious and patient, he would wait and see before acting.

Steeling himself a little more he turned his attention back to the scene in front of him.

The sheer number of wounds – starting at her left shoulder, all over her torso and continuing down her legs – were astounding. Many were clearly deep stab wounds made with a large knife. A few appeared to be shallower cuts, mainly around her breasts and on her inner thigh. Pearson eventually made himself look at her face. She was young, early thirties maybe, and even with the waxy, colourlessness of death and the teeth-baring grimace of her mouth Pearson realised she would have been very attractive in life.

'Took your time Fran,' Barrowdale said, turning his attention to the detective. 'Where's the charming DS Manning?'

'Headed here as soon as I got the call Douglas. Soph'll be here soon enough – she's doing some checks on the address before heading over. How long has she been here? And anything immediate you can tell me?' Pearson asked quietly.

'Two to three days. I'll know more after the PM. No need to look for the murder weapon – it was left on the bed,' Barrowdale said, nodding to a large canvas bag where the evidence was being collected. 'We'll examine every millimetre at the lab but I wouldn't like to bet there's anything on it apart from the victim's blood. There are no obvious fingerprints in the blood on the wall or the bedframe so my bet is we'll struggle to find any. There doesn't appear to be any blood anywhere outside this room. We'll check thoroughly of course, but I suspect the whole attack took place here. Blood spatter might tell us a little about the attacker, and the victim's clothes may offer something we can extract DNA from – fibres, hair or semen.' He waved the clear plastic evidence bag with the victim's underwear inside before dropping it into the canvas bag.

'Aside from that,' he continued with a shrug of his slim shoulders, 'as you can see it's not a big room and very little else seems to have been disturbed or moved. The front door wasn't forced so she let him in or he forced his way in when she answered the door.'

'There's little to no disturbance downstairs so I suspect she let him in,' Pearson said, his voice still quiet and subdued. Then, without turning his gaze from the bed and the woman on it he asked, 'Do we know who she is? Is there a husband?'

'Yes, she's Patricia Thorsten. Driving licence is in her purse in her handbag downstairs. She's married to Magnus Thorsten – there's a letter in the living room addressed to him. I haven't come across any other details for him as yet.'

Pearson drew a deep breath. 'Right, I'll get onto that immediately and leave you to carry on here. Is the pathologist on the way?'

Barrowdale nodded absently, his mind already back on the job.

'Nice to meet you Michelle,' Pearson said with a smile. 'Maybe next time he'll let you do some talking, eh?'

The young woman turned from the wall where she had marked up the blood spatters with numbered labels, smiled shyly and turned back to the blood and carnage she had chosen to make her career.

Chapter Two

It was Tuesday. Charlotte hated Tuesdays. She also hated the irony that it was, for her, the sort of day others would look forward to. She didn't work on Tuesdays, which was why she hated them. Where others would look forward to a day without work, at home and at their leisure to sort their day as they saw fit, Charlotte faced the dread of being alone in the house: the place was full of photos of Marcus, of his things, of anything and everything that reminded her that he wasn't there. At some time close to midday, she was sitting brooding on this over her fifth coffee of the morning when the doorbell sounded, making her start.

To her surprise, on opening the door, there was DC Handley standing in – or more accurately, filling – the doorway. Looking almost identical to when she had last seen him, the only detectable (she smiled to herself at the pun) difference was the colour of his shirt – green today, blue last week.

He cleared his throat then spoke softly to her: 'Mrs Travers, may I come in? I would like to talk to you...' Then clearing his throat again he added, '... in a somewhat unofficial capacity.'

Charlotte stood taking in the man – he seemed a little nervous or at least uncomfortable. She nearly laughed aloud when he shuffled his feet in an almost cartoon-like fashion.

What the hell did he mean by 'unofficial'? she wondered. Was he going to try to come on to her or something? But then, realising she would appreciate some company anyway and a break from the usual Tuesday hell, she moved aside and let him in.

He followed her a little awkwardly into the living room, declining her offer of coffee. He surveyed the room in the way Charlotte supposed policemen always did, appearing to take in every detail whilst never looking at anything for very long. Eventually he took a seat on the couch under the window, sitting back then immediately sitting forward again. Charlotte sat on the couch that ran at right angles to the window seat.

He looked at Charlotte intently for longer than felt comfortable to her and yet again cleared his throat.

'I realise', he began slowly, carefully shifting his gaze to the carpet, 'that our last meeting was not very satisfactory for you and that you feel let down by our efforts.'

She opened her mouth to talk but he raised his hand to stop her and continued, speaking more quickly now to make sure he finished what he wanted to say: 'I stand by our decision to officially cease investigating, as we can't afford the resources to continue looking at dead ends.' He raised his hand again to allay another interjection, then added, 'But...' He stopped and drew breath as though to speak but then didn't continue.

'But?' prompted Charlotte, when it became apparent he was either lost for words or had decided against what he had been about to say. He lifted his eyes from the carpet to her face and frowned slightly, clearly weighing up his next statement.

'But,' he began again, 'I wanted you to know that I'm not happy about this either. Your husband was, er, is ... I mean to say he doesn't strike me as the type of man who just ups and leaves. It doesn't somehow seem likely to me that he would leave his children without so much as a word – not to mention the fact that he was, is, a relatively senior civil servant and has left important work behind with no instructions or covering details. As I understand it, he was, ugh–,' he interrupted himself again, looking disgusted at his third blunder in a row, '–*is* an extremely conscientious man who enjoyed and was very dedicated to his work?'

She simply nodded at this, having no real idea where this little monologue was heading or what Handley actually wanted. Charlotte hoped fervently that he was not simply trying to clear his conscience for having handled their last meeting so badly or for getting nowhere with his investigations. She thought of asking as much then thought better of it; whatever he wanted he would get to soon enough, and if he felt the need to apologise or justify his actions, well, let him do so. It occurred to her that she might be able to use that in some sort of appeal to re-open the case.

'So you see Mrs Travers,' he continued, 'those details do not, for me, fit with a man who disappears from his whole life without there being something, some trigger or event or,' he waved his hand in irritation at not finding the right turn of phrase, 'or whatever, that has forced him away or led him to some form of extreme breakdown whereby he has simply dropped out of society altogether.'

Charlotte's patience ran out. 'These are the points I've been making all along, DC Handley,' she said hotly. 'If you think the same thing then why on Earth are you not keeping the investigation open? Why are you not still out there trying to find my husband?'

'Because there's no *evidence* Mrs Travers.' His reply was terse, responding to her aggressive tone. He took a long deep breath calming himself and held up both hands in supplication, his gesture saying, 'I will explain but please bear with me'. The gesture appeared to work.

When he continued his voice was soft and even again.

'The only facts we have to work on are those you gave in your statement, Mrs Travers, and to be frank my years of experience have taught me that people – especially those with a high degree of emotional involvement in a series of events – tend to mis-remember at best and at worst start to make the facts fit what they think *should* have happened. They want a particular scenario to be true so they tell their version of events with that scenario in mind, which can lead to the investigation taking all sorts of wrong turns. Other than your statement we have nothing, no trail to follow, no suggestions or insights from anyone that knew your husband well and certainly no hard evidence to tell us where he is or what has happened to him. So, you see, from a police investigation point of view there is nothing more we can do and hence the file stays open but active investigation stops.'

The look on her face must have betrayed her feelings and given the policeman a clue to what she would say next, as for the third time in as many minutes he raised his hands, requesting that she hear him out.

'However, I am, as I said at the door, here in what could be described as an unofficial capacity, although my superior knows I'm here, sort of. I would like to give this one last shot. Let's see if we can't pin down something we've missed or at the very least come to some sort of conclusion together that, hopefully, rules out anything untoward and so allay your fears on that point. I appreciate that this may not completely resolve the situation for you but, if we can find a reason why your husband might have left of his own accord, you could at least then be reasonably certain that your husband is alive and, therefore, at some point in the future might make himself known again.'

*

Handley had spent some of his morning writing reports to update his boss, his case files and the Crown Prosecution Service on various uninspiring and, in the main, straightforward cases. The rest of the time had been spent staring out the window or blankly at his screen. Occasionally he would frown to himself or sigh quietly. He was a man with something on his mind.

DCI Malcolm Tanner, the boss of Handley's team, was not – he admitted it himself – very good at recognising when a member of his team was distracted by something outside of work. He was, however, very good at spotting a lack of productivity. And detested it. As a result, he had decidedly had enough of watching Tony Handley look like he was trying to write a magnum opus rather than a few straightforward reports. He rose from his own desk at the other end of the room and strolled over to where Tony was sitting, yet again staring blankly out the window.

'Right Tony,' he said in his best 'The Boss' voice, 'either get those reports finished or bugger off and deal with whatever the fuck it is you think is more important.'

Handley looked up, startled, and stared blankly at his boss for all of 30 seconds.

'Er, yes boss. I mean there's nothing I think is more important, sir – than the reports I mean.'

Tanner grunted and shook his head. 'I won't have you moping about my bloody office making the place look like a fucking library where students and dossers pass their time. So, piss off and sort your shit out, but–' Tanner added, raising a 'not to be negotiated with' finger, '–those reports will be finished and filed with copies on my desk before five, understood?'

'Er, right, yes sir,' was all Handley could think of to say.

After he had locked his screen and put paperwork back in the correct folders, he pulled on his jacket and headed straight out of the station.

As he drove, Handley considered what he was going to say to Charlotte Travers. He also considered what the hell he thought he was actually going to do and how and when.

He found a coffee shop and sat staring out the window, absently stirring his cup of cappuccino; he always had cappuccino, mainly because he hadn't a clue what anything else on the menu was. The Travers case had been eating at him since it landed on his desk. Firstly, there was little to no evidence. And secondly, after following all the usual routes and procedures there was still a lump sum of zero to go on. Also, despite the fact the boss had eventually shrugged and said that that was that, nothing else could be done, the guy had probably run off with, as Tanner had put it, 'a richer, sexier, younger bit of stuff,' Handley felt that there was something that had been missed somehow.

The assumptions being made didn't make sense. This guy, who by all and every account was the dictionary definition of upright: a model father, doting husband (if you believed the wife, which – for no reason he could give – Handley did), a dedicated and professional man in his workplace (the Foreign Office, for God's sake) and a man whose habits and manner were predictable and stable. Would this man walk out on his life without any explanation or indication to his loved ones that anything was wrong? This just did not sit with what Handley felt he knew about people and especially what he felt he knew about Marcus Travers.

Then there was the mysterious letter he had received the day before disappearing. It hadn't been found so there was no way of knowing what it contained. It could be entirely irrelevant or it could be the answer to the whole case. Handley knew that when there was nothing but speculation around a piece of evidence, the only thing an investigating officer could do was ignore it. But Handley couldn't help himself. He wanted to know what was in that letter.

Even with all those unresolved questions and dead ends, and against his professional view that his boss was probably right – at least about there being nothing else to be done, if not the reasoning behind Marcus Travers' disappearance – Handley had, somehow, come to the conclusion that he needed to try again. That for his own peace of mind, if nothing else, he needed to try and see the 'evidence' differently. He'd missed something, he was sure, but had no idea what. He also had no idea how a police officer went about 'unofficially' investigating a case, or whether they should and more importantly were actually allowed to.

Handley felt very conflicted as he mulled this over. He was, he prided himself, a very professional police officer, always empathetic yet detached with victims, and straight and unemotional with those he arrested. He knew procedure and stuck to it religiously. This was his professional face and demeanour. But that was part of the problem – it was a face, a mask, one he had invented and developed over a number of years now. It hid, and hid well, his general and overriding insecurities and self-doubts.

He was conscientious – this came naturally – but he questioned everything else he did. Had he covered all the bases? Explored every angle and thread? He always felt that he hadn't or at least that his efforts were simply not good enough, and that for whatever reason he had failed, would always fail, that he just didn't have what it took and would spend the rest of his career as a detective constable or, at best, a detective sergeant. And this added another layer to his anxieties. He was ambitious, he wanted to achieve. He had a passionate and driving desire to be better than he was, hence his invention of a professional face and the persona to go with it. At least with that face on he could *look* the part even if he wasn't feeling it.

When he thought about this, the final piece and probably the crux of the problem arose in his mind. He feared he would be found out. He feared that somehow his boss or some other high-ranking officer would see straight through his professional demeanour and would know – simply by looking at him or assessing his reports or, why not, with black magic for all he knew – that he was not a good detective, just a, plodding, unimaginative good old-fashioned copper, only good for shoe leather in bigger investigations and for carrying the load of 'minor' incidents for the rest of the team.

And this weighed on him. It made him feel inferior and awkward around authority figures. Even Tanner who he had worked under for the last two years or more made him feel tongue-tied, sweaty and nervous. The only solution he could think of for all of this was to somehow impress his superiors, to make his mark and therefore lose all the baggage that he lugged with him every day.

And finally, he thought with a sigh, his last meeting with Mrs Travers had not exactly gone the way he had hoped, his attempt at reassurance had come across as glib and by-the-book. To say she had been unhappy with the meeting would probably have a good chance of gold at the Understatement Olympics.

Still undecided on exactly what he was going to say or do he got back in his car and headed for the Travers' home address.

*

Tanner watched, shaking his head as his young detective meandered out of the office. He would have to get that lad focused somehow. He was good and enthusiastic and always threw himself at whatever job he was given, but that would always be to the detriment of his other duties – filing reports being a prime example. Well, he thought, he's out of my hair for a bit anyway.

'Not that there's much left to get out of,' he muttered ruefully, running his hand over his balding pate.

'Boss?' The nearest officer must have heard Tanner's muttering.

'Nothing Davie. I was quite literally moaning about nothing.'

Ignoring the quizzical look from his DS he strode back to his desk. As soon as he reached for his next piece of 'bloody paperwork' his phone rang. Looking at the phone's display he saw it was his boss, Detective Chief Superintendent Pearson. With a sigh and a heavenward glance he lifted the receiver.

'Sir?' He attempted a respectful but extremely busy tone of voice, but didn't convince himself – never mind his boss.

'Malcolm, I know you're busy, aren't we all, but I need a word. Something's come across my desk that I need you to look at.' Pearson's voice was rough and rasping – smoking 30 plus a day did that to a voice.

'No problem, sir. Give me five and I'll come up.'

'Ah well, in that case I'll see you in the car park in one minute.'

This raised a smile from Tanner. Fran Pearson could smell a cigarette break from 1000 yards and never missed an opportunity for a smoke.

Precisely one minute later they were both stood huddled against the wall as a cold breeze did it's best to improve their health by driving them back inside. So far it had failed miserably.

After a couple of minutes of general catch-up and chat, Tanner decided he should prompt his Super onto the reason they had come out in the first place.

'So, what's this interesting bit of info then Fran?' Tanner asked between puffs.

They had known each other for years now, so when outside the office or shut behind a closed door with just the two of them they would revert to first name terms.

Pearson took a final drag and carefully put his cigarette out in the tray mounted to the wall. 'Do you recall The Charmer case?'

Tanner puffed his cheeks, pulled his collar up around his neck – signalling for the move inside – and looked at his boss with a questioning frown. 'Yeah I remember it alright. I was only shoe leather at the time but even a wet-behind-the-ears DC like me knew it was massive. Has something turned up then?'

Tanner had asked the last question with a slightly distracted air; he was recalling his part in the huge manhunt for The Charmer. He knew his boss had played a prominent part in the investigation. Over ten years ago now, a serial killer was thought to be responsible for at least a dozen murders stretching back several years. The investigation had continued for five years with no results. The murders had continued although more sporadically as time went on. Tanner had always assumed someone, somewhere, was still investigating and in all likelihood further victims were still cropping up.

The killer had been dubbed The Charmer by a national newspaper, after an unguarded comment from Pearson on how the killer appeared to be able to charm his way into the homes of his victims. This was soon pounced on by the rest of the media. His victims were all women aged between 20 and 38 – all relatively comfortable financially, some married, others not. There was no forced entry to any property and all the victims had been stabbed multiple times – brutally, as the newspapers put it, which always seemed odd to Tanner as the police were rarely involved in 'gentle' stabbings or 'friendly' ones for that matter.

His nose wrinkled at the stench that suddenly filled the little clearing in the scrub and trees. It was quite dark now so he struggled to see what had happened.

'God, has she shit herself?' he murmured quietly to himself, looking down at the very thin young woman lying sprawled on the ground as he sat back on his haunches to gain a better view.

The girl and surrounding ground were covered in blood – as, he noted, was he – but in the failing light it all appeared to be dark, glutinous, globs of 'stuff'. Now that he looked at the gore on his arms and torso, he could feel it cooling on his skin and worse still hardening in his hair.

He looked again at what was left of the girl. She was almost entirely covered in blood from her ankles to her neck, legs and genitalia slashed and cut, abdomen just a mass of clots and slowly oozing wounds. Then he looked more closely and as he did so he realised his error. At least two of his 'insertions' had punctured so deeply as to penetrate her bowels, causing two deep rents in the stinking, gelatinous organ now lying, visibly exposed, on her stomach. Both had spilled vile, dark smears of excrement over her belly and lower body.

Deep revulsion filled him as he realised he must also be covered in the stuff. He rose from where he had been kneeling and moved a few metres away where he retched violently, holding himself semi-upright with one hand pressed against the trunk of a tree. He was relieved they were all dry heaves, as at least there would be less to clean up. He knew that traces of the girl were everywhere but they were irrelevant. The police could know all they liked about who she was but what was important – nay, vital –

36

was that they had next to nothing of his traces. He knew he would never clean the area of all clues and was also comforted that even if they did somehow find a tiny trace of his DNA, or a fibre or any other 'clue', they would still have to catch him and match it first. There was certainly no trace of him on any records; he had never been arrested, never even been inside a police station, so no – they couldn't trace him from this mess and they were highly unlikely to catch him now, were they?

But as immune as he felt he was, he had to clean up this disastrous, pathetic mess. This was, for the third time now, nothing like what he wanted – not at all the beautiful transcendence he had been looking for. Instead, it was just a shit-filled space in some waste ground with a useless, unattractive, and, more to the point, unfulfilling bitch who'd had the temerity to soil his skin.

With a last hack that cleared his throat and mind he got to work.

He began by roughly grabbing the girl by the ankle and dragging her several metres to the near-vertical sides of the old quarry set in the middle of this piece of waste ground. There was water filling the bottom and the banks continued their steep descent long after the water line was reached. She would, with any luck, simply disappear without trace … not that anyone would probably report her missing anyway – cheap, filthy, drug-riddled, whore that she was.

Then, he returned to the clearing. There was no point worrying about the blood and shit on the ground; the rain would come soon and wash all of that away, and very few people would come through here and see it, if it stayed dry. He collected the cheap kitchen knife he had bought from Woolworths not too many hours ago, and then retracing his steps he tossed it after the girl.

Next, he gathered the clothes he had been wearing when they had come into the woods and shredded them, ripping each item into rags and unrecognisable bits of material. Taking these, he returned to his backpack which he had carefully left outside the clearing, well away from any potential contamination. From this he removed a large black bin liner and touching only this he emptied out an entire change of clothes (very different from those worn before – casual clothes became suit, shirt, tie, brogues) and then placed the rags into it. Finally, he could reach for the bottle of alcohol cleaner and the swabs he kept at the bottom of the bag and thoroughly wiped down every last inch of his body.

Freshly dressed and walking back out of the rough, abandoned woodland he had chosen as a temple, he chastised himself. Mistakes had been made, bad ones. Never again would he turn to whores or druggies to fulfil his quest. That was a big mistake, because although they appeared to be life's victims, they tended to be feistier and strangely cling on and fight with real venom. And, besides, there was no way he was going to find The One among *them.* The scene was far too hard to control: failing light, lots of opportunity to leave traces and potential weapons lying around for those chosen to be Delivered to use against him. That last thought raised a smile – the pathetic souls he had chosen so far posed no physical threat to him. And maybe that was the rub? He should aim higher, a lot higher … grand and classy from now on.

Yes, he was not stretching himself enough. He had to set his sights on a higher goal, hone his skills a little more. After all, it was barely a challenge to lure these guileless, unsophisticated women to the places he wanted. Yes, it was time to use his natural charm and step up the Quest.

Time to find some real women.

With that, his thoughts turned back to reopening talks with the rest of Europe about BSE-riddled beef and gaining the release of Brian Keenan from Beirut. Apparently it was important that he be freed although he could see no real reason why some little Irish pleb should be of any importance. Still, work was work and it was comfortable, easy work after all.

When he was nearly home, he found a neighbour's bin, conveniently awaiting collection, to dump his rubbish bag into.

This done, and now safe in the knowledge he was home and dry yet again, he straightened his tie and began whistling quietly to himself.

Strange, he thought, that the closer to home he dumped his detritus the safer it was.

Chapter Three

Tanner was brought back from his recollections of The Charmer case when his boss replied, opening and holding the security door for Tanner to enter, 'It'll be easier to show you up at my office. Couple of things have come up that might or might not be connected. And your lot are handling one of them.'

Tanner remained silent as they made their way back up the stairs and along to Pearson's office. He or his team were handling a case involving The Charmer? Surely not. There was nothing 'on the books' that he could think of that he could remotely connect to a series of killings from 10 to 20 years ago. There were a number of killings they were dealing with but all were straightforward cases – as far as he could recall – with most culprits either already in custody or being sought. None that he could think of were still open with no prime suspect.

They entered the office and Pearson gestured for Tanner to sit in the chair opposite his desk, taking the more comfortable chair behind it himself. Tanner waited patiently while his superior was apparently collecting his thoughts.

'Two things have come to my attention over the last couple of days,' he began at last. 'Firstly, yesterday I had an interesting email forwarded to me from Belgium.'

Tanner raised an eyebrow. Belgium? Where the hell was this going? But he said nothing, allowing Pearson to continue.

'It seems a Police Fédérale Investigating Officer – I think that's what they call themselves anyway – reckons she is working a murder in a town called Leuven, which I hadn't heard of but turns out to be a fairly large town, maybe a little smaller than say Chelmsford. Anyway, she's working a murder from about a month or so ago and in the course of her investigation was reminded of The Charmer case over here. It was pretty big news everywhere at the time and she has noticed some potential similarities.'

As Pearson paused, Tanner began thinking of questions and objections to this somewhat far-fetched 'connection'.

'She's sent us the details and highlighted what she sees as the similarities – I'll forward it all to you once we're done. I have to say she's been really thorough and the evidence she puts forward is pretty convincing, although all circumstantial at this time. I for one think there might be something in it, although frankly I have no idea if it can really be the same killer.'

Tanner sat for a moment thinking and Pearson knew well enough to leave him to it, holding back the second point he was about to make.

'So, before I spend time going through this Belgian report and then doing a full comparison with the files from The Charmer investigation,' Tanner said eventually, 'why not give me an outline of what she has to say so I can give you an initial assessment? Saves some time.'

'OK, that's a fair call Malcolm. Basically, the victim was found in her own home. She was a 32-year-old banking manager and was stabbed 15 times using one of her own kitchen knives. No sign of forced entry – forensics are going through the property with a fine-tooth comb but so far nothing usable has been found. The victim was last seen in a bar. She appeared to be waiting for someone, then received a call on her mobile and left. The caller used a pay as you go number, untraceable.'

'Right, so that has some similarities,' said Tanner, 'but a lack of evidence isn't a good place to start a comparison is

41

it? I mean the circumstances sound similar but there's nothing there to say it's actually anything more than that – similar does not necessarily mean the same as.'

'Malcolm, there was bugger all to go on in the first place. We never found any forensic that was of any use for The Charmer – you probably weren't party to the full forensic reports but they were all but useless. There was loads of cross-contamination, DNA from several individuals and hair from yet another set. Aside from the MO and what boiled down to a gut feeling on my part, there was nothing to actually confirm those killings were even really a series carried out by the same man. When I started this investigation CCTV coverage was minimal and of poor quality, so I thought I might get a break as it started to improve. But he's even got around that somehow, though God knows how.' Pearson's voice had become more gravelly as he spoke, obviously reliving the frustrating and fruitless past investigation.

'However,' he continued, 'you have to agree that this case from Belgium bears some similarity, so I still think you should compare it to our files. You're probably aware that the murders tailed off a few years ago and with nothing new to work on the investigation ground to a halt. Makes me wonder if our man switched to a different country. The only reason this was sent to me was that Belgium were looking at old newspaper reports and so on, and my name came up as Senior Investigating Officer – which technically I still am, although frankly there haven't been any significant developments for several years. The file is still open, of course, but I haven't really seen the point in putting another team onto it. I figure they'd wind up the same place I did, which is nowhere. I suggested another team look at it, maybe one out of my remit – you know, a fresh pair of eyes and all that. Top brass weren't having it, so I'm the expert apparently and it stays with me. Christ, nearly 10 years of trying to catch that bastard and I'm still nowhere near, so I need your help on this Malcolm. I need you to start afresh as though it were 10 years ago, step into my shoes as it were, and then see if this Belgian connection takes us anywhere.'

'Not being funny Fran but, I really don't want to be put in the shoes you had to wear 10 years ago. They'd stink for a start and I already have a headache,' Tanner grumbled. 'I don't need that turning into a need for a head transplant.' He sighed and rubbed his eyes with thumb and forefinger then pulled them down over his cheeks, 'Ok Fran, I'll take a look. You said there was something that was already on my desk?'

'Ah yeah, might be nothing but since the whole Charmer thing has reared its ugly head at me again, I had an initial search done, checking for names mentioned in the case files against any travel to Belgium or recent activity. Didn't expect to get anything back and yet weirdly I did. One of the people interviewed in The Charmer case, a Marcus Travers, has – I believe – gone missing and your lot are dealing with it?'

This raised an eyebrow from Tanner. Yeah DC Handley had that one. Odd, as there has been no trace of him at all – no body, no financial activity we can find and no sightings. And totally out of character ... by all accounts he was a pretty straight-up-and-down guy. Why was he interviewed?'

'We'd got pretty desperate by then, admittedly, but one thing that came up was that there were Government conferences, meetings, training sessions – you know the type of thing, generally Foreign Office and Home Office civil servants on a shindig. Anyway these were going on at the same time and in the same or nearby towns as some of the killings. Like I say, all a bit tenuous and desperate, but we traced and interviewed all those attending and Marcus Travers was one of them. In fact, he had been to at least four of them. His alibis were confirmed, however, and the interviewing officer reckoned, and I quote, "He was a really decent sort who answered honestly and truthfully". It could all be nothing but I thought it worth bringing to your attention since you're going to be looking at The Charmer files anyway, and he's Foreign Office so he would be very likely to travel to the continent, especially Belgium.'

Again, Tanner appeared to be thinking deeply about what he had just heard, this time running a hand gently over the smooth and shiny dome of his head. 'Hmm, that is…. interesting. OK Fran, let me have everything, as well as full access to the Charmer files. Does that mean the case is officially on our books? Just thinking budgets, you know?' Tanner gave a half smile knowing damn well what the answer would be.

Pearson chuckled, a sound rather like a small elephant crunching through gravel: 'No Malcolm, no chance. The Charmer review is a result of a request from an external force and as such is not yet officially handed over to me. It's just a review being conducted at my request. It won't require any extra manpower, other than yourself, so there's no need for additional budget. There could be a need, however, if you find that there is a connection. Then we may well be looking at official handover and, yes, budgets.'

Tanner laughed with his friend and superior. 'A well-rehearsed line, Fran. Fair enough, I'll have a dig and see what I can find. I'll let you know about the Belgian case as soon as, OK?'

Sitting back down at his own desk, a few moments later, Tanner blew out his cheeks and let out a long and noisy breath. Well, no point hanging about and fretting over it. Let's crack on, he thought, moving the mouse to open the email from DCS Pearson.

'06

The Urge had been too strong.

It had been many months since he had last worshipped a woman, shown her what true love was, that everlasting, eternal bliss and release. He had ached for that feeling of control mixed with abandon and then the sheer exhilaration of pushing the blade into her again and again. But he had to be careful, had to have self-control – his Quest could last many years yet. He had to keep going until he found The One, the one woman who was just perfect, who fulfilled him in every way. Then, and only then, would it stop.

The police, however, were upping their investigations. They had realised there were connections between a number of the Events and had declared that they suspected one man was responsible. That meant he must be very careful. He had hoped the disparate nature of the locations and variety of women chosen – all of a particular type of course, if you looked at them carefully enough, but with enough differences to keep even a keen investigating officer from spotting a pattern – would not have created links on the Police National Computer system, and that each case (especially those from a number of years ago now) would be handled locally and seen as a series.

He had also hoped that the chaos caused by the Buncefield oil terminal exploding last year would have given him some breathing space. The Home Office, in its wisdom, had placed the only back-up server to the PNC right next door to the huge oil depot, and it went up in smoke amid the largest fire in Europe since the war. He had laughed long and hard when he heard the news; the colleague who told him obviously assumed he found the HO's error funny and had no idea of its real significance.

Still, those clever IT boffins at the PITO had kept things running and then an upcoming DCI happened to notice a couple of similar Events, one in Brighton and the other in Manchester. This naturally led to several connections being made and eventually the DCI decided there were 10 'murders', as he called them. There were more of course – so many more women he had loved and cherished and Delivered, stretching back over a decade or so now.

He felt aggrieved that the DCI had described his deeds as something so crass as murder; had he not seen the nuances, the clear demonstrations of love and care he had shown these women? Still, the fact remained that they were now looking for one man, and that made his Quest all the more precarious.

Naturally they had no idea who they were looking for, but still, homing in on one suspect meant a concerted effort in investigatory activity and forensics. That could lead to a lucky break which might put him in a very dangerous position. A modicum of comfort to him was the chaos he caused with the forensic evidence: with so many different strands of DNA, hair, semen and occasionally saliva, it was almost impossible for the police to pinpoint any one individual. But if they did ever think to test him then they would find matches. He couldn't avoid leaving some traces and also knew that the police worked on the premise that you could not be anywhere without leaving something behind.

His evasion techniques had evolved further recently, as CCTV had become ever more present and pervasive throughout society. His use of wigs, hats and other props, as he'd used on this particular occasion, had very likely hampered any efforts to identify him.

He did not fear capture or its consequences but he did fear the ending of his Quest. He knew he would never be released if they caught him – he would die in prison or in a secure hospital and never see the end, never have the relief of finally Delivering the perfect woman, the perfect facsimile of *her*.

Yes, he thought, more restraint needed in the future, old chap. In the UK at any rate. He was pleased with himself for turning his attention to Belgium. It hadn't happened every time he had visited Brussels but a number of times now – was it two or three? Yes, three Belgian women had now been Delivered. Very satisfying. The chances of those particular Events being linked to any in the UK were remote indeed. The downside, of course, was that although his trips to the home of the European Union were viewed as a natural part of his work, they were not always frequent enough to sate The Urge.

He sighed as he took a last look at the lovely on the bed, the crimson blood covering her almost completely. Beautiful, at peace, fulfilled … she would never savour an experience so enlightening again.

But still she wasn't perfect. She wasn't The One.

'This might have to be the last for a while,' he said quietly to himself, trying to force his mind away from the Quest.

The Urge would have to wait.

Feeling a little melancholic as he left the flat she had so obligingly let him into, he raised his spirits by whistling quietly to himself.

Chapter Four

'OK', was all Charlotte could think of to say. DC Handley had asked the same questions in different ways over and over again across the course of the last three months. She could think of nothing else she could add and was not sure she wanted to go through that round of questions again. As much as she wanted answers she was, quite frankly, bored with repeating herself.

'I don't really want to wind up repeating myself, Mrs Travers,' Handley said, apparently reading her mind. 'So, on the way over here it occurred to me that the questions we should explore on the surface of it may seem ...' He paused, looking at the ceiling, obviously trying to find the right words. '... irrelevant, or maybe that we should look at the little things, the things you took for granted in your day to day life with Mr Travers?'

Charlotte remained silent, clearly waiting for Handley to elaborate or at least ask a question she could begin to formulate an answer to. Little things? Irrelevant? If they were little and irrelevant then how the hell was she to recall them off the top of her head?

Handley took the cue and continued, 'So, as you've told me, Mr Travers was an open and – as far as you are concerned – an honest man. Hard working and caring. We don't need to go through all of that again. Let's simply chat about day-to-day life here in the house. When Mr Travers was home from work in the evening or at the weekend, what kind of things would you do together? What would he do on his own?'

Still Charlotte remained quiet – her mind, for some reason, had gone completely blank. What did Marcus do on his own? They spent much of their time together with the children when he was home, and then very often the evening would be spent with a bottle of wine and the TV, whilst chatting about their respective days. All very normal. They had what they rather laughingly called an office in the small box room at the back of the house. Marcus would occasionally disappear up there to, as he said it, 'pootle on the net' or idly play a game. The police had of course already gone through the computer, to no avail. There was nothing really in the room except that and a desk; there was a cupboard which contained mostly junk and old, generally-defunct CDs of software.

Suddenly her eyes widened, 'His box!'

Handley looked at her and blinked, 'Pardon? His what?'

'His keepsake box. It's an old wooden box, you know with a clasped lid. He kept old photos, his degree certificate and that sort of thing in it. He's always had it – I rarely, if ever, saw him look at it. It's in the back bedroom. We call it the office as we have the computer in there. It's one of the few places Marcus would be that I wasn't … maybe he has something in there that would help?'

'Well,' said Handley in an even tone, 'at the very least it's something we haven't looked at before so let's fetch it down and have a sift through it.'

Charlotte rose quickly – at last something new she could pin a little hope on. She virtually ran up the stairs and along the landing. Once in the office, she reached to the top of the cupboard where Marcus' box always sat. It was not particularly large, maybe 50 by 50 centimetres wide and 30 or so deep. It wasn't particularly heavy either, containing mostly paperwork. Before returning back downstairs she had a look around the little room. There was nothing else that might prove useful. Clutching the box to her chest she headed down the stairs.

Whilst Charlotte was upstairs, Handley took the opportunity to take a look around the room which, contrary to popular crime fiction, he hadn't managed to achieve on his arrival. The room would have probably been described as well-appointed – neat and tidy with good-quality furniture, but otherwise unremarkable. His eyes fell on the family photograph hanging on one wall, a well-taken portrait, clearly done by a decent professional photographer. It showed the Travers and their two children, obviously taken a few years ago gauging by the age of the children. Marcus Travers was standing behind the rest of his family: tall and darkly handsome, smiling proudly at the camera. His face was as familiar to Handley now as his own face in the mirror. He had spent many a time over the last few months studying the picture Charlotte had brought in for him at the time of Marcus' disappearance, never gleaning any more information than the first time he had looked at it.

Handley looked up expectantly as Charlotte re-entered the living room, and watched her carefully place the wooden box on the coffee table, hooking a strand of her shoulder-length, very light brown, almost-blonde hair behind her ear. Handley had seen her do this on a number of occasions but still couldn't decide if it was an unconscious habit or a sign of irritation or nervousness.

'I'm surprised you haven't looked through this already,' he said mildly. 'It's a common response to losing or missing someone, you know, using old photos or possessions to try and get a sense of them or some sort of reconnection?'

'To be honest,' Charlotte replied, 'I'd forgotten all about it and had never really felt inclined to look through it even when Marcus was here. He rarely seemed to bother with it so it's just sitting gathering dust.'

As she finished speaking, Charlotte reached over to the box and quickly opened the clasp, while Handley shifted over on the couch to gain a better view.

The lid swung back easily enough on old but little-used hinges. Looking inside, they could see more or less what they'd expected – a jumble of pictures and certificates.

Slowly they began sifting through the pieces of paper, taking each one out, glancing at it and placing it carefully onto the coffee table.

'Hm, a degree in Politics from Edinburgh and then an MA in International Political Economics from Manchester University,' Handley noted, impressed, as he placed the two ornate certificates on the table.

'Yes, he was, *is* a smart man … that's why he was so respected at the Foreign Office,' Charlotte said distractedly as she looked at an old photo dulled by age, the colours now washed out, although she suspected they were never very good in the first place. It showed Marcus aged about 10, standing a little awkwardly next to his father. They were standing slightly apart, neither of them looking like there was much of a bond between them. Marcus was clearly not enjoying having his photo taken and his father was standing straight-backed and stern-looking, almost Victorian in his demeanour and dress.

She had never met his parents – both were dead before they had married and Marcus rarely, if ever, talked about them. She always had the feeling his childhood had not been a happy one.

She placed the photo on the growing pile of life's little mementos with a sense of sadness that Marcus had not experienced the affection he so readily gave his own children.

They were almost finished, Charlotte realised with a sinking feeling. This was going nowhere.

Handley lifted another much older and plainer certificate from the box, this one for swimming 50 yards. Mr Travers had obviously been very pleased about that little achievement, Handley thought, with a small smirk.

Then his eye caught some newer-looking pieces of paper at the very bottom of the box. He grunted and reached for them. His experience told him that newer-looking paper would, logically, only be found at the bottom of a pile like this if it had been deliberately placed there – in other words, hidden. Perhaps old Marcus was not quite the paragon of decency and uprightness that his wife thought and he had been led to believe?

'These might be of more interest,' he said quietly as he lifted what he could now see were notes of some sort, four of them, all handwritten and on reasonably good paper.

Charlotte, who until that point had been staring blankly at the pile of paperwork on the coffee table, now whipped her head up and looked intently at Handley. He read the first couple of pieces of paper in his hands and then quietly handed them over with pursed lips that Charlotte took to be a rueful expression.

Unsure what to make of his reaction she took the notes, hands shaking slightly and read the top one:

Marcus,
I must see you again, today or tomorrow, as soon as possible. Leave a message in the usual place and let me know when you can make it. I'll book the same place as last time when I know.
Julia

Charlotte's eyes were already welling up as she turned to the second note Handley had given her:

Marcus,
I thought the last time was really good. We seem to be thinking the same things and seeing 'it' for what it is. I will be out of the country for a few days but we must catch up again after that.
Julia

Her tears were flowing freely now as she looked up at Handley who had clearly been watching her intently as she read the notes. As he spoke it seemed to her that he had somehow become very far away. She could barely hear him as he let out a long breath through his nose and began to speak.

'I am sorry Mrs Travers, I really am, but it does appear that your husband was having an affair or at least some sort of relationship with this Julia. Do you know anyone of that name?'

She couldn't bring herself to speak – so simply, slowly, shook her head.

'Do you recognise the handwriting? Maybe from the letter your husband received before he disappeared?'

She would be forced to answer now, she realised, and yet was still not sure she could speak. How could this be right? She had been sure, no, certain, that Marcus was not involved with another woman. She was sure that she would have known, spotted little changes in his behaviour that over time would become significant and lead to her suspecting something. And Marcus was just not that opaque. He was incapable of hiding even simple, innocent truths. She always wound up knowing what he had bought for her birthday and Christmas and for their anniversary – always found out that he had a surprise planned or had done something stupid and wanted to hide it. She thought of the time he had ruined several expensive dresses in the wash; he had simply binned them and hoped she wouldn't notice. She had realised within a few days that something was up and with very little prodding he had confessed. So, how could she have missed an affair?

Handley had kept his eyes down as she cried. She was clearly in a world of her own. He was surprised himself, but the notes did seem to point in the direction of an affair. He decided it would be best to leave and began thinking of a suitably mollifying exit line when his eyes fell on the two notes still in his hand. He had been shuffling these nervously from hand to hand for the last few minutes and now the bottom one was on top.

His brow creased as he read it and re-read it.

Before coming to any conclusions, he decided to quickly scan the other one. It was much the same as the first two – 'must see you', 'we need to talk' etc, etc. Of course, he had no idea what order any of these notes were written in; there was no date on any of them, but he felt sure this one could be placed alongside the two that Charlotte Travers still held loosely in her hand. But the fourth and final note, and he was sure it was number four in the sequence, that one was different.

'Hmmmm,' he murmured. 'Mrs Travers I have to go back to the station now – may I have those notes? They're needed for my report.'

'What? Oh yes of course, er, what will be in your report DC Handley?' Charlotte asked quietly as she meekly handed over the two notes she held.

'I'm not entirely sure right now, Mrs Travers, but I will be in touch again soon.'

With that he rose, accepting the proffered notes, putting them together with the two he now held firmly in his hand, and headed for the door.

Charlotte could think of nothing to say so simply returned his departing nod and closed the front door.

'18

Recollections

She recalled one of their earliest dates. A picnic in Hyde Park, followed by the tube down to Westminster and a gentle stroll along Victoria Embankment, and finally into a cosy little bar somewhere behind Embankment station. It had been a glorious summer's day, clear skies with wispy, cotton-wool cirrus wafting lazily here and there, hot but tempered with a cooling light breeze.

They had talked almost constantly throughout the afternoon and into the evening. She remembered finding it amazing that a man with a lot to boast about – a very good job, his own flat and car, a good education – could be so self-effacing and modest. She was especially taken by his ability to listen, never interrupting, allowing her to tell him as much, if not more, about herself than he told her about himself.

He was also handsome, with dark brows framing brown eyes that twinkled with humour; too gentle in nature to be seen as rugged, but with strong features – jaw not quite square but still strong and proud. She remembered being impressed by his large strong hands, which somehow seemed at odds with the cerebral nature of his work at the Foreign Office. She had fallen for his sing-song Scots burr from the moment they'd met, so by the time they were sitting sipping wine, close together on a comfy bench, she felt she would melt every time he said her name.

It was strange, she thought now. She had heard him say her name a million times since that day and yet the way he had said it back then was still so fresh in her mind; it brought a smile to her lips even now, the rolling R and strong T at the end — she had never heard Charlotte pronounced so beautifully, or sexily.

That had been the date they had first slept together. Had that been the third or fourth one? — she now wondered. It had been quick by both their standards; they had admitted that not long after, but it had seemed so completely right and natural that neither had felt any angst or guilt. It had in fact cemented something they had both realised would last, in all likelihood, forever.

She remembered how gentle he had been, and how she couldn't decide whether he was a very attentive lover or simply very nervous that his inexperience would show. Either way it was apparent he hadn't exactly been a gigolo, and sometimes she wondered if she hadn't been his first one. It had been something in the way he had appeared so keen and looked at all times for reassurance that he was doing everything right. And as a result, she fell in love with him there and then.

Recalling the look on his face during that first night's lovemaking made her think of a different aspect to his nature. It brought to mind the times, even back then, when he would go distant and quiet. He would be staring into space, not seeing anything other than the inside of his own head; his jaw would clench and relax in a rhythmic, almost metronomic way, and his hands would curl, not quite clenching into fists but clearly under the same sort of tension. At the time she thought it kind of endearing, that he was obviously wrestling with a knotty problem from work or some such and needed to disappear into his own mind in order to work through it. She had consequently come to admire, as she saw it, his quiet determination and will to succeed.

She had seen that look many times since then, that faraway-ness that sometimes seemed to come from nowhere. She had always put it down to an intensity of thought and a deep caring for his work, for her and for their family's well-being.

A thought brought her flying back from the past to the present. She wondered, now, whether those moments had indeed been the way she had always interpreted them, or were they symptoms of something else, something he had never told her? Were they his escape from her and their world, taking him away to the life he would rather be living? Or, taking him to the life he was already living part-time and wished to have all of the time?

She might never find that answer out now and wasn't sure that she really wanted to.

Chapter Five

Handley rushed back to the office. He had to see his boss – that last note was, he knew, an important clue to the reasons behind Marcus Travers' disappearance. He had felt all along this wasn't a simple 'mis per', and here at last was some evidence to justify that feeling. Handley liked days like these.

As soon as he was spotted by his boss, Tanner nodded towards the 'private office' where only a day or so before Handley had told Charlotte Travers that the search for her husband was being wound down. Maybe now he would be able to phone her and say it was back on. It all hinged on whether his boss accepted the last of the notes as a lead worth following up.

As soon as he started shutting the door Tanner began speaking, 'What do you remember of The Charmer investigation, Tony? You would have been pretty young when it was at its height.'

He had indeed been young; in fact, he'd been at school during most if not all of it. He was, however, familiar with the investigation. He'd seen plenty on the news as a kid and his father had been a copper at the time in London; he was uniform but had been involved in some door-to-door enquiries and had told the young Tony all about it. He described all this to Tanner.

Tanner accepted it with a nod. 'Well, there have been a couple of things that have come up – one doesn't really concern you, but the other does.'

Handley raised an eyebrow at his boss. Tanner took his cue and filled him in on the enquiry that had come in from Belgium and, of more interest to Handley, Marcus Travers' connection to the old investigation.

'That,' said Handley when his boss had finished, with a note of triumph in his voice, 'is very interesting, given what I found this morning.'

It was now Tanner's eyebrow that raised.

Handley continued, his voice rising slightly with excitement as he produced the notes from his jacket pocket. 'I found – well actually, Charlotte Travers found these this morning.' He handed over the first three and continued: 'Now these three seem to back up the theory that Marcus was having an affair and has simply run off with another woman.'

Tanner nodded as he read the three notes, a hint of 'I told you so' on his face which then descended into a frown.

'There's a "but" isn't there?' he said, his voice getting gruffer as he spoke. He had seen something about the three notes and Handley suspected it was the same thing he had spotted.

'Yep, there is and it's quite a big one ...' Handley now spoke with real passion in his voice, the chance to impress his boss driving him on to state his case. 'I think you've noted the same thing I did, that if these are notes from a lover, why so short and to the point? But more importantly to my eyes, where are the kisses at the end? And where are the terms of endearment?'

'Uh-huh, I'd started to think that but maybe they were just not that type or were concerned that others – Mrs Travers, for one – might see them?'

'That's a fair point, Guv, but I still think it's a little odd. And *then* ...' There was almost a flourish in Handley's voice, like a magician about to say ta-da!. '...there's this.' He handed over the fourth and final note.

Tanner took it and glanced at this new piece of paper.

61

He had expected to see something very similar but this note, however, caused him real pause for thought. He sat stock still reading the small slip of paper a few times more. This one had no name at the top and no sign-off underneath, but the handwriting was exactly the same as the previous three – it was certainly from this Julia woman. The contents, however, were very different. It simply said:

I think I know what you've done, we talk today or I go to the police.

Tanner raised his head slowly to look directly at Handley, his brows raised, eyes wide.

Handley, who had already been staring at his boss, also raised his eyebrows, this time with an unspoken question framed in the gesture.

'Right,' Tanner said in a decisive and authoritative tone. 'I think you'd better drop everything else and get to finding Mr Travers and this Julia woman – whoever the fuck she is, don't you? I'll let DCS Pearson know what's going on.'

'95

That was damn close, he thought as he waved to the retreating back of the police constable. He watched her return to her colleague already seated in the patrol car pulled in tight behind him, with its blue lights still flashing.

He left his window down as they manoeuvred around his car and carried on into the night, making sure he was looking intently at the ticket he'd received as they passed. Nothing more than a concerned individual having just received an extremely rare ticket for a minor motoring offence. He had stupidly failed to check his brake lights and one had failed.

A trickle of cold sweat ran down his back. He had, after all, not 15 minutes before, Delivered another one. She would likely only just be cooling in her Newington flat. He would smell of her perfume, could potentially have some fibres – connecting him to her or her flat – on the clothes in the bag in the boot. Fingerprints weren't so much of a problem; he wore gloves for most of the Delivery and the points where he was unable to (it would be very strange keeping gloves on as he entered a house) he used his prodigious memory to recall anything he had touched – simply wiping down any appropriate object before he left.

He breathed deeply to calm himself, then tried to think a little more rationally. He was a respectable member of the public, was – as he'd said to the constable – simply driving home, which was entirely true. He had just neglected to state from where. He hadn't touched any alcohol and had also been courteous in the extreme to the young officer. He had given, as far as was possible to ascertain, no indication that he was in any way agitated or nervous.

But the officer could easily have decided to check the car over, maybe even have wanted to check the boot for a loose wire or to check the spare tyre. That would have been too close for comfort. She was unlikely to want to check his belongings, but still, the thought that she *could* have was disconcerting in the extreme.

His position helped of course. He could drop the FO into conversation fairly easily and as such would draw any suspicion further away from himself. But it wasn't immunity, and he knew if this happened again he would have to be extremely careful about what he said and did.

Another piece to work on and ponder – he had to ensure he could very convincingly explain where he had been and where he was going. He would have to do some mirror work to perfect what he was already thinking of as his 'police face'. And perhaps more importantly, try not to get stopped again. It was simple mistakes and happenstance that he knew were the most likely to lead to the end of the Quest.

He returned to the thought of hair and saliva which could yield DNA, and that fibres could easily be matched to those of his clothes or car, or anything else of his that he hadn't even considered. That thought really bothered him. Obviously, they would have to catch him and get samples in order to be able to match those with anything from the scenes, and he was certain he wasn't on the police database, but again that was a risk too far. He needed a means to counter that eventuality, to find a way to muddy the waters.

He resolved to start on his new homework as soon as he got home. Further research would be required on forensic evidence gathering, how results were obtained and what flaws there were in the processes.

But first, he had to dispose of the clothes in the boot and vacuum the carpet in there and the rest of the car – to be sure. That would be the highest priority. He was unwilling to rely on leaving it and having the car valeted in the morning.

Breathing a final sigh of relief, he turned the ignition, straightened his tie and pulled the car back out into the road, whistling quietly as he did so.

Chapter Six

Handley stood outside the very imposing Foreign and Commonwealth Office's main building on King Charles Street in Westminster. He had never been near here before, working mainly around the East End and Romford areas. This was actually City of London Police's patch and to Handley felt a very long way from Stratford! Taking a calming breath, he walked up the steps and entered the main atrium.

Having introduced himself to the officious individual at the main desk, he was asked to wait to one side and an aide to Sir Frederick Derringham would be along shortly.

He perched on the – to him – ridiculously small and fragile chair and prayed it wouldn't break.

Sir Frederick Derringham! Jeez, talk about elevated! Handley fidgeted nervously with his collar and straightened his tie. Sir Frederick was Director of European Political Affairs, just a couple of rungs below the Permanent Under-Secretary for Foreign Affairs. Essentially, he ran one of the largest departments in the Foreign Office and was Marcus Travers' boss.

After his meeting with Tanner, Handley had written up his initial report about his latest discoveries and those newly realised connections to The Charmer investigation. Meanwhile, Tanner had rushed up to DCS Pearson's office to, presumably, gain more budget and clearance to up the hunt for Marcus Travers. Travers was not exactly a suspect for The Charmer case but was, in the parlance, 'a person of interest' and Handley had to admit, he could see no reason why he shouldn't be a suspect.

Tanner had eventually returned and gestured Handley back into the little office. Handley had been –

metaphorically and at times literally – sitting on his hands waiting for instruction from his boss. He wanted to be active, he wanted to be part of something bigger than common assault and bag-snatching from old ladies. He worked those incidents hard and diligently, but ... Handley had dreams and ambition. Handley wanted to be on the 'one to watch' list.

Inside the small, bare office yet again, Tanner had outlined their course of action. Handley was to visit the Foreign Office and talk to Travers' boss, Sir Frederick Derringham, and confirm that Travers had indeed been on the training courses, team-builders and conferences that were of interest. He was also to try and ascertain Derringham's thoughts on Travers' reliability, and whether the 'Knight of the Realm', as Tanner had put it, thought Travers might – just might – have bunked off.

Tanner, in the meantime, was assigning some of the team to see if they could track the Julia woman, although he admitted they were probably flogging a dead horse. There was literally nothing to go on except some handwritten notes and maybe a little (and by *a little* Tanner meant *miniscule*) forensic they might glean from those notes.

Handley had sat quietly while Tanner proceeded to swear for a full 10 minutes about the size of the case file he had to go through, and that he was expected to play the happy 'we're all in it together' schmuck with the Belgians.

Following on from Derringham, Handley was to speak to whomever he felt was appropriate at the FO that might shed more light on the subject. Handley had already had telephone contact with everyone who had worked with Marcus Travers, but – he conceded – it could do no harm to loom over them in person. And maybe they might remember or, better still, even know this Julia woman.

And so, Handley tried to keep his ample weight off the flimsy chair and process all that had happened since he had left Mrs Travers on her doorstep with tears running down her face.

Two days of nothing much had passed since then. Apparently this was the earliest *Sir* Frederick could possibly do, and of course he was *always available* for The Met but *sure* the young DC understood that duty called. Handley had already formed an impression of Derringham: smallish, round, bow tie-wearing and assuredly posh and public school. Pompous, was a word that came to mind when Handley thought of Sir Frederick.

Not that Handley had met Sir Frederick in person yet; when he had called the last time to discuss Marcus Travers, he had spoken to a secretary who had asked him to email his queries directly to her. Sir Frederick was, understandably, very upset at the disappearance of Marcus, as were all the staff, but at that time he was 'distressingly busy' and could not afford the time to see DC Handley in person.

This time, however, DCS Pearson had applied whatever pressure he could bring to bear in order to secure a face-to-face interview with Derringham.

As he sat, Handley tried not to think about the fact he was about to meet one of the most senior civil servants in the country. This was way more terrifying than being in front of Chief Superintendent Pearson – after all, Derringham would almost certainly report back on his conduct and professionality. He fervently hoped his mask wouldn't slip at a crucial moment, like as soon as he was in Derringham's office. The chair creaked a little when he shifted position slightly, stopping him dead in his tracks. He determined to sit as still as possible whilst trying to summon every last inch of his professional persona.

Eventually, a very slim, middle-aged woman in a very smart blue suit – skirt precisely at knee length, hair dark brown and immaculate – approached Handley where he sat.

'DC Handley? Sir Frederick can see you now – please be aware he has only 10 minutes to spare and then he must leave in order to attend to ... matters of State.'

Lunch, more like – thought Handley as he rose from the chair, being careful to push down on the arms so as to avoid bringing it with him. He followed the prim and proper secretary down the corridor she had approached from.

After what felt like an interminable journey through one ornate corridor after another, they came to the outer office of The Director of European Affairs, presumably where Ms (definitely a Ms) Prim and Proper worked. She hadn't introduced herself and had spoken only to direct him on their travels, but Handley was sure it was her that he'd spoken to and emailed previously.

'Please wait here a moment,' she said as she moved to the inner door, knocked and entered.

After a moment or two she re-emerged and held the door open with a gesture for Handley to enter.

The first thing Handley noted on entering the office was its size. It was vast. The Met would have housed five officers in there, plus various filing cabinets. Predictably, the walls were all wood-panelled. There was a built-in bookshelf on one wall, stacked with large tomes, none of which Handley could see the titles of. Then his eyes fell on Sir Frederick's desk, a huge wooden affair that was immaculately tidy and devoid of any paperwork. Yeah really busy, thought Handley, seeing in his mind his own paper-strewn, note-festooned mess back at his own office.

Finally, he looked at Sir Frederick Derringham himself, rising smoothly from behind his monolith of a desk. He was not at all what Handley had expected. Tall for a start, maybe only an inch shorter than Handley's six feet four. His hair was dark and well groomed – surprisingly dark for a man in his fifties, dyed maybe? – with a square chin and wide, full-lipped mouth. There was a slight paunch around his middle but otherwise he looked like he kept his broad frame in trim. He wore an extremely expensive suit, with a light blue shirt and understated tie. His eyes, brown and clear, were conveying warmth and welcome as he stretched a strong hand towards Handley.

'DC Handley,' he said as he shook his hand with a strong and dry grip. 'I must again apologise for not seeing you when you first approached my office, and I wish to make it clear that I was and still am deeply upset and concerned at Marcus' disappearance. I am afraid, however, that the world and therefore the Foreign Office just does not stop, for anyone.'

His voice also surprised Handley, it was rich and full of character with a tuneful quality suggesting a strong tenor singing voice. Although it held the wide vowels and clipped consonants of a public-school accent his tone was warm and held not a trace of the pompous bluster Handley had expected. There was the barest hint of Scots to his accent. Handley was already warming to the man.

'I completely understand Sir,' Handley replied, trying to keep any trace of deference from his voice, 'and I'm pleased you could afford the time to see me on this occasion.'

Derringham waved this away with a quiet 'Anything at all to be of help.'

He gestured to a set of seats on the other side of the office from the book shelf. They were low, wide and leather clad – four of them sat around a neat, glass coffee table.

After seating themselves, Handley declined the offer of a hot beverage and decided to launch straight into his questions, being aware of the time constraints that had been placed on him.

'Sir Frederick,' he got as far as saying before he was interrupted.

'Frederick, please,' Derringham said. 'I don't hold with titles – all my staff call me Frederick so I don't see why you shouldn't. So, er, it's Tony isn't it? Your superior gave your full name when he called me. May I call you Tony or would you prefer a more formal form of address?'

'I think at this stage, Sir Frederick—' Derringham held up a wagging finger causing Handley to falter slightly which he then covered by clearing his throat before continuing. '*Frederick*, I think at this stage I would prefer DC Handley if you don't mind.'

Derringham smiled a radiant, white smile. 'Of course DC Handley, I do understand.'

Handley could feel the conversation slipping from his control already, Derringham seemingly effortlessly gaining the upper hand by controlling the terms of address. With a force of will Handley pushed his professionalism to the very forefront of his mind, focusing hard on the job in hand.

'I'm here, sir,' Handley said, deepening and slowing his voice as he spoke so as to project a serious and purposeful air, 'to ask if anything further had occurred to you since I

71

emailed my questions regarding Marcus Travers' disappearance?'

Derringham shook his head. 'No, not really ... as I said in my earlier reply Marcus was, *is*, a dear colleague I have known for many, many years. In fact he was instrumental in my gaining such, ah, elevation, one might say. I socialised with him on occasion, although less so since he married. Us free spirits tend to move in different social spheres' – a half smile crossed Derringham's mouth as he said this – 'although I know his wife and children well, of course, but apart from that I knew little of his private affairs in recent years.'

'You're not married yourself then sir?' Handley knew this was entirely irrelevant but couldn't help but ask.

'No, DC Handley, never have been. Just haven't seemed to find the right girl.' Derringham honoured him with one of his dazzling smiles. 'I don't see a wedding ring on you either Tony – bit of a kindred free spirit yourself, eh?'

Handley felt himself begin to blush a little. 'Ah, no, I'm not sure I'm a very free spirit but like you I just haven't found the right person.'

To hide his unease he cleared his throat and continued straight into another question. 'You say you've known Mr Travers a long time – how long would that be? And perhaps if you can give me your thoughts on him as a person?'

'Oh, we go way back,' Derringham said, stringing out the "way" longer than was entirely necessary and waving a hand to further emphasise his point. 'We met at the Scottish Office, same department. I had been there around a year when Marcus arrived. Turned out we had both been to Edinburgh, again only a year or so apart, and that we had similar backgrounds. Similar in that we were both from the north east of Scotland and both from quite staunchly Presbyterian families. We would often share a chuckle over a pint of eighty whilst poking fun at our rather strict and stony-faced fathers.'

Derringham sat back a little in his chair with a wistful smile on his face and faraway eyes. Handley stayed silent, allowing Derringham his moment of reminiscence. Then his mouth formed into a small moue and his eyes became a little unfocused, staring above Handley's head and clearly weighing his next words.

'My thoughts on Marcus as a person?' he said eventually. 'I have to say I thought very highly of him, both professionally and personally. He was excellent at his work, dedicated and professional, superb with his staff and others in the office, and had all the potential to rise to the very top of the civil service. On a personal level, I have already said we got on very well – I consider him to be one of my closer friends. If I were to offer any negatives at all I would say he was a little given to introspection which could lead to his being overly quiet at times. Oh and –' Derringham added with a short chuckle – 'he was also a bit of a scruffy bugger. I was forever brushing stray hair of his jacket shoulder or reminding him his top button was undone.'

Looking at Derringham's immaculate attire, Handley could see how Marcus' scruffy appearance would rankle him. He resisted the urge to ensure his own tie was straight.

Derringham sat for a moment, that half-smile back on his face, an expression that Handley realised made him look almost boyish. After a second or two his face returned to a more serious expression as his brow creased.

'Your Detective Chief Superintendent intimated on the telephone that there had been a development, is that how you chaps put it? That it was now rather more important that I see you, in person, as soon as possible. Is there something? Is there something more, er, pertinent you wanted to ask, DC Handley?'

Handley felt a little chagrined that his boss had apparently spilled the beans over the phone – giving the impression, he felt, that he was nothing more than a note-taker. He drew a calming breath before continuing.

'Well, yes there have been some developments and it has become more important that we locate and can hopefully talk to Mr Travers. There is an outstanding case that recently threw up some information that we would like to check. It's an investigation from some time ago that remains unsolved and until recently had had no further lines of enquiry. Marcus Travers may have some information that could shed light on certain matters. Also, we would be interested to gain information on certain aspects of his work that might help move the investigation along. The information goes back a number of years but we'd hoped the Foreign Office would keep diligent records on the sort of things we want to know.'

Derringham lifted his clasped hands up towards his face, his index fingers pressed together and extended upwards so that they just touched his slightly pouting lips.

'So somehow you have connected Marcus to an old case? Is that correct?' Derringham's tone was schoolmasterly, like a senior figure requesting clarification from a junior. Handley suspected that tone was heard a lot in this office.

'Can you tell me any more, DC Handley? It may help me track down the information you're looking for, or at least make my efforts more, er, relevant?'

'I can't say any more on the case in question, sir, only that it's a very serious matter and Mr Travers may hold information vital to that investigation.'

'I see. I take it from what you say that this case has now been re-activated?'

Handley simply nodded in response to Derringham's probing, refusing to be drawn by it. Instead he simply proceeded to outline the information he wanted – which conferences Marcus had attended and where they were, especially those covering specific dates. Derringham produced a slim leather-bound notebook and a very expensive-looking pen, jotted down some details and asked some questions on specifics like dates, double-checking the year every time Handley gave him one.

After Derringham had stopped writing Handley felt it was time to ask the more pertinent question: 'Is there any way that your records could track whether Mr Travers was in attendance for the entire duration of these events?'

Derringham sat back and smiled whilst running a perfectly manicured hand through perfectly styled hair and eventually said with a small laugh, 'I may well have been on a couple of those jaunts myself, Detective Constable.' He gave a slight, barely perceptible wink as he said this. 'And even I have been known to disappear from the odd interminable conference. I wouldn't be at all surprised if Marcus had done the same. In answer to your question, however, no we don't have any means to track that sort of thing.'

As Handley tried to think of another question, Derringham spoke again: 'Now you have my confession that I have done a runner from several of these conferences, will you be investigating me too?'

Handley smiled in response. 'No sir, your name did not come up when this was first looked at, so it's just Mr Travers I would like to know about.'

Derringham simply returned the nod with a tight smile. 'Good to know, couldn't have my excellent name besmirched now, could we?' The smile became a slightly lopsided grin.

'Well, they are all quite some time ago,' he continued, 'but I wouldn't bet against Agatha having kept something somewhere, probably relating to expenses. We have credit cards for this sort of thing – that should suffice don't you think?'

Handley, who assumed Agatha was Ms Prim and Proper in the outer office, nodded in agreement again.

'Well, if that's all DC Handley, I really must be getting on. I'll have Agatha email you the details as soon as we have them.'

'Thank you, sir,' said Handley, shaking Derringham's hand as he rose. 'Actually, Sir Frederick, there was one more question I wanted to ask.'

Sir Frederick made a 'fire away, but make it quick' gesture, one that should have been a complex set of hand signals but which he turned into a simple flourish of one hand.

'We discovered some notes amongst Mr Travers' possessions from a Julia. We're not sure if they were work-related or personal, so I wondered – is there a Julia here? Or have you ever come across the name in connection with Mr Travers?'

Derringham thought for a moment then shook his head. 'No, Detective, I can't say I have – we all get rather a lot of visitors and I'm afraid I am often far too busy to keep track of all or indeed any of them. Sorry.'

As he spoke Derringham was gently but firmly guiding Handley towards the office door. The interview was now officially over.

The two men shared an amicable nod and Handley headed through the now open door into the outer office.

When Handley had passed Agatha and reached the outer door, Derringham spoke again.

'Detective? How on earth is this information going to help you find Marcus?'

'Well sir, frankly I have no idea at this time.'

With that he exited the outer office and started on the long trek back to reception, hoping fervently that he wouldn't get lost on the way.

*

Derringham stood looking at the now closed outer office door for some time, obviously deep in thought, his normally smooth and handsome brow rutted by a deep frown.

Agatha watched her beloved boss silently, waiting for him to either speak to her or ignore her presence and simply return to his own office – either of these actions were equally probable.

Eventually, Derringham's brow cleared and he turned to her. 'Agatha, the young police officer requires the following information – I assured him you would certainly have something tucked away that will assuage his rather strange curiosity.'

He handed her the notes he had taken in the meeting, then appeared to have a second thought.

'And when you've completed that, dig out whatever you have on file for Julia Metcalfe.'

'96

He watched the boy's back arch and smiled at the muffled scream as the needle pierced the scrotum. Every muscle in the boy's body tensed as he pushed the needle further in – searching out the epididymis – and there was a higher, although still muffled, scream when he found his target. Deciding to enjoy the torment a little longer he left the syringe where it was and casually checked the bonds tying the boy's wrists behind his back and the rope that led from there to his ankles. They were, of course, very tight. The boy was sobbing now, in fear and confusion. He could feel the wracking sobs shaking the body beneath him.

Before he began the work he needed to do, he took a look at the young, very lean and track-marked body lying tethered on the damp, mucky concrete of this disused builder's yard. The boy was young, maybe 20, and would probably be called handsome – although his judgement on such matters was poor. It had been easy to get him there; he was a rent boy after all and like most rent boys and prostitutes he was already desperate for his next hit so any 'trick' would do. It also meant there was no faff in getting the boy undressed – he had done that for himself as soon as they were out of the car. He was, after all, expecting sex.

He hated that part most of all – the pick-up and drive to wherever he knew would be secluded and safe, the feigned interest in the young man's body and the talk of what he would 'like'. Homosexuality disgusted him, had done since childhood. He had heard his father's sermons enough times, in and out of church, for it to be quite literally beaten into him.

But this was essential, vital to the Quest – a necessary evil, he thought. But then there was no reason he shouldn't take at least a little enjoyment from the unsavoury task.

Leaving the syringe firmly lodged in the tissue below and behind the boy's testes, he reached for his briefcase. It looked like many, many others seen in towns and cities all over the world; a business man's briefcase, full of work to be done at home and tomorrow's important documents. But this case had no paper in it, had nothing that he would use at the office.

Using his small pocket torch, he double-checked the surgical gloves he was wearing for holes or tears. Satisfied there would be no cross contamination he returned to the task ahead.

With exaggerated caution he removed three small, glass vials from the small pockets lining the inside of the lid and placed them on the hard, cold concrete next to the boy, removing each lid as he did so.

The boy had not stopped trying to scream, sob and beg through the thick gag in his mouth and he decided he had had enough of the noise and pathetic whimpering. Lifting the cosh that he had used earlier to subdue the young man, he viciously swiped it across his ear and jaw. It shouldn't kill him but would hopefully shut him up for a bit. He didn't want him dead yet. He needed his heart to be still pumping blood, keeping the tissues and cells healthy for a little while yet.

Returning to his case he picked out another syringe and needle, both still in their sterile wrappings, and a small pair tweezers. These were placed neatly next to the vials.

Ensuring his gloves were securely on, he moved to the syringe with its needle still sticking into the boy's scrotum.

He chastised himself for playing games now, as the needle had moved during the boy's sobs and struggles. He quickly re-located his target and pushed the needle into a fresh area of the epididymis. He pulled back on the plunger, extracting the semen that this thick mass of tubes stored ready for ejaculation. Pulling the needle clear with a great deal less care than he had inserted it, he emptied the contents into one of the glass vials and closed the lid. Only a weak whimper made it out of the gag.

Whilst picking up and assembling the second syringe and needle he searched for a clear spot on the boy's legs and back. He needed an area where blood vessels were close to the surface but not destroyed by drug use. There were not many spots, the boy was clearly a heavy user. Luckily the boy was skinny and he found he could raise the vein which ran over the ankle enough to insert the needle. He extracted as much blood as he could and put this into the second vial.

Finally, he took up the tweezers and carefully pulled out a number of hairs, both pubic and head. On a whim he also pulled some hair from an armpit. Each of these were carefully placed into the third vial. All three vials were then quickly but carefully placed back into their respective pockets. The syringes were dropped into a plastic bio-hazard tub he had purloined from a local hospital – ready to be thrown into the incineration bin back at the same hospital. Pulling an anti-bacterial wipe from the pack sitting next to his box of gloves, he wiped down the tweezers and secured them in their appropriate place in the case. He snapped the case shut and secured the locks with all the verve of a CEO concluding a very lucrative deal.

Leaving the boy for a moment, he returned to his car. Once the case was safely stowed in the boot, he lifted the carpet near the spare wheel and pulled out a large kitchen knife, recently purchased from Woolworths. He also picked up a large brown paper bag and a pair of comfortable-looking brogues.

Closing the boot, he returned to the prone, quietly groaning body of the young man.

He killed him cleanly and quickly. There was no ritual required here, no message or markings were needed.

Turning the body over he grabbed it roughly under the shoulders and hauled it across the short piece of waste ground that separated the builder's yard from the River Tyne. The river was pretty deep here but still held a reasonable current. Finding weights for the body had been easy, there were plenty of bricks and other heavy objects left lying around. He pushed the boy's body out as far as he could using a long, rusted pole he'd found in the scrub, and watched as the young man – whose name he had never known but who he would offer a little word of thanks to at some point in the future – sank below the dark waters. With any luck he'd never be found. If he was, there would be scant evidence left on the body. Either way, he knew he would be the last person on the list of the Northumbria Police Force. The knife was thrown as far out as he could manage.

Finally returning to his car, he removed the overalls and cheap trainers he'd been wearing, revealing the very smart suit below, and placed them into the paper bag with the needles, to go into the hospital incineration bin.

Having slipped on his brogues and then dropped the bag in the passenger footwell, he made his way around the front of the car, straightening his tie and whistling quietly to himself.

Chapter Seven

Malcolm Tanner adjusted his shirt cuffs as he strode down the stairs to the main entrance of the station. His 'guest' had arrived and he was keen to get this meeting over with. It wasn't that he had dismissed what the Belgian detective had had to say during their phone call earlier that day, but frankly – why they had to meet, on her insistence, he had no idea. He could have said all he needed to say over the phone, although he realised that he also hated his phone, but still! Pearson had said it would be for the good that they meet – cross-continental co-operation and all that.

Opening the security-coded door, he caught his first sight of Jacqueline Montreux, Inspector Principle of the Belgian Federal Police. She was tall and slim with an athletic look about her. Her shoulder-length, brown hair was neat but not showy or overly styled, and her trouser suit matched it with its tidy, business-like look. Her eyes were made larger by the thick glasses she wore.

'Inspector Montreux? Malcolm Tanner, it's a pleasure to meet you.' Tanner said.

'Detective Chief Inspector Tanner, the pleasure is mine.' Her voice was soft with the lilting French accent he had been struck by previously over the phone. It was a pleasant voice and yet it had a professional steel to its undertone.

'I have to say, Inspector Montreux, I am still surprised you wanted to come all this way to discuss what, to us at least, is a very old, albeit unsolved case. There has been some recent activity but very little, although I appreciate you feel there are similarities with a much more current one of your own.'

'Please, Chief Inspector, call me Jacqueline. But no, it is not so far. There are many flights from Brussels that take only a few hours. I stayed in a pleasant hotel last night and will fly back tonight – it is just as easy for us to meet face to face. And, I feel that we may be more...' She pursed her lips and frowned, searching for the right word. '... aha, productive if we can sit together and look at the evidence, yes?'

Tanner smiled. She made sense – despite his grumblings he had to admit that he found face-to-face meetings were often far more productive than telephone calls or worse still bloody emails.

'Indeed Inspector, I can't help but agree with you. Please follow me, I have one of our meeting rooms set aside so we can spread out a little and discuss the files in as much detail as necessary.'

Turning, he led her back through the security door and towards the meeting room he had booked.

After settling into the office and receiving the coffees Tanner had gruffly ordered from a passing PC, he gestured for Inspector Montreux to begin the meeting.

'Well, Chief Inspector, as I have already outlined in my email, when I began to look for cases of similarity to the killing in Leuven, I discovered five cases spreading across the last eight years. All are women between the ages of 28 and 35, four were married, one was single. They were all found in their own home, with no sign of forced entry or disturbance to the rest of the house outside of the bedroom. All were stabbed multiple times over their entire bodies. All very similar to your Charmer case. Forensics found at the scene were next to useless. It is fascinating that a connecting feature to all five cases is that the samples of hair, blood and semen that we managed to isolate as not being the victim's were all from several different people.'

84

She paused and looked pointedly at Tanner. 'I note that there is no forensic evidence mentioned in the file you sent me, Chief Inspector?'

Tanner appeared to be deep in thought, his brow furrowed and his hand absently rubbing over the shiny skin on his scalp. Eventually he looked up, nodding.

'Yes, there was an addendum at the end of the file I'll confess – I deliberately neglected to include it. It basically says that there *was* forensic evidence found at each of the scenes in The Charmer file, but it was essentially useless. It's what our science people call 'irrevocably cross-contaminated'. In other words, there are several different DNA profiles present – some male, some female – and at the time of the tests it was virtually impossible to separate them or make any real coherent sense of which strands were actually present at the scene. It was the one detail I was waiting to hear from you before I made any further decision on whether we might be looking at the same man. And, Inspector, that is starting to look like a probability we should consider.'

Inspector Montreux smiled. 'You are a very careful man, Chief Inspector. *Might, maybe*, and a *probability* that we are looking at the same man? Surely this information is the last coffin nail?'

It was Tanner's turn to smile. 'Nail in the coffin, Inspector? We say the *final* nail in the coffin. Anyway, yes, I am a very cautious man. I find it pays to be cautious, more often than charging in does. So, your forensics were the same as ours – a mixture of lots of different profiles? Have you managed to isolate any? Make any identifications from them?'

Montreux nodded. 'Yes we did. It was a woman – a prostitute. We matched the DNA as she had been arrested several times before, but more interestingly – she was reported missing several months before the killing where we found her DNA. That was three years ago now and she still hasn't been found.'

Tanner nodded slowly. 'Hmmm, yes. A few years ago, certain DNA profiling techniques had improved and other victims had been added to the file. So there was a review of all the evidence. A sample taken from semen found at one scene in Manchester turned out to be a rent boy from Newcastle – enquiries showed he hadn't been seen for several years, no one knew where he was. But the main upshot was that at the time of the killing he would have been no more than 21, way too young to fit the rest of the pattern.'

Opening the thick file on the table in front of him, Tanner pulled out the two reports he had been talking about, handing them over to Inspector Montreux.

'OK,' he resumed, after allowing her a little time to read. 'It seems to me, Inspector Montreux, that we are getting somewhere here, do you agree?'

Montreux simply nodded. She had finished skim-reading the two reports and was now reaching for her own files. As she began to remove them from her briefcase she paused and looked quizzically at Tanner.

'You said there were more victims added to the file?' she asked. 'So, you believe this man is still active in the UK?'

'Yes,' replied Tanner. 'The additional killings are more recent, but less frequent. Without solid evidence to the contrary, we have to assume it's the same killer. It could, of course, be a copycat, but we think not. One assumption for the drop in frequency was that he had been arrested for something else and had been serving time, but none of the DNA or other forensic tests matched anyone with a record. Now, the fact that your investigation has led you to our door may well mean that he switched his attention to Belgium during those periods.'

'That is a distinct possibility,' Montreux said, finally pulling her files from her case.

'So,' Tanner continued. 'It seems that our man is extremely forensically aware and, more than that, knows exactly how to flummox our boys in the lab. But more to the point, it's starting to look like our boy has more than the – what is it now? – 15 or 20 murders to his name between here and Belgium. Right, well that might give us something to work on but it'll take a lot of resources and computer hours, I suspect. So, is there anything your lot have come up with that maybe we've missed?'

Montreux was looking at him quizzically but still nodded, 'Yes, we have. But first, Chief Inspector, *flummox*?'

Tanner laughed – a full, open-mouthed and very loud guffaw. Collecting himself he explained the word to her, smiling all the while.

'Does that mean I'll have to repeat my last four or five sentences, Inspector?' he mock-reproached.

She grinned back at him. 'No, Chief Inspector, you do not. I am not quite so easily distracted as to be derailed by one word I do not understand. And please, I have said to call me Jacqueline – I grow a little tired of our respective ranks being bounced back and forward.'

Another smile from Tanner. 'No indeed, Jacqueline, and yeah Malcolm will be just fine. So?'

'Yes, we may have found something that you have not spotted. One minute while I find the relevant photographs,' she said, fishing in the files in front of her and pulling a picture from each. 'These were spotted by a particularly keen-eyed pathologist.'

Tanner took the pictures and studied them closely. Each showed a close-up of the inner thigh of a woman – a melee of slashes, cuts and stabs covered what looked like the whole area on view. If someone hadn't circled an area in red pen, he would never have spotted anything that particularly stood out. Even with the circles he still wasn't sure what he was looking at, and he indicated as much with a look at Montreux.

She was quick to respond. 'They are almost impossible to spot if you don't know what you are looking for. This particular pathologist has an unusual hobby. He enjoys visiting churches – not because he is fervently religious, but because he says he just likes the décor.' She shrugged as she said this, a very Gallic gesture as far as Tanner was concerned, then continued. 'So he is very familiar with all sorts of iconography and religious imagery, useful sometimes no?'

Tanner nodded absently, he was still staring at the photographs trying to pick out any sort of pattern in the cuts and slashes that were circled. There were certainly no crosses or obvious religious symbols there.

'You have to turn the images slightly, like so, then look here.' She pointed to a particular set of shallow cuts. 'And then look at this.'

She pulled out a further piece of paper, and on it was a printout of what looked like a stylised drawing of a tree that was on fire. The tree was reasonably intricately drawn, with a short trunk and many branches snaking up off it. The roots below were knotted around each other in a way Tanner felt he should recognise but couldn't quite place. The flames, although more stylised, were clearly just

88

that – flames. He looked at the image and back to the mortuary photos. If he concentrated, he could see – albeit more crudely – something similar in the cuts. Montreux was right, it was almost impossible to spot.

'It is, apparently,' Montreux continued, 'a fairly common symbol of Protestant churches and particularly of the Presbyterian Church. It's called the burning bush. Our pathologist had visited the church of St Andrew in Brussels and remembered the design he had seen on a tabard cloth draped over a lectern.'

'So, he might be Scottish?' Tanner asked, plundering his very limited knowledge of churches and church organisation. Then the thought occurred to him – Travers is Scottish, isn't he?

'Not necessarily, I am afraid. When this was noticed, background research was of course completed and it would appear that Presbyterianism is, if not prevalent, then at least common around the world, from New Zealand to Europe and even Africa and India. Having said that, yes, the majority of Presbyterians are to be found in Scotland.'

'Great,' was all Tanner could think of to say. It was like trying to pick up water from a pond, he thought – thinking you were gaining something, getting just a little closer to at least a profile or something tangible and then it all just slid through your fingers, back into the pond, joining a myriad of possibilities and potentials, none of which were useful or even tightened the search parameters.

He sighed and rubbed the top of his head, looking off to one side of the room. He stayed like that for some time then looked back at Montreux.

'So,' he said slowly and carefully. 'We could be looking at a religious motive or someone related to or working in the church. Probably the Presbyterian church.'

He thought again of the Travers investigation – did Travers have any connection to the Presbyterian Church? He didn't know but made a mental note to ask Handley when he saw him. And if Handley didn't know he would kick his arse back out the door to go find out.

'Yes, that would seem a good avenue to follow.' Montreux nodded her head in a very definite affirmative.

'Right,' he said, a decisive note to his voice. 'I'll get my lot to take another look at the PM photos from The Charmer files – may I keep this printout?' He indicated the picture of the burning bush and Montreux nodded. 'It could also be useful if our respective labs take a joint look at all the forensics found both here and in Belgium. There might be DNA or hair or something that matches in all cases that might still not help – it's likely they'll be from some poor sap that's missing, presumed dead – but it might just be that one matching strand could be our man. At the very least, if there are matching sequences then we can say it's highly likely they were put there by the same person.'

'Agreed,' Montreux stated assertively. 'Can I suggest that we set up links between the two teams, here and in Belgium? I am fairly sure I can persuade my finance department that I now need some resources to hunt this man.'

'Yes, good call,' Tanner replied. 'I'm also pretty sure my boss'll be releasing some funds my way too so there should actually be 'a team' in place when you're ready.' Even if that team consists of just me and Handley, he thought, but didn't say.

Tanner paused for a moment, thinking, then said, 'I'm beginning to think we need someone in to help profile this guy, although I'm pretty sure it was done first time around. But, I'm wondering if this new information and a fresh pair of eyes might not be a bad thing. Have you had anyone look over the files in that way?'

'In a way,' Montreux said, 'unlike the Americans, we don't have an FBI to take on such tasks, but we do have a number of officers trained in criminal psychology. They have come to the conclusion that the man we are looking for is very likely from the UK, and that you have possibly already encountered him, maybe even interviewed him in the course of your enquiries.'

Tanner raised an eyebrow. 'Why do they think that?' he asked.

'Because of the pattern – there were no such crimes in Belgium until much more recently. It is possible he has switched his locale as he felt you were if not close then at least now aware of him.'

'Hmmm, yes, that would make sense,' Tanner replied. Travers again, he thought but instead said 'What else did they come up with?'

'Not much else, really. They, like you now, see a religious element. Maybe he believes he is on a mission from God or perhaps holds a grudge against the church and wishes for them to be blamed. Besides this there appears to be no connection between the victims, apart from being reasonably well educated and comparatively affluent.' Montreux finished her sentence with that Gallic shrug Tanner had noticed earlier.

Tanner sat for a few moments, slowly nodding his head and pursing his lips.

'We may have someone that fits at least one part of that bill, in that he has been questioned before on the subject of The Charmer, albeit in a very minor way and from a bit of a dead end line of enquiry. However, it is interesting that your psychology guys have made that observation. We are currently looking for him, and whilst we're not considering him a definite suspect at this stage, we are keen to speak to him.'

'You·cannot find this man?' Montreux asked.

'No, he disappeared a few months ago. That was why his name came up in connection with all of this – we were initially just investigating his disappearance then a connection was made, but again I say it's a fairly tenuous one at the moment.'

'I see,' Montreux said. 'I wonder, Malcolm, do you have this man's DNA on file? That might help either implicate or exonerate him.'

'No, this man is a civil servant with no previous police contact. He would be considered a pretty upright, well-to-do citizen.'

'You have access to his house?' Montreux asked, a small frown creasing her brow.

'Yes, of course, we have been liaising with his wife regularly and the officer assigned to the case has been there on several occasions, as well as our Family Liaison officer.'

'Then you could, perhaps, with his wife's permission, see if you can find something that your laboratory could extract DNA from? Perhaps a hair sample from a comb?' The small frown stayed in place as Montreux spoke.

'That is a good suggestion, Jacqueline ...' A small, half smile appeared on Tanner's lips. 'Sneaky maybe, but good all the same. We could present it as an exercise in elimination, or in order to ensure any bodies found are not Marcus Travers.'

Montreux returned his smile with a much brighter one of her own. 'A-ha,' she laughed. 'I was wondering if you were going to give me a name. I can have a search done to see if this man has been in Belgium of late.'

'Yes, you could,' replied Tanner, 'but, let's see if anything comes of the forensics first before we go chasing around Europe for a someone who turns out to be simply a *mis per.*'

Montreux accepted this with a nod.

Suddenly, Tanner brought his hand down sharply on top of the files, making Montreux jump a little.

'Now Jacqueline, I think it's time I bought you lunch,' he said with a broad smile.

Montreux smiled and stood. 'That, Malcolm, is the best idea of the morning.'

With an extended arm and an exaggerated bow, he led her out of the station and down the street towards his favourite pub.

'86

He realised she was inviting him to bed and the usual panic swept over him. She was lovely, slim but with curves in all the right places. How could he turn her down without it seeming a monumental snub? More panic now as he realised he would have to say something to either put things off completely or to buy himself some time to gather his shredded nerves.

It wasn't that he was unwilling or, heaven forfend, unable. He was simply terrified that at the crucial moment everything would flood back to him and his only option would be to run, either that or face crushing – never to be recovered from – humiliation. And there was no way he would face that again.

His mind drifted back to his 16-year-old self and the fear, the embarrassment but above all the humiliation he had felt when *she* had laughed at him. The memory burned, crystal clear in his mind, and even now – six years later – left him seething with shame.

He could not, would not, put himself through that again. He wasn't sure what he would do if he faced such a scenario, if a woman laughed at him again the way *she* had. Would he simply burn again and walk away head down? Or would his rage take over, making him do something stupid? Or would the depression he would feel afterwards lead to him becoming yet another young man to take his own life?

No, he wasn't willing to take the risk.

She was talking to him again, flirting maybe. He hadn't heard anything she'd said, hadn't been listening at all. She touched his arm sending a shiver down his spine, was that pleasure or fear? Or something else entirely? He wasn't sure. What he was sure about was that he had to leave, had to get out and be away from her, these people, this party.

Then an escape came to him. He would feign illness, a sudden feeling of nausea, stomach cramps or perhaps just a general feeling of being unwell.

He turned to her and tried to arrange his face in such a way that conveyed illness but at the same time utter disappointment at having to miss out on what would have been really fun.

'I'm so sorry Nancy. I would dearly love to come back to your place, but I'm feeling rather unwell all of a sudden. I think I should just go home, maybe get some fresh air on the way. I hope you can forgive me?' He smiled at her as he said this and raised his hand to cup her cheek.

'Oh,' she replied, confused by this sudden turn of events. 'Oh, you poor thing.' She pressed the back of her hand to his forehead, frowning a little. 'Well look, why don't I walk with you, I'd be as happy at yours as mine. I could put on a nurse's outfit and take care of you?' she said with a wicked grin.

He laughed, remembering to make it sound a little weakened. 'Well, that is very tempting. But no, look I'm a terrible patient and, frankly, I just want to curl up in bed right now. I'll be fine tomorrow I'm sure – I'll call you or something then. And it's such a good party, I'd hate for you to miss it in order to suffer my grumblings.'

In order to curtail any more argument, he kissed her gently on the mouth, enjoying the sweet taste of her lips and the scent rising from her neck. His anxiety and fear rose to another level. He had to leave. Many of his long-held thoughts and fantasies were surfacing. She was too much – and this was now dangerous territory.

He caressed her cheek, smiled and made for the door without another word. He didn't turn to look back until he was outside the tenement block, then allowed himself a last baleful look up at the second-floor window – still emanating the lights and sounds of the party that carried on without him – and the thoughts and feelings that were now screaming in his mind.

He reached his own flat, a comfortable but small one-bedder in Edinburgh's New Town, having kept his mind as blank as he could throughout his walk. Thoughts would occasionally intrude but with a furious self-restraint – that meant he all but ignored road crossings and passers-by whom he barged into at regular intervals – he managed to suppress them. He was acutely aware that this made him appear, by the various comments he heard, either a 'fucking arrogant cunt', 'a fucking student wanker' or 'a posh tosser'.

As he was sitting, reclined on the leather sofa in his living room, he considered these insults and the evening's events.

Was he any of the descriptions he'd just heard? No, he most certainly was not. Whilst aspects were true – he was a student and he could be arrogant – he was not 'posh' or 'a cunt' and certainly not a 'wanker'. But then, did the opinion of everyday, low-intelligence nobodies really matter to the likes of him? Again, no, they did not.

Was he different? Above the general mass of humanity? Yes, he absolutely believed that he was.

Did he care what they or anybody else thought? Or felt? No, he absolutely did not.

So, what did he care about? That was an interesting question with an equally interesting and complex answer.

What he cared about was stopping the feelings of shame and embarrassment he had felt earlier that evening and for all of his young adult life. What he cared about was having something akin to intimate relations with a woman. Specifically, he wanted intimate relations with *her*, although he knew that was a distant and unobtainable dream. What he cared about was being free from his past and free from the crippling thoughts that plagued his dreams.

And again, it came back to *her*. He could not excise *her* from his mind or psyche. *She* loomed large whenever he came close to any form of actual sexual contact. He could kiss a girl, that was fine, he could stroke her arm or even her neck, but beyond that *she* reared *her* beautiful, angelic, innocent head.

And then *she* laughed.

And then, unbidden, the thoughts he'd been avoiding all evening – at the party, after the party and indeed during every sleepless night for close to six years – raised their ugly head. They disturbed him and yet at the same time elated him. They took him somewhere he felt he could never go – although if ever questioned he was not sure why he felt he couldn't go there. They transported him to a place where *she* was laid to rest. Where *she* – hah! – was put to bed. Sent away with a finality that meant he could rest, relax and maybe even forgive.

Could he forgive *her*?

Did he have the capacity – the level of projection and feeling, the required forethought to see *her* as *she* would be now? Could he bring himself to talk to *her*, try to explain, maybe even allow *her* to explain? Was there an ounce of forgiveness left in him that would allow him to simply let go and end his nightmare?

And the answer boomed in his mind.

NO.

No – there was no forgiveness, no reconciliation and no rest until *she* was expunged entirely.

She would pay.

There were, of course, others. She was not the sole reason for this, not the whole story. There were his father and mother, whom he couldn't bring himself to think of as his parents. Parents loved and nurtured their children. Parents cared for their welfare and worried over their future wellbeing. Parents hoped that their children would become well-rounded, happy and capable of making their way in society. But, not his…. not his…. begetters. They would pay thrice-fold, they would pay in tears and shame and doubt – exactly as they had poured it, unrelentingly, on him.

His hatred and anger rose to a pitch he had never experienced before. Yes, those three would pay and suffer and *feel* what he was now feeling. He would wipe them from the Earth, and he would cleanse his soul with their suffering.

And then the final piece fell into place. They would burn, yes – but burn with guilt and horror at the suffering of *others*. There would be proxies. They would take *her* place and when they did, they would feel all of his torment. He would Deliver them up. They, these others, would be the sacrificial lambs which would cleanse his soul.

And he would not rest until he had Delivered the ultimate image of *her* … and Delivered it in a way that his pathetic, cruel and deluded begetters would recognise as their own. He would make sure that they knew, understood and then felt the same shame, guilt and humiliation. He would score this into the very thing he could not bring himself to touch, the very flesh of woman.

He would carve it into them all.

AND THEY WOULD ALL BURN.

That night in his dreams *her* laugh was crueller and more mocking than it had ever been. He woke to it ringing in his ears and knew that unless he acted, *she* would never stop.

Chapter Eight

Fran Pearson was sitting at his desk, an untouched report in front of him, lost in thoughts from many years ago. As he accrued his years in the force, he had become proud of his ability to disassociate from the cases he worked on, the aftermaths of vicious crimes he had witnessed, the victims and the predators, the lambs and the jackals that – given the slightest chance – would devour them. He was bothered by them at the time of course, who could feel nothing when faced with the dead face of an innocent young girl, who by chance was in the wrong place at the wrong time? Who could not feel hate for the man that had killed her?

But despite all this, Pearson didn't carry that hate or remorse or guilt along the way with him. He knew intrinsically that he would do his best for every victim, he would work their case until there was simply nothing left that could be done. And then, if no one was apprehended, if they could not find the man or woman responsible, he would file the details away in a part of his mind set aside especially for those 'unsolveds'. And, if anything ever came up that sparked one of those memories then woe betide the person who had done the sparking!

Still, it allowed him to move on and not be weighed down by all those files, all those memories, all those ghosts.

Except one.

The Charmer.

He hated the name, had hated it when it was coined. It made this monster, this cold and calculating psychopath, sound like a roguish Lesley Phillips type character – getting into scrapes and capers but never really meaning any harm. That was most certainly not The Charmer. Pearson himself had seen the results of this man's 'charm'. The women ripped and torn on their beds, the cold and calculated way he covered his tracks, the casual disregard for human life. Not just the lives of the women he killed but the lives of those they had touched, those who had loved them and in a number of cases had relied on them for care and safety and life. He knew of one young girl whose mother had been an early victim, and at the tender age of 14 – unable to live with knowing the nature of her mother's killing and that she was in the house at the time (all be it as a babe in arms) – had taken her own life. That victim, the one The Charmer probably knew nothing of, that was the one Fran Pearson was determined to get him for. It was the death of that young girl that he would nail through the heart of that bastard.

When he found him.

If he found him.

It hadn't weighed on him for some time now, day-to-day monotony had taken care of that, but now it had reared its ugly head again. When the old reports and case files were brought back up to his desk, he dusted off the front covers along with all the old thoughts and feelings in his mind.

If he found him.

He had been proud of being astute enough to go looking for similar killings to the London ones he had attended. Had felt elated when specific searches had resulted in cases in Manchester, Birmingham, Southampton, Edinburgh and York all having a high probability of being a series of crimes committed by the same man. Had been even prouder when he was asked to head up the nation-spanning team being put together to hunt this man down. The teams would all remain in their respective areas but would report all findings to him and his team. He was to lead one of the biggest manhunts in the history of policing. It earned him a promotion from DCI to Detective Superintendent.

And yet, all those people, all those teams, all that information hadn't got them anywhere near the man responsible. Early apparent breakthroughs, forensic and otherwise, had all turned into red herrings left by the killer or had simply turned to dust under closer inspection.

He always suspected that his much slower climb to Detective Chief Superintendent was because of his failure to capture this man or even get close to who and where he was.

Now he had a chance to lay to rest his only demon. The one ugly, deformed excuse for a human being that he knew would haunt his every waking and sleeping hour, for the rest of his days, unless he took this second chance.

If he failed this time, he hated to think what he would do.

If he failed this time, he knew that would be the end of his policing career; he couldn't continue in the job if he failed again and would never be able to look himself in the mirror and convince himself he was up to the job.

With a faraway look still in his eyes, he shut down his computer, pulled on his jacket and slipped quietly out the building.

'18

Recollections

She remembered how the months following Melissa's arrival had probably been the hardest and happiest of their lives. Neither of them came from big families or had any experience of babies and their needs and demands. Night after night of next to no sleep, spending hours trying to work out what she was screaming about – was she hungry, cold, needing a nappy change or simply awake and wanting her parent's attention? And those times when one of them thought they had worked out the reasons and settled her down, only to despair when – as they crept back to bed – she had started to wail again.

But they had both adored her, doted on her and smothered her in love. She was to their eyes the most beautiful child in the world and they had talked about how, when they looked at her, they both felt their life was now replete. Marcus had at all times carried his share of parental duties, regardless of whether his work demanded he needed to rise early. He had organised it so that he wouldn't have to travel or be away for more than two days at a stretch, during the first six months of Melissa's life. Often, in the middle of the night, she found he was already rising from bed as she awoke to the familiar sound of the baby crying. Every evening, when he returned from work, he would immediately take the baby from her and tell her to go rest and relax and that he would take care of things for the next few hours.

She laughed aloud when she remembered the first time he had had to change a particularly full and pungent nappy, how he had gagged and coughed his way through the whole thing. And when eventually he sat back from the changing mat, proud at having survived the whole horrendous ordeal, his look of dismay on realising he had put the nappy on back to front. Then his look of resigned horror as Melissa had promptly filled the new nappy and he had to gag his way through the whole procedure anew. But he never shied from changing her, even after that particular ordeal.

Charlotte's love for Marcus had grown every time she saw him with Melissa. When he had cradled her in his arms, she looked so small and vulnerable whilst he had looked so huge and strong and protective and at the same time gentle and adoring. She saw a fierce protectiveness in him and realised it was part of the love a father showed his child, that he would kill or be killed in order to keep her safe, and her heart melted every time she saw it.

He had been the same when Callum had eventually come along – every inch the attentive, loving father, all the while ensuring that Melissa never lacked for attention or love.

As she thought about this period of their lives, she realised that all their attention had been directed towards the children and not each other. It was strange that whilst in many ways they had seemed closer than ever before they were also slowly drifting apart. Their conversations, once long and rambling, had become short and perfunctory, mainly centred around the children or the requirements of the house and their day-to-day lives. Sex, when it occurred, was utilitarian, simply serving a basic need and not forging bonds or living up to the tag of making love.

Maybe that was when it had started – whatever 'it' was. Had that been when he had finally drifted away, when he had started the affair, if affair it was, with this Julia? Or had it begun much, much earlier than that? Had Marcus simply not found the way or the courage to end their marriage before it was too late and they had had children? And had he only stayed after that because of them?

How could she reconcile the images and feelings associated with this man that she loved – and that she had also watched love their children – with a man she now believed had been lying to her, for God-only-knew how long?

As with all her recent recollections, she had become resigned to their bittersweet nature and the love and betrayal that surfaced with every one – that toxic mixture that formed in her mind whenever she tried to recall Marcus and the way they had been, the way she had thought they were still.

They were a blessing, though, these mixed feelings. They were driving her on to find that point in time, the very moment it had all gone wrong: the month, the week, the day or – if necessary – the second it had all changed, when Marcus had gone from being hers to someone else's, or when his life had changed so irreconcilably that he had to leave and run. Then she felt she might know, through this process and through using her insight and intelligence, she might know the answer to the most important question of all. She would know the reason why.

Chapter Nine

Handley sat looking at his screen without taking anything in. This, it seemed, had become his default work position of the last few weeks. Seemingly getting somewhere, in reality getting nowhere. Cycling round the same problems, orbiting around a cluster of assumptions and probabilities but never getting any closer to the answers. They were still no further in finding Marcus Travers. Julia was equally elusive – more so, in fact, as they didn't even have a surname for her. The re-investigation into the Charmer also appeared to be stalling with, as yet, no forensic or profile coming up with anything that might help find the man, even after the new light shed by their Belgian colleagues.

Then all the unanswered questions came back to mind: was Marcus Travers the killer, or was he running scared, having been complicit in some way? Or was all of this a blind alley, nothing whatsoever to do with the Charmer? Was Marcus Travers simply a man who, for whatever reason, had had enough and walked out on his life?

And then there was the Charmer himself – why suddenly appear in Belgium, if indeed he had? Just what sort of man were they looking for? Clearly very intelligent, forensically aware and always, always a non-entity. None of the re-tested DNA, blood, hair or fibre samples had thrown up anything new. Those that had been identified in the past had been removed in the hope that their man had been arrested for something else since, but none of the remaining samples had matched anyone on the database. Some of these samples matched each other but not all, so again it was impossible to pinpoint a profile that could be placed at every scene. And even if there were a single matching profile in all cases, there was still the possibility that this wasn't their killer but just another planted red herring.

Given the mismatch of forensic evidence, the latest theory was that the killer didn't appear to ejaculate when he killed. This explained why semen samples didn't match – they were all from different people. He may, of course, have used a condom or avoided ejaculating onto or inside his victims, enabling him to clean away any usable evidence.

There was also the fact that he made sure, as much as was possible, that he removed his own hair from the scene before replacing it with hair from other people – or perhaps he wore overalls similar to those worn by SOCO, ensuring no hair contaminated the scene. Hours had been spent comparing hair samples found at the different scenes; some matched in a number of cases but without a suspect to compare the matching samples to they had nothing.

They couldn't even pinpoint a locale for him. The killings were so diverse in location – Belgium, for Christ's sake – that there was no identifiable locus. He could be anywhere in the country or, now, abroad, anywhere in the rest of Europe. In fact, that was the one thing they knew – he could travel extensively and not rouse suspicion. But then countless hours spent by tens of officers trawling the obvious occupations – reps, lorry drivers et al – had drawn a total blank. Not that anyone expected a Ripper-style, freak arrest when a car is stopped for a minor misdemeanour and suddenly a plethora of evidence emerges.

This, Handley knew, had been why it had taken so long in the first place to identify that they were indeed looking for one killer. The murders had been so far apart that each force worked the cases as isolated incidents, perpetrated by a local – there had been no obvious pattern and no recurrence in any given area. It was only when the then DI Pearson spotted a link between two and then three cases that had taken place in and around London that any links were even considered.

Handley, like his boss and his Detective Superintendent above him, was at a total loss. They couldn't trace the killer without evidence but they wouldn't have any evidence until they traced the killer – a Gordian knot, one that didn't allow them to use scissors to solve.

He realised with a start that his phone was ringing and probably had been for a while. He snatched up the receiver.

'DC Handley,' he said, summoning the best impersonation he could of someone who was hard at work, someone who hadn't – until that moment – been sitting apparently idly worrying over problems they couldn't solve.

'Ah, DC Handley, so glad I've caught you. It's Frederick.'

Handley sat for a second, eyes wide – the expression on his face the universal one made by every human on the planet desperately trying to identify a voice on the other end of the line – as he thought, 'Frederick? Frederick? Do I know a Frederick?'

Three seconds of silence were stopped when the person at the other end of the line qualified, 'Frederick Derringham,' and then the voice, tone and intonation all clicked into place.

'Oh, Sir Frederick ...' Handley found himself sitting up straighter in his chair and clearing his throat. 'Um, it's good to hear from you. How can I help?'

'Well, old chap, it's more how I can help you.' Sir Frederick sounded somewhat smug and a little triumphant. 'Firstly, however, an apology, it has taken Agatha a little longer to gather the information you requested but I am pleased to say I shall be emailing it to you forthwith. I hope the delay hasn't been too inconvenient?'

'Not at all Sir Frederick, I'm very grateful for your organising it. I realised I was asking a lot, so to be honest, I wasn't expecting it so soon.'

Handley tried to keep his voice even, conveying a laissez-faire attitude to his desire for that information, while his hand was already moving the mouse to open his email in anticipation.

'Very gracious of you DC Handley, I must say. Anyway, you shall have it, as I say, imminently. However, that is not the primary reason for my call.' Sir Frederick was clearly enjoying his moment of revelation and Handley stayed silent, allowing for the inevitable dramatic pause.

'I may have found your Julia,' Sir Frederick continued.

Handley sat forward now, his hands automatically grabbing his pen and pulling his notepad over.

'Really? That's excellent news, Sir Frederick, please tell me what you know.' Handley was struggling to keep the excitement from his voice but a large slice of urgency still made its way into his tone.

'Well, this may not be who you are looking for, but, on more than one occasion Marcus appears to have signed in a Julia Metcalfe. As far as I know she is an investigative journalist, but I have to confess – I have never fully understood what that is, or indeed, how they manage to make any sort of living as such. Anyway, I have nothing to explain why she should be meeting Marcus but I thought the name was too much of a coincidence to not mention it.'

Handley was silent for a moment as he jotted down her name and wrote several question marks after it.

When he did speak it was in a calmer manner than before. 'Thank you, Sir Frederick, that could prove to be extremely useful. Could you tell me – how many times did Mr Travers sign her in? And when was the last time he did so? Also, any other information he might have given?'

Sir Frederick gave a short, barking laugh. 'I'm one step ahead of your questions, Detective, I have it all here. Marcus last signed her in nearly six months ago. Prior to that she was here three times – on each occasion he listed the reason for her visit as 'research' and then added 'The Guardian' but without any further explanation.'

Handley scribbled down this information. His mind must have wandered as he processed this information on Julia, as he suddenly realised Sir Frederick was still speaking. He felt his cheeks redden as he lied to the senior civil servant, pretending that for some reason the line had broken up a little (entirely unlikely these days, he thought, unless Sir Frederick was in Mozambique using an old Nokia via satellite and standing precisely in said satellite's only black spot) and would he kindly repeat what he had just said.

Sir Frederick's voice dripped with indulgent patience as he replied, 'Technology is still flawed, DC Handley, no need to apologise. I was simply saying I took the liberty of calling on an old friend at The Grauniad ...' He chuckled at the use of the old nickname for the newspaper. 'And he told me that Julia Metcalfe was indeed a freelance reporter for them, but whatever she might have been working on at that time, it didn't involve them or the Foreign Office. And,

110

perhaps of more interest to you, they haven't heard from her in several months now.'

Handley sat very still for a moment, trying to calm the rush of thoughts going through his mind. Julia Metcalfe, if indeed it was the Julia they were looking for, had disappeared at the same time as Marcus Travers. But where to and how were still complete unknowns. And the biggest question was still – why had they disappeared? More questions with no answers. He gave himself a beat to halt the flow of questioning in his mind.

'That, Sir Frederick,' he said, slowly and quietly, 'is extremely interesting – thank you very much for bringing it all to my attention. Could you send me the details of your friend at The Grau… er, The Guardian, in case I need to ask further questions? I would like to follow this up straight away. Is there anything else you can tell me?'

'No, no that's all I can tell you DC Handley, but I sincerely hope it is of use. I am so very worried for Marcus, especially now there appears to be a great deal of interest from you chaps. I do hope you can find him hale and hearty, and soon. I'll put my friend's details at the bottom of my email if that's acceptable? Now, I'm afraid duty calls. Please let me know of any news on Marcus and rest assured I will be in touch if there is anything else that springs to mind. Goodbye.'

Before Handley could respond in kind or thank him, Sir Frederick had put the phone down. He continued to breathe slowly and calmly for a few minutes, mentally treading water, allowing his mind to absorb the extra oxygen and start actually doing some work.

So, Julia Metcalfe was some form of investigative journalist. He now knew her surname and that she had in the past worked for The Guardian. Plenty to go on there, he thought.

A number of questions immediately sprang into his mind. What had she been working on that appeared to involve Marcus Travers? Was it actually related to The Charmer case or were they all simply jumping to false conclusions? It was, after all, still possible and even probable that they *were* having an affair and had simply run off together. This would explain the secrecy and deceptions and why Marcus had tucked those notes from her so carefully away?

These questions led undeniably to a simple and obvious conclusion: they still knew next to nothing about the relationship or dealings between Julia Metcalfe and Marcus Travers. They had the notes she had sent and these certainly suggested that he had at least replied, but more likely was that they had met and discussed whatever she was working on and that this had happened more than once. However, they could equally be read as notes from a mistress determined that he leave his wife and family for her, and again that they had met on more than one occasion to talk this through.

And now he knew she had visited the Foreign Office on at least four occasions, which would, to Handley's mind, suggest that it wasn't a relationship of the illicit, romantic type. It seemed very unlikely Marcus would tolerate his secret lover coming in to his place of work. It felt too indiscreet, too open, after all they could have simply met for lunch outside the office. Handley smiled as it occurred to him that the Foreign Office, during the day at least, was not somewhere you could easily invite a lover to then sneak into the nearest broom cupboard for a quickie. And what's more, Marcus Travers simply didn't fit the type who would do so.

With the scant evidence available to him, Handley had to conclude it seemed more likely that their relationship was platonic – based on something Julia had been working on or was interested in or had come across during the course of some sort of investigation.

He mulled this over for a while then decided on a course of action. First on the list was to find out as much as possible about Julia Metcalfe, which meant checking the electoral register, DVLA records, land registry and the PNC. Then, a visit to The Guardian, to see what they knew of her work and what she was generally interested in and might therefore have been working on. This, in turn, might tell him something more about the connection between her and Marcus Travers.

Feeling better for having a clear plan of action, he jotted down what he intended to do. He would have to run all this by the boss and felt more prepared to do so if he had written it all down while clear in his mind.

As he rose to leave his desk and find DCI Tanner his email chimed. He glanced quickly at the sender, keen to be getting on, and saw it was from Sir Frederick. He sat back down and opened it. There was a Word document attached, the email simply saying 'Hope this is what you needed, F.' Sir Frederick's details were embedded below, under which were the details of his contact at The Guardian, clearly added after their conversation.

For a second or two Handley considered leaving the email until after he had instigated his searches into Julia Metcalfe, but his self-preservation instinct kicked in. Malcolm Tanner would hang him by the balls if this were really important and he had neglected it for something else – so he sat back down and opened the attachment.

It was immaculately laid out and contained a number of inserted Excel sheets with various notes underneath each one – the whole document was clearly Agatha's work. The first of these tables was entitled 'Assigned engagements requiring overnight stays'. Handley wondered about the meaning of this heading, especially the word 'Assigned'. Wouldn't Marcus have all his appointments assigned to him by his superior? Scanning to the next heading, 'Instigated engagements requiring overnight stays', it became clear that Marcus had more autonomy than Handley had thought. He chastised himself for somewhat naively ascribing his own lack of autonomy to Marcus Travers' position at the Foreign Office. Marcus could, it would seem, simply inform the office that he would be away on business directly associated with his work – presumably, although not necessarily, with clearance from Sir Frederick. Handley added this to his to-do list and wrote 'check with Derringham' next to it. Then there were credit card transactions and expenses claims and finally absences, which Handley took to mean sickness and such like.

Each spreadsheet was very long and contained a lot of information. Handley's shoulders sagged as he realised he would be sitting for hours, trawling through all of this data. Still unsure what should take priority, he decided to print out the document and – whilst it was printing – find the DCI and defer that decision to him.

As he hit the print button it occurred to him that he may as well print the relevant lists of dates, times and places that the new information would need to be checked against. He went to the appropriate folder on his desktop and opened the file containing the list of murders attributed to the Charmer. He was about to hit print when one of the dates on this list caught his eye. Frowning, he clicked back to the Foreign Office list.

He doubled-checked twice, then checked another date on the two lists, again twice. He knew he would still have to go through every entry on the spreadsheets but, with a smile that veered between self-satisfied and grim, he now knew exactly what should take priority.

'10

Brussels ... a place he found both interesting and boring in equal measure. Boring because work – copious, tedious amounts of work – was never far away when he was there. He was, after all, only meant to be in Brussels when he was working. Interesting because all sorts of new opportunities to further the Quest presented themselves, as they would again very soon if all went to plan.

He was in the foyer of a moderately expensive hotel, not far from Grand Place and Gare du Nord station. The official reason for him being there was to attend a function hosted by an NGO promoting business links between various elements of the technology market across Europe. He was attending in order to represent the British Government and its concerns. He had already spotted a number of contemporaries from other nations, most notably the representative for the German government. He fervently hoped that they had not spotted him.

The unofficial reason he had agreed to come was the lovely, young lady sitting not far away in the bar area. He had come across her a couple of times in recent days, always looking a little like an outsider, lost and unsure how to gain access to the clique she needed to join. He recalled that feeling from his own past. These days he was always confident and often the centre of attention; he hadn't felt like an outsider for more than 25 years now.

His interest in her had been piqued immediately – she was so similar in looks and manner that his insides had leapt. He knew immediately that he could not let her slip through his grasp. He had made some discreet enquiries as to her name and position, where she was likely to be over the next week, which seminars, which shindigs and meet-and-greets, and slowly discovered all he needed to know.

Her name was Adele and she was an independent PR consultant based in Brussels. She was just making in-roads into the IT and technology industries and was trying to pick up contacts during this week-long conference and networking event. She was intelligent, erudite and most importantly unattached, romantically, as far as anyone knew. Perfect, he thought.

And now, in this hotel foyer, was the chance he had to meet her, to assess the likelihood of her actually being The One or close to that, at the very least. He'd already noted as he'd entered the hotel that she was sitting alone and apparently not actively seeking anyone out. There was no time to waste, he didn't want some smarmy little shit moving in before he had a chance to. He walked swiftly into the bar area, then moving to the bar itself he ensured he was standing with his back to her, precisely opposite where she was sitting. He ordered a malt and, once served, lifted the glass and turned, seemingly as though to survey the room. He allowed his eyes to wander for a few seconds and then settled them directly on her, holding his gaze until she looked up at him.

She lifted her head in the way people do when they instinctively know they are being stared at and stared straight back at him. He felt the tingle of anticipation as she did so. 'Yes, she will most certainly do,' he thought as he held her gaze. He allowed a small smile to form on his lips and creased his brow slightly as if questioning whether he knew her or not. Before she could look away, he walked over to her.

He usually found the first five minutes or so tricky, introducing himself and formulating an appropriate reason for having approached. On this occasion it was easier – he had only to say that he had seen her at a number of events but hadn't had the pleasure of encountering her at previous conferences so thought he ought to introduce himself. She, it turned out, had also spotted him and so was glad he had approached. He had spoken French whilst negotiating the introduction and it had the desired effect. She was impressed at the quality of his vocabulary and grammar, though joked that his accent needed considerable work. He joined in with her chuckles. They then switched to English – it transpired her native tongue was Flemish, so to avoid any further 'faux pas' he thought English seemed the most neutral language, which she also spoke fluently.

He gave her a false name, just to be on the safe side. One of the boons of being a civil servant and not a politician was that his name and face were not widely known outside of his sphere of influence, but he liked to minimise the risks.

After a couple more drinks and a general laugh at some of the other delegates in attendance – the nerds, boffins and others who appeared to speak a language entirely their own – they decided to move to a different bar. She lived in a suburb of Brussels called Sint-Agatha-Berchem, to the north of the city, and wanted to move somewhere a little closer to home. He knew a small bar at the north end of the city so suggested they go there. 'Two more drinks', she told him, and then she would be ready for home. With a casual air that he hoped came across as simply curious, he said, 'Do you know, I've been to most areas of Brussels at one time or another but I don't think I have ever been to Sint-Agatha-Berchem. Why don't I escort you there? If you

118

know of a local bar you like to frequent, I'll buy us a nightcap and you can tell me a little about the place.'

Smooth enough, he thought. Just the right amount of charm, interest and non-threatening language. She was definitely warming to him, he could tell, but right now he couldn't decide whether she was warming enough. Still, he had his briefcase with him so perhaps it wouldn't matter.

It took a little persuasion. She said she was tired, and had probably drunk too much, etc. etc. But eventually – with the promise of just the one drink and the pledge that he simply wanted to see her get home safely or at the very least on home turf – she relented and they headed out to find a cab.

It was getting later in the evening and being a Wednesday, the roads were fairly quiet. It took just under 20 minutes in the car. He noted the route as they went, always aware of escape routes and alternative places to pick up or call for a cab back to the city. Always careful, always planning.

When they reached their destination, it turned out to be a smallish bar situated on the corner between two streets. It was a cosy little place, typical of many little cafés to be found throughout Belgium and beyond. The barman or owner, he couldn't tell which, greeted her with a flurry of arms and a staccato, machine-gun delivery of Flemish. She returned the welcome and presumably explained that her companion was British and had very little Flemish because he immediately began to speak in slightly faltering but perfectly understandable English. He liked the place immediately, it was comfortable and homely. Shame I can never come back, he thought.

He persuaded her, with the help of their enthusiastic host, into having two more drinks, by which time she was starting to show the effects of the alcohol. Her words slurred slightly and she became more tactile and flirtatious. During these drinks, she explained that she lived just around the corner and that the area was known as 'the village' in the city – it was quiet and residential and had some pleasant green spaces. Perfect for his purposes, he thought. He decided that after he had finished, he would use Google maps to make his way through one of these parks before calling a cab.

As a third round of drinks arrived, this time unasked for, he excused himself and headed for the gents. Once safely locked in a cubicle he pulled a small vial from his inside pocket. Earlier, during one of her toilet breaks, he'd slipped it out of his case and placed it in there ready for later use. This was why he had wanted her close to home, Rohypnol acted quickly and dragging a semi-conscious woman into the back of a cab in the middle of the city would attract far too much attention. He palmed the vial and headed back out to the bar.

As he'd hoped, she decided it was her turn to visit the toilet and making sure the barman wasn't looking he slipped the drug into her drink.

He didn't always use this method to subdue his women, they were often too far from home to risk them falling unconscious on the way. He had several methods he could employ, perfected over the years. He now had them all down to a fine art. For example, he had a small cosh in his case and could quickly and precisely render a woman unconscious as soon as they were safely locked inside the front door. There were also a number of other sedatives and drugs that relaxed inhibitions and had women dropping their natural guard when with a stranger. He had realised, however, that these would be unnecessary with this one, the drink was doing most of that work for him.

Rohypnol took roughly 30 minutes to fully act on the body and render the recipient if not totally unconscious then in a state of almost complete paralysis, unable to move anything save perhaps their eyes. In the intervening time, the drug had the effect of making the user appear very inebriated. It had the added advantage of being virtually undetectable after a couple of hours in the body.

She took less than 15 minutes to succumb and begin to look as if she had had that one drink too many, the one that tipped her from tipsy to outright drunk, giving him the perfect excuse to make apologies to the barman and offer to escort her home safely. She readily agreed.

Her apartment was indeed nearby, only a five-minute walk from the bar. He had to prop her up as he unlocked first the outer door and then the one into her flat. Once inside, it took less than a minute to discover the bedroom and dump her on the bed. Moving swiftly, he went back out to the hallway and opened his briefcase. First, he removed his clothes and placed them neatly by the front door, then he donned the paper overalls that had been folded neatly in the bottom of the case, and finally pulled on his surgical gloves. He had long ago realised he didn't need to physically touch his women in order to fulfil the Quest. Once suited, he headed for the kitchen in order to find a suitable knife.

He took his time, she wasn't going to scream or fight, so he could carry out his work with quiet efficiency. He enjoyed it far more when he wasn't rushed or hindered by flailing limbs. He took satisfaction from the little grunts of pain and slight twitching of her arms and legs – she was clearly at least semi-conscious – as the knife carved The Burning Bush into her thighs.

He allowed the pace to increase over the final half an hour or so – cutting, slashing and stabbing in an ever more frenzied and brutal fashion, with each thrust of the knife delivered with more force than the last, thrashing at the flesh and hitting bone and sinew. Eventually he threw his whole body behind every stab and cut such that the blood frothed and boiled beneath him.

Finally, he fell on the knife as it sunk into her torso just below the sternum. With a sigh of contentment he was finished – sated for now.

Dropping the knife on the bed, he went back into the hall to his briefcase, his kit. Carefully removing several items he returned to the bedroom. His first job was to remove any stray hairs that might have made their way onto her body, paying particular attention to her hair, both head and pubic. Using a nit-comb he went through each area with care and precision. Satisfied he had removed as many of these as possible, he used tweezers to pull several hairs from one of the vials he'd placed on the floor next to the bed and then placed them on and around her body. Deciding against using the semen from another of the vials on this occasion, he instead inserted a syringe into a vial of blood, and added this to the wash of already congealing blood all over the bed.

Happy the job was done he returned to the hall, removed the blood-spattered overalls and placed them inside a plastic bag in his case. Before pulling on his clothes he found a convenient full-length mirror in the hall and checked everywhere on his body for blood. Happy he was clean, he pulled on his clothes and let himself out the door.

Back outside it was easy to locate one of the local parks. Heading towards it he mused on how odd it was that men seemed to not notice his features – other than the obvious dark hair, dark eyes and an approximate height – so he knew it was highly unlikely the barman would remember enough about him to aid the police in their search. And even with a decent description he would be long gone, back in good old Blighty.

He wondered idly how long it would take for her to be reported missing and for her body to be discovered. Not that he really cared – he now knew she wasn't The One. She hadn't assuaged The Urge, so the Quest would have to continue.

Arriving at the park, he was relieved to see it wasn't yet gated and locked.

'Pleasant evening for a stroll,' he murmured quietly to himself as he entered the park, and allowing himself a small, satisfied smile, he straightened his tie and began to whistle softly.

Chapter Ten

Charlotte had turned the home office upside down searching for any further letters from Julia that Marcus might have hidden. She had virtually dismantled the wardrobe that his case had been sitting on top of, had lifted the carpet and turned out every drawer of the filing cabinet. She had to restrain herself from ripping the cushioned chair open, electing instead to examine it minutely, using the angle lamp from the desk to gain extra illumination, to try and spot any flaws in the stitching or covering.

Her whole afternoon's efforts had yielded precisely nothing.

There was nowhere left to look in the room. Her frustration grew and morphed into the anger and hurt she had felt on discovering the existence of Julia. Lifting the lamp she still held in a white-knuckled grip, she smashed it against the edge of the desk. It broke at the hinge that allowed the top to be manoeuvred around. With so little destruction wrought on the lamp her frustration grew further, but she could see nothing else she could take it out on.

Like a retreating tide the desire to smash everything in the house slowly ebbed away. She stood with head down, still breathing hard but at least a little more evenly, with the broken lamp still in her hand. She stayed like that for what felt like an hour or more but in reality was only maybe 10 minutes. Gradually, she felt an element of calm return. The anger and sense of betrayal, the anxiety and frustration were not so much dispersed but more hidden. They were what she felt a psychiatrist would call 'supressed'. They were still there, as they had been every day since finding the notes, but were now a roiling, shapeless and directionless mass somewhere at the back of her mind.

The whole fruitless exercise had been sparked by an earlier visit from DC Handley. He had shown up at her door with what turned out to be one of their forensics team. Her initial reaction was one of confusion and horror. What on Earth were they looking for? It all seemed a little over the top for a missing person.

DC Handley had quickly assuaged her trepidation by explaining that it was simply for elimination. That should they find anyone with a resemblance to Marcus they could determine relatively quickly whether it was him or not. She relented and let them in.

The forensics officer, whose name she had been given but had forgotten almost immediately, had then scoured the house. He appeared to bag certain items, most notably Marcus' comb and razor. DC Handley had then asked if there was anything in the house that Marcus tended to handle that she did not, explaining that they may be able to gain fingerprints. The only thing she could think of was the toolkit under the stairs. Although she used some of the items in there it had been Marcus who undertook the majority of the repairs and DIY around the house. Handley had seemed satisfied that that would likely do. Finally, he had the forensics officer take her fingerprints, in order to differentiate hers from Marcus'.

They had eventually left, apparently satisfied with their finds. The exercise, however, had set her to thinking. She hadn't really thoroughly searched the house herself. The police had a few months ago when she first reported Marcus as missing but they didn't know the house like she did. Maybe she would spot something they hadn't. And so

125

her trawl through every room, ending in the office, had begun.

Her internal clock, so common to many mothers, chimed – the children would need collecting soon. Placing the lamp carefully back on the desk, she began to mentally collect herself.

She never wanted the children to see her distressed in any way. The problem was, of course, that she *was* distressed. So in the time since Marcus' disappearance she had found she had become a consummate actress as soon as Melissa and Callum were in sight, acting out a part and yet feeling very different inside. With this realisation, she found her thoughts turning to Marcus' actions in the weeks, months and years prior to his disappearance. Had he been doing the same – playing a part while hiding what was really going on? She realised she had no idea, and not for the first time in the last few days she wondered if she had ever known her husband at all. On current evidence, it would seem not. She found this incredibly hard to reconcile in her own mind. They had been together for the best part of 12 years; a part of her felt she knew him in a way that was instinctive, that made her feel she could almost read his thoughts. She felt she should have been able to predict even his most erratic of behaviours and, perhaps, his deepest thoughts.

And yet, as with every time she had tried over recent months to reconnect with the details of her married life with Marcus, her mind simply went blank.

Returning downstairs, she sat for some time in the living room trying to clear her mind and relax a little before collecting the children. As she did so various random thoughts began occurring to her. These were vague at first – just jumbled half memories and feelings, small and inconsequential things that lacked any coherence or, even, relevance.

Slowly, however, she found certain elements started to coalesce into something approaching coherence or maybe a sort of logic that wasn't logical. She tried to dismiss them – they still didn't make complete sense – but her mind kept pulling her back to them. She began to feel rather than think that there might be answers in there somewhere. That sub-consciously, at least, her strongly analytical and intellectual mind had quietly been pulling the information it craved from the deep, long-forgotten recesses of her memory. And now, it was starting to share its conclusions with the conscious part.

Her thoughts continued to swirl around for a little while and then began to form into something verging on the tangible, only to slip away again, back into the general whirl of thoughts, like a wisp of smoke merging back into the plume from a fire. These odd fleeting moments of clarity led her to believe that there may be something in this after all. That perhaps she needed to let her brain work this through, allowing it to eventually present its conclusions in a way that would be relevant and meaningful.

For that she needed time and space and peace and quiet. She called her mother – hoping she would be able to collect and keep the children with her, possibly overnight – claiming to have a severe headache, very likely from stress, and just needed to rest for the remainder of the day. Her mother agreed without question or protest. She knew how much the last few months had taken their toll on her.

With the children taken care of she decided to sit back, try to relax and let her brain simply carry on sorting through whatever it was trying to get at. She did her best to not interfere, not attempting to latch onto any thoughts or feelings that welled up in her mind, but allowing them to pass into whatever region of her mind they needed to, simply allowing this process to take its course.

It became a rather surreal experience – a strange wander through her own psyche, almost meditative. She was an observer in her own mind not an active participant. She started to notice things happening; there was a slow but steady stream of memories moving through her mind as though her brain was replaying them, sorting and selecting or discarding them as it saw fit. Another part of her brain was working through half-recalled feelings, picking out those that had felt uneasy, unsure or questioning of a situation. The whole process appeared to be centring on a single point, coming together to form a series of conclusions and generating further pertinent questions. This might be a long list, she realised.

She glanced at the clock on the wall – an hour had passed already. She started to feel restless, needing to get up and walk around a little. An aimless wander around the downstairs of the house didn't make her feel any better. In fact it made her more restless. Finding herself standing in the hallway, she reached for her coat, bag and keys and headed outside.

Once outside and down the drive she realised she hadn't a clue where she was going to go. Maybe just around the block, a walk and fresh air would be all she would need. As she walked, she passed the bus stop near the corner of the road. She went to continue past it, but something made her stop. Turning back, she pulled her phone from her bag and checked the app that gave bus numbers and times from any given stop. There was one due in five minutes which would be stopping at the tube station. On what felt like a whim she decided to wait for the bus, with still no clear idea as to where she was going. She was still considering this when the bus hove into view. As she extended her arm to hail it her final destination sprang into her mind, with no warning or forethought, just a clear and certain idea of where she should be.

The bus took only 10 minutes to reach the station and from there it was a 30-minute tube ride into central London and Embankment station. After a short walk around the corner she was in front of the cosy little bar where she and Marcus had shared a number of pleasant evenings together since that early date she recalled so vividly.

She hadn't been there for several months now. It was probably six months ago that they had persuaded her mother to babysit and come here before going on to eat at an over-priced and not particularly good Italian. That was three months before Marcus had disappeared. She felt that perhaps sitting where they had sat then – just the two of them, feeling they were the only two in the bar when in reality they were surrounded by office workers all noisily enjoying a post-work drink – might just bring other recollections to mind.

Six months ago, they had found a small corner table and sat side by side, Marcus turning his chair so he was facing her with his back to the rest of the bar. The babble of voices and movement of people had seemed to vanish, as if a smoked glass window – like those in the back of a limousine – had descended from the ceiling and cut them off from everything else. They had talked quietly for an hour or so, although she couldn't now recall what about – work probably, the children certainly and maybe thoughts and plans for the future. *Had* they talked of the future?

The bar was very different at this time of day. It was only just three o'clock, after all, and there were only six or seven people in, mainly sitting in pairs plus one customer on his own. The couples were huddled over their tables, conducting muted but rapid conversations. The lone drinker, a middle-aged man looking careworn and worn out, was sitting propping up the far end of the bar, nursing what looked to be a large gin or vodka. She realised she could be making a big assumption and it could just be water in his glass but she doubted it somehow.

Due to the lack of people, and also because not one of them had so much as glanced up as she had walked in, she felt comfortable enough to head to the bar, get a drink and sit on her own – something she would never normally countenance.

The barman looked vaguely familiar as she approached him. She couldn't be certain but she was fairly sure he had been one of two working there on the last evening she had been in. She smiled to herself as she thought about how she stereotyped DC Handley as having a look that could only say 'policeman' and wondered if there was a look that said 'barman'. If there was then this guy would probably fit the bill. He was youngish without being baby-faced, with a mop of unruly brown hair and a haze of got-up-too-late-to-shave stubble on his chin and cheeks.

He smiled the professional, warm smile of a bartender comfortable in his niche. When he asked what he could get her, she realised she hadn't a clue what she wanted to drink. Embarrassed, she stared blankly at the back shelf and then the optics behind and above the bar.

She almost settled for the clichéd woman-on-her-own drink of G&T or a white wine spritzer, but then noticed a bottle of Glen Mhor and recalled how Marcus had extolled its virtues the last time they were here, dismissing the more recognisable single malts on offer. She even remembered how to pronounce it correctly and smiled when the barman had no idea what she had asked for. Still smiling she directed him to the correct bottle and ordered a double with no ice.

As he set the drink down in front of her he said with a chuckle, 'I wouldn't have put you down as a whisky connoisseur, if you don't mind my saying.'

'Oh? And why is that?' Charlotte replied. She couldn't, at first, work out why she felt so pleased that he had spoken to her until it dawned on her that she hadn't had a simple, pleasant and meaningless chat with another adult in what was probably weeks but felt like years.

'Well, your accent was a bit of a clue,' he replied with a shrug, 'and frankly, you just don't look the sort.'

Her smile broadened a little as she asked, 'And what sort are whisky connoisseurs normally? The Scottish thing is pretty lame – plenty of English people enjoy whisky, you know – and if you're going to pull the racist card why not the sexist one as well? Women are also capable of enjoying a good whisky and determining which ones they like.'

He grinned and gave a short 'hah' of a laugh and raised his hands. 'Fair cop,' he said. 'You're right, of course, but it's just the vast majority of whisky buffs I get in here, and there are a few, tend to be middle-aged, pompous men who wax lyrical about their choices, naming the town where the distillery is located and even the water source, and so on and so on....' He waved his hand in a circular motion and pulled a face that very articulately indicated the tedium of it all, before continuing. 'I have to say,

131

though – not one of them has pronounced that one in the way you did. How do you say it again?'

'You pronounce it something like glen-vawer, although I confess I'm probably making a mess of that. My husband's a Scot, from the same part of Scotland as the whisky. He told me how to say it.'

'I'll remember that for the next time the pompous arses are in,' he said with another grin. 'Anyway, enjoy.' With that he turned away and headed to the lone customer at the end of the bar. 'Ready for a top-up Charlie?'

Charlotte lifted her drink and headed for the table she thought of as her and Marcus' and deliberately sat exactly where she had before.

She sat there for some time, nursing her whisky, and realised the last hour or so of travel and then the simple small talk with the barman had distracted her from the main reason she had left the house in the first place. She hoped the coalescing mental processes she had begun to experience earlier were still whirring away in the background. She did her best to relax a little, closing her eyes and allowing her mind to go blank.

It took a little while and a few false starts – she would feel she was just about to grasp something and then her mind would jump to something irrelevant or silly like 'must remember to buy milk'. But slowly and surely, she found she was regaining the state she had connected to back at the house, with a part of her separating from the rest and watching closely what was happening in the rest of her brain.

Letting the process take its course, even when ordering another whisky, and feeling that the alcohol was helping her relax and therefore concentrate better, she gradually began to unravel the message her sub-conscious had been trying to convey all along.

When it finally came it didn't explode into existence like the thought equivalent of the big bang, or even wash over her like a wave of emotion. In fact, none of the clichéd phrases or metaphors for a personal revelation could be applied. Nothing sprang, leapt, dawned or even suddenly occurred to her. It was something more organic, that started very small and grew slowly and steadily until she could see the whole of the picture she had been trying to grasp. And once she could see it in its entirety, it was a single simple statement that had a whole series of emotional and logical attachments that held the central statement aloft, supporting and underpinning, until there could be no argument with the truth of it all.

Marcus had lied to her, not once or twice but on several, if not many occasions. She had known it at the time or more accurately had felt it. She had realised that what he had said or not said to her hadn't, for a whole host of reasons, rung true. His tone of voice, a certain look that crossed his face, his body language and then the creeping feeling at the back of her mind that something did not quite fit between his telling of events and her memory of the day or week in question. She had ignored it all at the time, generally accepting that everyone had slightly different recollections of events and times, and that there could be a plethora of reasons why someone spoke or acted slightly out of the ordinary.

But now her mind had started to put them all together into one coherent pattern. Long, long forgotten memories were attaching to equally obscure ones, and she could see now why she knew he had been lying to her. An immediate list of examples presented itself.

Firstly, she would often complete his mileage returns for his expenses – it saved him time and meant he was not sitting working at home so much – and she recalled now more than one occasion when the numbers had not quite added up. She would as a matter of course Google the mileage between home and his destination, to check for any obvious errors. There were several occasions where he appeared to have done more miles than Google maps had suggested. She had even questioned him once, receiving the answer that he had had to take a detour because of an accident. Eventually, she put the inconsistencies down to her not quite getting the correct destination or that he had taken a slightly different route. But now, it seemed to her that there were too many examples for them all to be simple mistakes, so why had she dismissed them so readily?

Then there were a number of calls between Marcus and the office – some to Sir Frederick Derringham, others to his team. They had seemed innocent enough at the time, just general office catch-ups and to-do lists for the next week, assignments and so on. These often occurred the evening after returning from a trip away as he frequently took a day off or worked from home after trips of more than one or two nights – ostensibly so he could spend a bit of time with the family. So, again, they didn't seem out of the ordinary. She had always found it a little odd though that these calls hadn't taken place whilst he was away. She eventually decided that perhaps he was constantly in meetings, and afterwards in informal talks over dinner or drinks or whatever, and so hadn't had time to call the office – especially since he only seemed to manage quick, snatched phone calls to her of an evening.

All very normal and understandable, she had thought, until details of some of those calls began to return to her. More than once she had heard him say things such as, '...much better thank you' and 'I'm sure by tomorrow I'll be back in, hale and hearty', a phrase she knew Sir Frederick used. A strange choice of words to use after a Foreign Office trip, and when she had thought to ask, he would say he had felt like a cold was starting or that he had had a dodgy stomach after a dinner or other such reasons for the office enquiring after his well-being. But if the office knew he had been feeling unwell then he *had* been in touch with them whilst away, so why the catch-up call on his arrival home? And why had he never mentioned to her that he was feeling ill on his calls home?

There was also a conversation she remembered having with Sir Frederick himself. It was at a FO soiree for those in management roles, under the guise of a management meeting and team builder, although wives and partners were invited – something Sir Frederick had explained with a wink and a 'Oh I'm sure we can say that we're just keeping everyone's peckers up', followed by an uproarious laugh.

She had at some point mentioned a piece of work Marcus had spent hours on, having just been away for a week in Brussels, often bringing it home to continue into the evening. She had mentioned it for a couple of reasons, partly because she had been more than a little chagrined that Marcus had been away for Melissa's birthday so wanted to say, in a roundabout way, that she felt Marcus was sent away too often and for too long. She also wanted to let him know that she felt he worked Marcus too hard, expecting reports and follow-up information and

135

recommendations to be completed almost immediately after the trip with an extremely tight deadline.

Sir Frederick had looked non-plussed for some seconds after this; she had at the time assumed he was trying to remember which of the many junkets and meetings she had been referring to. Now his reply came back to her almost word for word.

'Oh good Lord yes I recall, another bloody round of bloody Brexit talks and shenanigans, or should I say *Schengen a gones*.' He had given one of his barking laughs at his own pun, clearly feeling the wine he had been steadily working his way through all evening. After a minute of chuckling he had continued: 'Yes that was a bugger of a trip. Meetings until all hours of the night, the hotel couldn't cook a decent steak to save their lives, the German interpreter was taken ill so it was a good job the old boy from the Auswärtiges Amt could speak excellent English, and the only thing it achieved was to generate more paperwork than it did solutions. I remember calling Marcus to warn him of the ridiculous amount of work he would have on his plate after my return. All for what would amount to bugger all.'

Funny, she thought. Her memory of that conversation had until now contained the phrase '...after *our* return.' Was this another assumption she had made that had turned out to be more than a little awry? Was her memory turning the statement into one that fitted with that assumption? Marcus had been away for that week so she had figured he and Sir Frederick must have taken the trip together. Now, with her new clarity of recollection, the obvious inconsistency became clear. Sir Frederick appeared to have made the trip alone or at least with a different team and therefore without Marcus. After all, if

Marcus had been there why would Sir Frederick call him? And why had Marcus only talked about his work on that trip and not mentioned Sir Frederick at all? Most importantly, if he wasn't there then where the hell had he been for a week? And doing what?

These memories, now so clear and bright that they could have been of yesterday's events, were combined and intermixed with strands of feelings and what she could only call twitches in her sub-conscious. They were telling her the little things she had picked up on at the time but subsequently ignored – subtle but pertinent changes to Marcus' tone of voice, the looks away from her face as he said or explained certain things, a quiet nervousness afterwards. There had been a furtiveness to his demeanour during these periods that she must have picked up on and then dismissed, or perhaps had not even registered at the time.

These revelations, experienced over half an hour or so, brought her sharply back to the present. She realised she hadn't noticed the bar or its patrons for that entire period and it had got a lot busier. There were now the ubiquitous office workers filing in slowly from nearby businesses, so ubiquitous in fact that she felt she recognised a number of faces from six months before. The sudden rush of noise as she came out of her reverie almost overwhelmed her. It was time to go.

Downing her drink, she quickly exited into the chilly, late-autumn evening with still very little idea as to what to do with her new insight. One thing she did know, however, was that she would be taking things further and she would get to the truth.

An obvious course of action would be to take her thoughts to DC Handley, but she knew he would dismiss them as being, well, obvious. Naturally Marcus had been lying to her, that was plain in the fact that he had managed to pull off a complete disappearing act, which could only be achieved with careful forethought and planning – all of which he managed to hide from Charlotte. No, DC Handley would want more than just her new-found insight. He had probably been waiting for the moment the penny dropped and she came to see Marcus' disappearance for what it was.

The street was busy … those office workers not heading for the bars were heading for the tube and the commute home. The bustle and noise began to irritate her as she tried to make her way back towards Embankment station. The fourth time she was jostled by a passer-by made her mind up for her, she would go find somewhere a little quieter and have another drink. It had been years since she had had the time or the freedom to go out by herself. She needed to give herself more time to think and formulate a plan of action.

She was about to settle for the bar she had just been in, busy though it was, since it was still only 10 yards behind her and she would likely still get a seat by herself. Then she thought of a couple of places where she knew FO staff sometimes went after work – they were both much quieter than the surrounding pubs and bars, predominantly because they were off-street. Their entrances were closely guarded secrets – hidden up small alleyways, unlikely to be found by passing trade – while the bars themselves were situated on the first floor, one above a gents tailors and the other above a fried chicken outlet. Both were more like exclusive clubs than bars – all wood panels, discreet booths, table service and an unspoken agreement between all patrons that there would be no unnecessary noise. The exclusive members-only feel was reflected in the prices, another reason they retained an air of quiet seclusion in the heart of the overcrowded, heaving city.

Her feet had already adjusted her course and she allowed them to lead the way, keeping her head clear for further contemplation. Her starting point near Embankment station put her closer to the two venues than the Foreign Office, making the walk only five minutes or so. She had already decided on which of the two she would visit; Marcus had mentioned it more frequently and so she assumed he went there when he did stop for a drink before heading home. Her logic was that this would be the bar where she was more likely to 'bump' into one of his colleagues, those that knew him best at work, those that might let slip some information – information that could provide a more solid foundation to her thoughts.

She now craved the insight she simply couldn't get through her own cognition – it had to come from somewhere else, another viewpoint or perspective. The people that Marcus worked alongside would very probably see a different man to the one who returned home in the evenings. And, more importantly, perhaps know if or when he had used the freedoms afforded a senior manager to cover other activities.

As she walked, she affirmed and reaffirmed the belief that she – without any training or understanding of the processes required, and without the authority of the likes of DC Handley – would be able to unpick and unlock these workplace secrets. By the time the last corner was being turned she held every conviction that she would meet just the right colleague, that particular person who had covered for Marcus once too often, or who was jealous of his freedom of movement and noticed he wasn't always on company business as he claimed, or some other combination that would unlock the whole affair.

Snarling internally at the unintended pun, she pulled open the lower door that led to her chosen hunting ground.

'04

DCI Pearson's head ached. His back felt like it would never straighten out again and his eyes were so bloodshot he had begun to believe that someone had taken sandpaper to them. It was fast approaching midnight and he had been in the office since eight that morning – 16 hours of reading files and collating information. He had nearly given up several times, but knew he was getting somewhere. He'd needed to call round a number of other forces to track down investigating officers and request additional information. He'd waded through hundreds of scene of crime photographs and lengthy PM reports as well as forensic evidence reports. The forensic reports had been sent to his own team to contrast and compare, while the PM reports had gone to the pathologist.

Sitting back in his seat, ignoring the roaring protests from his head and back, he looked over at the board on the far wall. It was, he admitted it himself, a little old-fashioned now to be using a board to pin information, photos and any other material pertinent to an investigation. But Pearson liked to have one – it allowed him to visualise several incidents and their potential connections. Now, with the weight of information that had come through to him, he realised he would need a bigger board. A smile crossed his face as he thought of Jaws and the famous line about needing 'a bigger boat'. I know how you feel Officer Brody, he thought, I'm drowning here too.

He puffed out his cheeks and put his hands behind his head as he stared at the board trying to correlate the information up there with the new information he had collected throughout the day. There were some connections between them and he had placed these files to one side for the time being. Those that appeared to have similarities also had inconsistencies, but these could be put down to differences in the direction each investigation had taken or simply the language used by the report's author.

He had suspected a single killer had been involved in two murders he'd worked on back in 2001. The cases remained unsolved and there had been no further murders on or around his patch that bore the same hallmarks. Then, by chance, he had come across another case in Kent a couple of months ago. He happened to be good friends with a DI down there and they met for a pint or two one evening. His mate had been bothered by a previous case that he'd been unable to solve. When he outlined the details Pearson's ears pricked up, and he immediately saw the similarities between the three cases. They had discussed the particulars for the rest of the evening and by the time he left the pub Pearson was convinced he was looking at a serial killer operating in and around London.

Unfortunately, other unrelated cases and a generally overwhelming workload had prevented him from doing anything further with that information. Months had now passed since that meeting with his DI friend, but his inability to solve the murder of those two women in London and the case in Kent still ate away at him. They would fill his thoughts when he should have been focusing on other things. Finally, yesterday, having found it hard to think of much else and needing to resolve the issue, he had gone to speak with his boss. Although sceptical, his boss had eventually admitted there was the possibility that it was the same man and had given Pearson the next day to work through the cases afresh.

And so that morning, at eight o'clock sharp, he had begun the process of tracking down any similar cases in Greater London and the home counties. He found two more – one earlier and another later than the three he already had. He tried looking for a locus, a central point where the killer was likely to be based, but that proved to be unfruitful since the killer could be anywhere in the Greater London area. His enthusiasm had waned a little then, at the thought of 12 million or more potential suspects.

His next port of call had been MO – were there enough similarities between the cases to call them a series? Were they looking for one man or was it two or (heaven forbid) more men committing very similar crimes in different areas of the country? He decided to start from the premise that it was one man (or woman, he couldn't yet rule that out) and try to find enough in the evidence to show a consistent MO.

That had been relatively straightforward, he thought, stubbing out another cigarette and taking a swig of cold coffee. The one clear similarity was the lack, or confusion of, evidence. The forensics were all over the place as far as he could tell: bits from one person, DNA from someone else, semen from yet another. This, though, was starting to be telling. All the cases were the same in that respect and that could be seen as an MO. The lack of forced entry was also consistent across all five cases. Other similarities were the physical appearance and social standing of the five victims.

All of the victims' final movements had, as far as possible, been traced. Two had told friends they were going out on a date on the night they were killed, two had left work and were never heard from again, and the final one had been on a day off work. No real similarities there. After various public appeals, some witnesses had come forward to say they thought they had seen the women who had been out on dates. This had allowed the investigating teams to trace some grainy CCTV footage of the women waiting in bars – presumably for their mystery dates. But in both cases the women had taken calls on their mobiles and then left. They couldn't be traced after that. They had nothing on the other three.

By three in the afternoon, and with the beginnings of what was to become the mother of all headaches, Pearson had begun to consider that there could well be other murders around the country. The London and home county cases were committed cleanly and effectively – they were clearly the work of an established and practised killer. There would have to have been other killings – he had to have developed his methods. But Pearson's searches had turned up nothing else within the search parameters he had set himself. And so, he'd turned to the arduous task of calling other major forces around the country. This started to bear fruit.

By the time the clock hit six, he had seven other similar cases from all over the country: Edinburgh, Manchester, Leeds, Norwich and several places in between. There were slight variations here and there but all bore the hallmarks of the five he already had. The earliest he had was from the Newcastle area and dated back to 1999, the most recent was only two months ago in Brighton. It had occurred to him then that there may have been others, but they had clearly been lost in the mists of time. Still, as the evening wore on he had felt increasingly convinced that he was looking for one man who operated all over the country – and that he was prolific.

144

And now, frowning at the last cigarette in the packet, he realised that there was no set pattern in terms of time elapsed between each murder. There were several months between some in the sequence and then two in quick succession and so on. This was clearly a man who couldn't indulge himself on a regular basis or to any set pattern. No full-moon killer here. It could point to someone who had a 'normal' life outside of his murderous pastime; he was, perhaps, married with a good steady job, precluding him from venturing away too often. Maybe his job took him away occasionally and those were the opportunities he took to kill.

Shaking himself, Pearson realised he had begun to speculate. He needed to spend his time on the facts and the evidence not on theories about the nature of the man at this point. His eyes refocused on the board in front of him. He was tired in the extreme and realised that this was making his mind wander.

He checked the time. He had been staring at the board, reviewing his day's work in his mind, for over half an hour, but through the fuzz of tiredness he realised he had come to the conclusion that had evaded him for most of the day. He *was* looking for one man, and the MOs and similarities in the SOCO pictures and the victims all verified that – even without any forensic confirmation. He could put that in front of his boss and with a little luck get the go-ahead to begin the search for the man that had eluded him three years ago. A man he now knew was responsible for 12 murders across the whole country. A man that must be caught before that toll became higher still.

It was a daunting task but Pearson felt he could achieve his goal. He was convinced he was the right man for this job. He would catch this bastard.

'Right,' he announced to the empty room. 'It's time for home, Fran old son – big day tomorrow.'

*

It was not so much a big day as a big week that followed. Pearson's boss had immediately seen the connections and agreed that this was indeed one killer operating all over the country. He took this up the chain of command and before long the beginnings of a task force were formed. Various dedicated teams were set up in the key locations, all working their angles; they would report directly to Pearson who would be overall head of the national investigation. He was allowed to hand-pick five officers and a civilian support team. He was given a remit to bring in other officers as and when required. All forces were given the initial basic MO to look out for with the task force ready to respond immediately if anything crossed their radar.

Forensics had returned their conclusions: there were some matching hairs and DNA from two scenes, two others had matching DNA from semen, and the rest all had different profiles present. Because there were no definitive matches across all cases it was impossible to put one person at any given scene. Their advice was simple – catch him and they would do their best to match the individual to at least one or two of the scenes.

A forensic psychologist was called in to help profile the killer. Pearson suspected and was eventually proved right that this had taken them nowhere.

At the end of the week a press conference was organised. Pearson outlined all 12 cases, showing photos of the victims and appealing for people to come forward if they remembered anything at all from the final days and nights the victims were last known to be alive. He also outlined the killer's methods and the similarities across the cases. He omitted any reference to forensic evidence.

Near the end of the conference a young journalist from The Sun raised his hand and asked: 'Chief Inspector, how do you think the killer is gaining entry to the properties of his victims?'

At a loss for a full and reasoned answer – he really didn't know at this point – Pearson resorted to a glib and non-committal answer: 'I don't know, maybe he simply charms his way in.'

The following morning the headline in The Sun ran:

THE CHARMER
12 WOMEN BUTCHERED IN THEIR OWN HOMES
And so it all began.

Chapter 11

The St. Martin's Lounge was exactly as she remembered it from over 10 years ago. She had been here once before with Marcus; she had worked at a corporate law firm in the City at the time and they had met up after work. It had been a pleasant couple of hours being introduced to a number of his colleagues. The wood panelling was still in place alongside the subdued ambience. A decade between visits probably meant a thousand changes, large and small, had been made to the place but she could detect none of them. So her brain filled the gaps in her memory with the objects and décor that were in place now but likely weren't previously.

As soon as Charlotte passed through the door at the top of the stairs her feet hit lush, deep carpeting, which immediately deadened the sound of her shoes. As she made her way towards the bar, she wondered whether it had been laid deliberately to remind those entering that this was not the sort of place for loud football banter or across-the-room conversations. Two staff this time stood near the bar, both watching her approach with slightly suspicious eyes. They were not accustomed to or necessarily appreciating newcomers.

Just in time to avert any embarrassing exchanges with the bar staff she remembered that this place was table service only and quickly turned to look for a vacant spot, allowing her to survey the room properly for the first time. She was about to take a table by the window opposite the bar when she caught sight of someone sitting on their own in a far corner. She couldn't quite make out their face — partly due to the angle of their body, partly because an ill-positioned lamp was casting a shadow over that corner of the room – but the woman's bearing and demeanour were very familiar. Changing her mind, Charlotte headed for the corner and hoped she had correctly recognised its occupant.

Realising her approach would likely go unheard due to the carpet she announced her presence some way off from the table by clearing her throat. Its occupier didn't react at first but as Charlotte readied herself for a more forceful cough, the woman turned her head and shoulders towards her. To Charlotte the movement was so graceful she could only describe it as balletic.

With an inner sigh of relief at having recognised her target correctly, Charlotte smiled and extended her hand. 'Agatha, so nice to see you, how are you? I hope Sir Frederick is treating you well.'

Agatha had looked a little startled at Charlotte's approach but cleared the expression quickly and returned the smile, although it seemed somewhat strained to Charlotte's eyes. She had met Agatha on several occasions and knew Marcus liked and trusted her; she never used her position as Sir Frederick's PA for any personal leverage and treated everyone with the same pleasant, if aloof, manner. She was older than Charlotte by maybe 10 years, but held herself with such poise and elegance that she appeared, to Charlotte's eyes, virtually ageless. The general air of primness that she carried with her seemed a little diminished here, presumably as she was relaxing after work.

Charlotte began to feel a little sorry for her, sitting drinking on her own. No friends to unwind with or family to go home to? She was being hypocritical, she knew. What had *she* been doing for the last two hours, after all? And it was equally likely that Agatha had a packed and

149

fulfilling private life but had simply chosen to sit alone for an hour or two. Assumptions were dangerous things, Charlotte thought – something she found she had been reminded of on a daily basis recently.

'Oh, Charlotte, um, hello.' Agatha appeared to struggle a little with what to say next, looking around her as if for inspiration. Eventually her gaze settled back on Charlotte's face.

'I'm sorry – you were, I confess, probably the last person I expected to see behind me,' she continued. 'How are you, my dear? We are all so dreadfully worried for Marcus, and you and the children of course.'

Agatha had risen from her seat as she spoke and taken hold of Charlotte's hand with both of hers, squeezing tightly during the last sentence, then abruptly letting go.

With her poise fully recovered for a second time she gestured for Charlotte to take a seat at her table.

'Please join me, can I order you a drink?'

Agatha was all business for the next few minutes – ushering Charlotte to a seat, ordering a vodka tonic for herself and a Glenfarclas for Charlotte, then waiting quietly until the drinks were delivered to the table. Leaning forward slightly in her seat, she then spoke again, a grave and concerned expression on her face.

'How are you, Charlotte? It must have been so very difficult for you over the last three months.'

The two previous whiskies and the assertions she had made on her walk to the bar combined with her desire for answers now threatened to burst through the veil of polite just-met conversation. Charlotte found herself having to hold back from simply firing hard question after hard question at Agatha: *Where was he, and when? How can you know he was where he said he was?* These were the questions that vied and jockeyed for position as her opening gambit. Fortunately, she checked herself in time to remember she was the wife of a missing man, not some unhinged copper from a novel, and the woman opposite her was nothing more than a concerned colleague of that man, not a shady underworld henchman. More to the point, Agatha was clearly as concerned for Charlotte herself as she was for Marcus.

With a deep intake of breath Charlotte began recounting the last few months: the shock and fear, the depression and anxiety, the hurt and anger at Marcus' apparent betrayal, and finally the determination to get to the truth. Agatha listened patiently and in the most part quietly, with only the occasional sympathetic interjection or clarifying question. Charlotte found herself offloading all of her twisted and turbulent baggage on a woman she barely knew, realising all the while that Agatha was a far better listener and inquisitor than she would ever be.

After what felt like hours, but in reality was probably only half an hour or so, Charlotte ground to a halt. She had nothing more to add and found that all those pertinent questions she had intended to ask had simply faded away. Downing the last of her Glenfarclas and raising the glass at the barman to indicate another round, she looked directly at Agatha.

'What do you think is going on Agatha?' The question wasn't plaintive or pitiful, but direct and demanding, delivered with exactly the right tone to impress Agatha – and Charlotte could see it.

Agatha sat for quite some time, chin lowered, her usually unlined brow furrowed with a central thought line. She remained quiet as the waitress brought their drinks over, simply nodding to the girl and absently lifting the glass to her lips, sipping and apparently savouring the drink then slowly placing the glass back in exactly the same position on the table – all very carefully and deliberately.

Eventually she looked up, her face softening and a sympathetic smile crossing her lips.

'I can feel for you Charlotte, I really can. I lost my husband – he died I mean, he didn't disappear – nearly eight years ago now and yet I still look for him on every street and in every familiar place we shared. It is almost impossible to describe that sense of loss to anyone who hasn't experienced it. It is devastating and numbing and removes all sense of purpose and future one may have held – at least it does for quite some time. But, and this is the rub, my husband died – was killed actually. It took a long time but eventually I could accept that he was not coming back. I knew he wouldn't walk through the door one day as if it had all been a horrendous dream. There would be no happy ending for us. But you, you my dear, have to live with the hope that Marcus could come back, that maybe he is alive and well – albeit possibly in a dark place or suffering a life crisis or believing he is better off elsewhere with someone else. All the same, he *could* come back and for me that is more destructive than any absolute loss anyone can feel. Your hope is what is destroying you. You have, I think, a choice. Either you can spend the rest of your days wondering, searching and questioning, forever believing that he is just around the corner and one happy day he will walk back into your life or….'

Agatha paused, lifting her drink and sipping delicately. Charlotte, who had found herself hanging on every word – desperate to hear the alternative answer to the most moving and profound summation of her predicament she had heard – simply stared, wide-eyed and expectant.

'Or…' Agatha continued, 'you can say fuck it, leave the little shit to dip his tiny, cheating wick wherever he wishes and hope he catches syphilis or whatever the latest fashion in venereal disease is, and leave the twat to wallow in his own filth while you and your children get on with your own lives, only hoping you can catch up with the slimy ingrate to extract every last penny out of his miserable hide.'

Agatha sat back, still calm, still elegant, her last line delivered in the same even tones she had begun. Charlotte simply stared, unashamedly open-mouthed and speechless.

'83

Disgust, self-loathing, depression, fear, anger, shame, hate, terror, remorse and then steely resolve washed over him, wave after wave of each powerful emotion crashing against the inside of his skull. With each wave, a rush of sensations and residual, backwashed reactions seemed to double the intensity of the original feelings. He had been trying to sleep but his brain was throwing up images and vivid memories, both true and imagined, driving the whole cycle faster and further with each pass until he felt his brain would simply explode. As the whole episode reached its seeming climax, he began to wish that this would actually happen, so it would stop and he could rest.

He had been home from university for a week now, having completed his first term away in Edinburgh, and every night had been the same. All the reminders – constantly bombarding him – were almost unbearable in the daytime but at night, lying here in his old room in the manse, the rollercoaster terror ride would begin, spawned by the memories and emotions stirred up throughout the day. The village was so small he couldn't go anywhere without a building or a face or a road name sparking the same burning flashbacks, leaving him shaking and red with embarrassment and shame.

From the moment he arrived back he had been hit with the first of these intolerable reminders. The only bus stop in the village stopped outside the school. His final two years at that school had been filled with humiliation, sneering bullying, outraged disgust and abject, lonely misery. Even the teachers appeared to hold little sympathy or concern, leaving him thoroughly isolated and open to any abuses his peers could think up. Stepping down from the bus on his return he had looked up, straight into the face of the imposing, granite building – his own personal house of pain and torture. Things simply got worse from that moment on.

The following day he had been expected to attend the kirk – he had no choice in the matter, even though he was now 18 and should have the final say on whether he went or not. His only solace was that he could sit in the usual family spot at the front, meaning he was facing away from the rest of the congregation and their sometimes hard, sometimes sympathetic stares – all reminders of his humiliation. By the end of the service he knew he couldn't remain in the village and face another service in a week's time. As he stood to leave his legs were shaking so badly he felt they would give way below him, and his lungs were so tight he could hardly breathe, leaving him feeling faint and even more unbalanced.

Over the course of the next week the village had closed in around him, seemingly pointing and laughing and accusing. The people, who had all known him his whole life, avoided him where possible and when they had no choice their conversation was short, mumbled, monosyllabic and devoid of all eye contact.

Near the end of the week he had found himself several miles from home on top of one of the many hills that surrounded the village. The night sky was clear and the galaxy spread around him in bright, brilliant points of light. He had missed the stars during his time in Edinburgh and hadn't realised until he got there that the light pollution would obliterate so much of the night sky. Here, he could clearly see the axis of the Milky Way threading across the sky, surrounded by thousands of its other constituent stars. He wore only jeans and a thick jumper, no coat, and the sweat created from the climb had started to cool and turn to ice in the sub-zero temperatures. He had virtually run up the hill – seemingly trying to escape the village and its people, in reality trying to escape himself.

Turning his tear-streaked face to this awe-inspiring sight he screamed, cursed and raged at the stars until he fell to his knees coughing, hacking and retching onto the frozen shards of grass.

It was unfair, no, it was amoral. It was worse than either of those things combined. The humiliation had been bad enough but the thought of returning and facing it every holiday, over and over again, was completely unbearable. The demand that he attend the kirk was an insult to his already injured pride. His father's overbearing, humourless cruelty was starting to make his skin itch with the desire to punch him hard enough to put his fist through the old cunt's face.

All of it was becoming totally unbearable and he would have to face several years of this yet. Impossible, unacceptable, intolerable. It would kill him if he had to face this again. Either that or he would kill someone else.

Or he would kill someone else.

Kill someone else.

Kill.

He pushed that particularly disturbing thought to one side. That was unthinkable, went against everything he had been raised to believe. He still held the values of his parents. More to the point, he simply knew it was wrong to consider taking another person's life. Didn't everyone know that? It was basic instinct, wasn't it? And you certainly don't kill your own. What was it called? Natural Law? He didn't need his bastard father to tell him that, or anyone else for that matter.

Then he thought about *her*. She was long gone, had moved away while he was at Uni. But she was still there in his mind, still part of his dreams, desires and ambitions. What had happened to their becoming a couple at school and going to university together, living in rooms next to each other in halls, and then sharing a flat for the final year or two? What had happened to their life after university — marriage, children, the works?

All of it had turned to dust because of them — his parents, the kirk congregation, *her*. Gone because of what they did, how it was done and everyone eventually finding out, thanks to *her*. Why shouldn't he think of committing murder on these people, on all of them, the rest of the village and anyone else who had been involved?

He closed his eyes and tried to clear the horrendous thoughts swirling in his mind, the images of *her* and them ripped and torn, and the idea that he would be free if only he could be rid of them all. Cleansed of the guilt and humiliation he could get on with his life. His plans for the rest of his days could, would be fulfilled. He would have a chance.

He had to get himself out of this way of thinking. He could just move on, lose contact and get on with his life — never return here, never see his parents again and definitely never see, think or hear of *her* again. But the feeling and the hatred had stayed with him. He couldn't move on from the idea that they had to go, had to die. He was becoming a slave to his own desire for revenge and release and for them all to suffer.

Sobs still wracking his body, he screwed his eyes tight shut in a final effort of will to stop it all.

And then, unbidden into his mind, came her laughter.

She had laughed.

She wouldn't stop laughing until he stopped her. Permanently.

With that thought he threw up on the frozen ground, knowing that he was now trapped by his own nightmares.

Chapter 12

Charlotte couldn't shake her wide-eyed incredulity at Agatha's outburst but tried to hold together the small talk they had descended into. Agatha had switched seamlessly and blithely to enquiring after the children and Charlotte's work.

After half an hour or so of the inconsequential chatter, Agatha placed her drink meaningfully on the table. Clearly another change of subject was due, Charlotte thought, and this one perhaps of more import. Agatha looked at the table a moment, clearly weighing her next words.

'Are you aware the police were enquiring about Marcus at the Foreign Office a few days ago?' she asked in a quiet, almost conspiratorial voice.

'Well, yes I would imagine they would,' replied Charlotte, with surprise in her voice. 'After all, they are still looking for him and anything from work or home may help them.'

Agatha shook her head. 'No, not entirely, my dear. You see a young DC—'

'That would be DC Handley,' Charlotte interrupted.

'Quite,' continued Agatha. 'You see he spoke to Sir Frederick for some time. Now I wasn't party to what was said, but afterwards I was asked to find and send a lot of information about dates, absences and expense claims.'

'OK,' was all Charlotte could think of to say, still not really seeing where this was going. 'Again, surely they are just trying to trace his movements and establish a pattern as to his whereabouts.'

'No, Charlotte, you are missing something – I hadn't finished about the information. You see, they asked for details going back several years, which I was a little surprised about. I tried to discreetly question Sir Frederick about it afterwards but he wasn't very forthcoming. But from the little I could glean I got the impression they weren't just trying to find Marcus because he is missing, but more that they were very interested in catching up with him for another reason.'

Agatha paused and lifted her drink.

'Like what?' Charlotte asked.

'That, I'm afraid, I can't say,' Agatha replied. 'Like I said, Sir Frederick was less than forthcoming on the subject. But it really felt like there is some form of investigation going on that you are unaware of.'

'Hmm, well that might explain the hair and fingerprints DC Handley came looking for this morning,' Charlotte said, as if to herself.

'Hair and fingerprints?' Agatha asked.

Charlotte explained DC Handley's visit, along with the man from forensics, explaining she had been told it was for elimination purposes, should anyone materialise with resemblance to Marcus.

'Yes, that could be the case, but I now wonder. If you were to put these two pieces together along with a very minor hint from Sir Frederick, I think you should probably prepare for a difficult revelation from your DC Handley at some point in the not too distant future,' Agatha said quietly.

Charlotte sat for some minutes digesting this information. Agatha remained silent, allowing Charlotte space to think.

She was lifted from her reverie when Agatha tutted and muttered, 'Speak of the devil and he's sure to appear.' Then she said, more audibly this time, 'Frederick, you've finished earlier than I expected.'

Charlotte turned her head to see Sir Frederick Derringham approaching from the doorway, with a wide, white smile crossing his handsome features. The smile dropped slightly and a small frown creased his brow as he saw Charlotte.

'My dear Charlotte,' he said with genuine surprise in his voice, 'what on Earth brings you here?'

Charlotte returned his smile, taking his proffered hand, and in that very affected manner he made to kiss her knuckles without actually making contact.

He sat down and glanced quickly at Agatha. 'Yes, frankly Agatha, I've had that damn report up to my ears today,' he said. 'I've emailed number 10 saying they'll have to wait until the end of the day tomorrow before they get it. Damned if I'm going to spend all evening writing it for them when they're probably out enjoying themselves.'

Agatha allowed herself a half-smile at the back of Sir Frederick's head as he turned towards Charlotte.

'Well Charlotte, what has brought you here?' he asked, whilst waving at the bar staff. They clearly knew exactly what he wanted.

Charlotte explained about her attempt to connect with Marcus' frame of mind at the time of his disappearance, and how she had found herself heading to the St. Martin's Lounge as she had remembered the place from an early date with Marcus.

Sir Frederick listened attentively throughout then asked, 'And did you find the answers you were looking for?'

'Not really Frederick, no,' Charlotte replied. 'The only conclusions I can draw are that I'm not sure I knew Marcus as well as I thought and that there are some big holes in my knowledge of the sort of man he really was. I realised I know next to nothing about his past. I wonder, now, whether there was something I didn't know that led to him leaving – some family secret that raised its head. But then I could equally be totally wrong. I'm as lost now as I was three months ago.' Her voice broke slightly as she finished speaking and Sir Frederick placed his hand comfortingly on her shoulder.

'I can only imagine how terrible this has been for you my dear, dear girl,' he said softly, patting her shoulder gently.

'I have no more idea than you why Marcus has disappeared,' he said. 'However, I may be able to shed some light on a little of his past. We have been friends for such a very long time that I have picked up some of his story along the way. If you think it might help you?'

Charlotte nodded, 'Yes it may do. I suppose I won't know until I hear it but anything I don't already know could well be the key to what has happened.'

'Well, let me see,' Sir Frederick said, looking towards the ceiling and stroking a hand down the underside of his chin and neck. 'Where to begin? You know we come from the same area of Scotland?'

Charlotte nodded again, an affirmative and a prompt for him to continue combined in a single gesture.

'We grew up only a matter of miles apart,' Sir Frederick continued, taking the cue, 'but far enough apart that our social paths simply never crossed. When finally we did meet – both of us young men looking to build a career in the civil service – we quickly became firm friends and marvelled at the coincidence of our shared geography. We would go out together quite often back then so inevitably talk would turn to that of home and family.'

'He rarely, if ever, spoke to me about his family,' Charlotte said, trying to disguise the feeling of jealousy creeping over her – clearly Marcus had been more open with Sir Frederick than with her.

'No, I'm not surprised,' Sir Frederick said. 'It took quite some time for him to tell me anything. It was, as I understand it, not a very happy childhood – another thing we shared, unfortunately. You see, we were both raised in particularly Calvinist families. Strict does not begin to describe our respective fathers' rule of their families. Their word in the house was law, their authority absolute. They were both brutal and unforgiving men; affection wasn't just in short supply, it was non-existent.' His brows furrowed and his eyes darkened as he dropped his gaze to the table. He was silent for some time, the memories of a cold and unhappy childhood playing across his expressive face.

Eventually he looked back up. 'So you see, perhaps it's not so surprising that he didn't talk about his family to you. I suspect he was happy, as was I, to see them safely put under the ground and forgotten as soon as possible afterwards.'

'Yes, I can perhaps see that,' said Charlotte. 'I'm not sure I can see though how that connects to him walking out on us – unless the letter he received had something to do with them, but after all these years I find that hard to fathom.'

'The letter?' Sir Frederick asked, his brow furrowing further. 'I was unaware of any letter – what did it contain?'

'I have no idea,' Charlotte replied. She went on to explain that Marcus had received the letter on the morning of his disappearance. She found herself unable to mention the notes she and DC Handley had discovered, without really knowing why. Embarrassment, she decided in the end, and shame of course, with a healthy dose of disbelief and non-acceptance mixed in.

Sir Frederick considered this for a while with pursed lips.

'Do you know?' he eventually said. 'This talk of the past and your thought that it might connect to Marcus leaving somehow reminds me of a further point I had forgotten. You see, when Marcus' mother finally died – a few short years after his father, probably from relief at having got rid of the old goat – the house wasn't left to him. They left all their possessions including the house to the kirk. I recall being a little surprised that Marcus seemed rather unbothered by the whole thing. He said at the time that he was glad he didn't need to have anything to do with the place – that the church was welcome to it and that he hoped they would discover it required major renovation and would cost them a fortune to restore.'

Sir Frederick took a sip of his drink before carrying on, again perhaps considering the situation or remembering the loss of his own parents – it was hard to tell. Charlotte continued to sit in silence, her mind trying to find any connection between what she knew – flimsy as it was – and this new information. She could see none.

'I could never understand why he wasn't more annoyed by the whole affair,' Derringham continued. 'I mean they made his whole childhood and early adult life a pure misery. The least he should have expected was to make some money out of the old buggers. Mind, that was maybe me projecting my attitude onto him. It occurred to me some time later that he may have simply wanted to put everything from his past as far behind him as possible. Perhaps he wanted nothing to remind him, ever again, and so couldn't bring himself to even set foot in his old family home, even just to sell it.'

Agatha, who up to this point had sat silent and inexpressive, now interrupted, 'I don't see how this could possibly help Charlotte, Frederick. It seems to me you're simply reminiscing, not shedding any light on the matter.'

Charlotte was a little taken aback by Agatha's tone and abrupt words to Sir Frederick. She had always assumed his staff treated him with the same deference outside as he received in the office. Then it occurred to her that he and Agatha had worked together for many years and as a result had probably formed a greater bond than that of boss and PA. And, given Sir Frederick's lack of reaction he was obviously used to such reprimands, out of the office at least.

'Yes, yes Agatha,' he said, mildly enough, 'as usual you're quite right. I'm waffling on and not helping poor Charlotte here one bit. Only I had begun to wonder, after the mention of that letter – and I have to say I'm speculating wildly – that it may have been to do with this property or his parents or both. And like Charlotte, I'm now wondering – did it stir up something from that horrendous past I've described? Did Marcus, in fact, receive some communication about the house or his parents' estate in general that set a chain of events in motion that ultimately led to his disappearance?'

They all sat in silence for a while, Sir Frederick and Agatha allowing Charlotte the time to consider what he had had to say.

Eventually, she shook her head and said, 'I don't know Frederick, it's possible I suppose, but he's been gone over three months now. What on Earth could it be that has made him completely disappear for that length of time?

165

And why has he not been in contact? It all seems a bit implausible. I mean if it was as simple as some family issue, surely he would have said and let me know he would be away for a while. He would still have called regularly and I would know where he was and what he was doing and that he was safe and well. Instead I have none of those things.'

'I have no answer to those questions, my dear,' was all Sir Frederick could say in response. Then he added, 'I only wish I did, if only to give you some peace of mind.'

Charlotte could think of nothing else to ask Sir Frederick or Agatha; she realised it was now very late and she was acutely aware of the effect the alcohol was having on her. She felt woozy and her head was swimming. Too many new things to consider with no real resolution in sight and now she was struggling to think straight through the whisky. Time to go, she decided.

'Thank you, Frederick,' she said and heard the slur in her voice. 'I think I'll need time to consider what you have said and see if it leads me anywhere. Now, I think, it's time I went home.'

'Yes, me too,' said Agatha, rising from the table. 'Charlotte, tonight is on me.'

'Not at all,' Sir Frederick interjected. 'I would be affronted if you wouldn't allow me to pay.'

Both women accepted this with a shrug.

Once outside, it became apparent that they were all going in separate directions. All the same, Sir Frederick insisted that he share a cab with Charlotte to see her safely home.

They spoke little during the journey. Charlotte was silently considering how much the last few hours had cost Sir Frederick and then decided that he could easily afford it. Not far from her home, he turned to her and looked at her for a little longer than was comfortable. She squirmed a little under his gaze and determined to avoid looking back at him.

Eventually he put a hand over hers, which she realised was resting on her knee and as a result so was his hand, which only increased her discomfort.

'You know, Charlotte, that although – to my regret – we have not had the opportunity to meet each other with the frequency I would have liked, I have always held you in very high regard. Please do not misinterpret my words as some crass attempt at seduction – they most certainly are not.' He had clearly read the look on her face and interpreted it correctly. He didn't, however, remove his hand.

'I only wanted you to know that you, and Marcus naturally, but especially you are very dear to me.' He continued patting her hand. 'I have felt from the first time Marcus introduced us that there was something very special about you, although I don't think I could put it into words with any coherence.'

He stopped talking for a second and gave an embarrassed half-laugh. 'I am being ineloquent in the extreme and realise I have worried you further with my clumsy attempt to express my desire to see that you are OK. Nothing more. That you only need to ask and if it is in my power to do so I will be of every assistance possible.'

Feeling only a little less worried than a moment ago, Charlotte smiled weakly. She really was quite tipsy now and simply said, 'Thank you, you're a very kind man Frederick.'

He waved this away with a 'tsk' and a gesture she took to mean 'not at all'.

She was somewhat relieved when the cab rounded the corner into her street; she still felt a little uncomfortable at Sir Frederick's words and, as she saw it, over-familiarity – albeit well-meaning and obviously with nothing more than platonic concern.

As she walked more than a little unsteadily up the drive to the house, the cab idled at the kerbside and she had no doubt that Sir Frederick watched every step until she was safely inside.

'80

It had never bothered him until that Sunday – having to sit in the front row of pews alongside his mother and aunt. His father was the minister after all and his family were therefore expected to be at the forefront of the weekly worship. But this Sunday was different. This Sunday he desperately wanted to be able to see the rest of the congregation, or more precisely one member of it. He wasn't sure where she was sitting but he knew she was there, had seen her family enter the kirk and had watched intently as his father had welcomed them warmly into, as he put it, their 'new family in Christ'.

He had lost them after that, his mother slapping his knee and tsking at the unseemly craning of his neck and gawping at the congregation. As he reluctantly turned back to face the lectern there was a hissed reprimand from his mother reminding him of his duty as the son of the minister to behave with dignity and respect for their place of worship. He hadn't listened, he was too intent on trying to discern where she was just with the power of his mind, which he knew before he started was a waste of time. So he had to content himself with simply knowing she was somewhere behind him, could perhaps see him and might even at this moment be looking at him.

Her family had moved to the village a couple of weeks before – escaping what to them was the rat race of Aberdeen and looking for the quieter, everybody-looks-out-for-everybody-else life of a village. Her parents had presented themselves at the manse the day after they had moved in, telling his father over tea and scones (great doughy abominations with the odd currant in, that took longer to chew through than it had taken to cook them –

his mother insisted on making them and his father insisted on forcing them on anyone who came within 10 feet of the house) that they were deeply spiritual people and had felt their faith waning the longer they had spent among the Godless masses of the city. His father, naturally, had welcomed them to the village and spoken effusively on how most of the villagers attended the kirk every week, barring illness, and that they all held strong beliefs in the family of the church and that he was sure they would soon find their obvious and powerful faith returning once they were settled within the community.

He had sat, quiet and uninterested, whilst his father had droned on about his church and congregation. If he was home at the time of these visits – which, aside from school and the very occasionally allowed visit to a friend, he generally was – he was expected to present himself and sit with his father in what was rather grandly known as 'the receiving room' whilst they talked. It seemed to him that this was the closest his father could get to passing on the family trade to his son. It was an apprenticeship in banal conversation interspersed with the occasional tersely delivered tirade on the dangers of sin or the perils of treading too far from the sight of God and so suffering the agonies awaiting those who had fallen from His grace. He was not in the least bit interested in any of it.

He would generally spend this time daydreaming, creating cinematic scenes in his mind from passages in his favourite books. He would often find that by the end of one of these chats he had effectively watched an entire film in his head.

The part of his brain that always paid attention to the room, and especially looked out for when he was being directly addressed, had suddenly realised his father was

170

speaking to him. With some effort his mind caught up with the conversation and begun paying full attention to what was happening around him.

'You'll be happy to show Mr and Mrs MacInally's daughter around the school, won't you boy?' his father was saying.

His father had always called him boy, even when it was just the two of them, and always used the same gruff, stern tone of voice. There was never a hint of pride or encouragement in the way his father spoke to him, never did he hear anything that might resemble love or even mild affection. Everything his father said to him sounded, at best, like a superior talking to a troublesome and particularly slow junior, and more often like an admonishment waiting to turn into a full-on, invective-ridden, screamed rant. He was essentially a man from the wrong century living his life 100 years too late.

He had given himself one heartbeat to catch up – they had a daughter! That really caught his interest. His 15-year-old mind had been focused more and more on the opposite sex for the last half year or so, but living in a small village did not exactly allow for any experience outside of his own imagination. And due to the very small sample size his imagination also lacked for material. It wasn't that the girls in the village were particularly unattractive or that there weren't any with the requisite anatomy already-developed – they just all seemed very unapproachable in a sexual sense.

It had already occurred to him that he had known many of them since they were literally babes in arms. They had grown up together and he had seen every one of them in various situations that didn't lean towards a burgeoning sexual imagination – eating worms, peeing themselves and

171

getting covered in mud and coo shit did not feature highly on his list of sexy things a girl might do. He also knew that being the son of the minister excluded him from many of the more surreptitious activities that the others of his age got up to, especially in the woods by the burn. No one wanted his father to find out and so there was an element of mistrust towards him too.

But now there was a chance to get to know a girl he had never met – and to do that ahead of all the other boys who, like him, would no doubt relish the thought of a new girl in the village.

'Yes of course,' he had replied in his most respectful and polite voice. 'I'd be happy to, and perhaps, if she'd like, I could also show her around the village tomorrow so she knows her way around before going back to school?'

'I'm sure Ailsa would be grateful of some company her own age,' Mr McInally had replied. 'That's very good of you, I'm sure she'd be glad to be out and about.'

So, it was agreed he would call round the next day and have this new girl all to himself until their return to school. He had felt delighted, excited and not a little nervous about the whole thing. Over-arching all of this was the thrill of having the opportunity to 'get ahead of the game' when it came to getting to know this Ailsa girl.

The following day had gone well as far as he was concerned. She was pretty and kind of funny, and he felt they got on very well. They had chatted amiably as he showed her around the village – what there was of it – generally covering her life in Aberdeen, how the village was so small in comparison and how much she missed her friends. She bemoaned that she had had so many friends in Aberdeen and that she doubted there were enough kids in the village to replace them all. She talked for some time about the 'wild' afternoons spent in parks and other hang-outs where adults were scarce on the ground.

He had listened politely enough, not really knowing what to say. Eventually he had found himself defending his wee village, claiming they were a great bunch of kids, all of whom could be pretty wild and fun, and that there were loads of hang-out spots around the village where you wouldn't see an adult for hours on end. As he spoke he led her out of the village and took her to the various spots he had mentioned, hoping no one was there as he approached each one. There wasn't and so he relaxed into their afternoon.

He had found his feelings for her developing very quickly. He wanted to take her hand in his within 20 minutes and wanted to kiss her after an hour. He had felt a connection and believed wholeheartedly that they would become a couple over the next week or so before going back to school. He might even get to sate some of that sexual curiosity that ate away at him almost every waking hour. The very thought of that had him keeping his hands in his pockets to try and hide his very obvious excitement.

He was more than a little disappointed when he had finally walked her home and, on the doorstep, she had thanked him for a lovely afternoon and for showing her the village and then promptly turned and walked straight into the house. No kiss? He hadn't been expecting much but at least a quick peck wouldn't have gone amiss, would it? After all, hadn't she looked as though she had felt their connection too? Wasn't it obvious to her as well as him that they were clearly destined to be together? He had left feeling a little dejected and rejected, but on the walk back to the manse he came to the conclusion that she was simply shy and had hidden that by getting into the house as quickly as possible.

As he walked, he began to daydream – their first kiss, shy and tentative to begin with would become more passionate and confident as they continued, finally breaking away slightly breathless and both flushed with excitement. They would continue these illicit snogs for some weeks, talking in between and getting to know each other in a way that surpassed friendship and even family to become a deep and unbreakable love.

He had reached the manse just as his daydream had started to get more interesting, or at least more graphic as he imagined them moving on to what was known as heavy petting – he was determined to find out exactly what that entailed before he and Ailsa got to that stage – and by the time he had reached the front door the dream had begun to flash forward to their first full sexual encounter.

Closing the front door, he had run straight upstairs to his room, trying desperately to hold the imagery and sensations he had conjured in his mind. Closing the bedroom door and jumping onto the bed he immediately started doing what countless pubescent boys had done for many thousands of years, all the time praying his mother or father would not enter the room unexpectedly.

He had tried to call on her a few times over the 10 days leading up to the return to school and was always left disappointed. She had either found an excuse for why she wasn't available or had on two occasions invited him in only for them to sit in the living room having excruciating and stilted conversations with her parents. He felt she constantly contrived to avoid seeing him alone, but having already formed the opinion she was a shy and quiet girl these minor rejections were to be expected, he had supposed.

On the first day back to school, he had collected her as promised. On the walk there, their conversation was stilted and perfunctory – not at all the dazzling, rich and deep repartee he had imagined. Neither was there any gazing into each other's eyes, ignoring all others around them, or a hand-in-hand romantic stroll towards school. He had thought of nothing else for days and had in his mind's eye a crystal-clear image of how this should have gone. The reality was as far from the dream as Inverurie Loco FC were from the Scottish Premier League.

'You'll be in a different form class to me,' he had mumbled, as he trailed along beside her. 'It's done alphabetically so you'll be with Mrs Daniels and I'm in with Mr Proudfoot, but I'll show you where to go so you'll know for tomorrow.'

She had replied with a lacklustre 'Ok, thanks' and that was that.

That was the height of the walk to school. His disappointment was so strong he felt like he could reach out and touch it, receiving an electric shock in return.

Over the following weeks his disappointment had slowly morphed into resentment and frustration. It wasn't long before she was leaving ahead of him to walk with new-found friends, girls from her form class who were notoriously part of the 'cool' clique. They were soon joined by the boys from this set – football and rugby playing school heroes, all big-built sons of farmers, with fair-haired rugged good looks and the flushed cheeks common to many Highland lads that girls seemed to find so attractive.

He had watched enviously as she laughed and messed around in and amongst a group of people he rarely spoke

175

to, never mind had the gall to try and join. Most disheartening was the obvious way she had opened up. She wasn't the shy, introverted girl he had believed she was – she was energetic and vocal with a fun, carefree nature that the cool set simply lapped up.

Slowly, however, the dream of the life they would have together had re-emerged. He would lie half asleep at night and his mind would slowly concoct the story of their lives – predicting every move, twist and turn of their sometimes turbulent but always passionate and loving relationship all the way to their old age and beyond. So detailed were these dreams and imaginings that he could, had he the inclination or desire to do so, have written a full-length romantic novel to rival Wuthering Heights or anything by Joanna Trollope.

In his dreams, they would return to being friends – she realising that the kids she'd been hanging out with were shallow and ultimately uninteresting. Slowly they would come to realise, so the story went, that they were far closer in nature than their initial meetings had indicated. He was more open, funny and lively, she would turn out to have a great love of books and an interest in politics. They would spend hours either laughing at joke after joke or running about like little kids in a quiet area of the woods, shouting and shrieking as they fooled about. Other times they would sit quietly, under a tree on pleasant summer evenings, discussing a particularly good novel or what they would change if they were in government.

That tree would be the site of their first kiss, as they sat both reading from the same book. Their heads would move closer together, then they would turn at the same time to say something, their eyes meeting and shy smiles appearing on their lips and finally, with sighs of relief and

176

growing excitement, they would kiss. Both had wanted to for weeks but neither had plucked up the courage to do anything about it and now was the time. It was natural and unforced, with neither of them making the running but simply submitting to the moment.

The dream had become more fantastical from this point on. They would move quickly from kissing to touching and ultimately, naturally, they would make love in the woods where their relationship had been born. At this point he would always have to break off and relieve the ache in his groin, always being careful not to make too much noise or stain the bed covers.

Sated, he would lie back a little breathlessly and continue his internal narrative.

Realising the disapproval of their parents (they were too young to be so close, they had to finish school, get good grades, and so forth) they would hatch a plot to run away to Edinburgh. There they would find exciting and fulfilling lives, he as a novelist and politically-active commentator, she in PR or advertising, both of them rising to become leading lights in their fields. Their parents' initial horror and shock at their running away would soon turn into pride and admiration. Eventually, they would willingly give their approval to marriage. Children would follow and life would be bliss for the rest of their lives.

And so, the dreams would go on … night after night, becoming ever more real, more solid and then finally slipping from fantasy into a form of reality. They were no longer imaginings, they were – ultimately and inevitably – a map for how the future would look. It *would* happen, could happen no other way. There were no alternate paths, no twists or turns in the route. She would be his, and was meant for no one else. She would see that clear as day in the weeks or months to come.

He would make it happen.

And then *she* laughed.

Chapter Thirteen

Fran Pearson and Malcolm Tanner were sitting in the saloon bar of the Porters Arms, a good old copper's pub, one that had seen several generations of police officers sitting quietly discussing the job over a post-work pint or two. They had just come out of an 'inter-departmental liaison and cooperation planning meeting', the kind of stuff that would make even the most ardent fan of management meetings shudder. Both had moved at breakneck speed towards 'the Porter' at the end of the meeting without a word being passed between them as to their destination.

Police officers rarely talked about anything other than the job, and Pearson and Tanner were no exception. On the surface of it, it was just two colleagues chatting over their respective caseloads or certain managerial problems they were facing. In reality, it was an informal case review being conducted with two pints of Speckled Hen sitting between them.

'So,' Pearson said. 'Bring me up to speed, Malcolm. What are your thoughts in general about the evidence we have so far?'

Tanner took a healthy gulp of his ale and wiped the froth from his top lip before replying, 'Well, I'm not sure we have much, Fran.' He said this with a slight twist of his mouth indicating he was about to disappoint his boss. 'Any so-called evidence we have is purely circumstantial, at best. Handley has looked further into the dates and details from the FO – that was a good spot, that pattern he saw almost straightaway. Anyway, he reckons there is some correlation between the dates and locations where Marcus Travers was away on business and some of the murders we are attributing to the Charmer, but not all of them, it would appear.'

Tanner took another swig of beer then said, 'Good lad that, dedicated and determined. I need to work on his focus a little perhaps but he went through reams of the stuff the FO sent over. It may be that there's more to be gleaned from it all but I really need more manpower to cover all the ground. Although, I have to say, I'm not sure we'll get much further on that line. Some dates match, so what? Still doesn't really mean much – there's likely to be as many, if not more, where they don't.'

Pearson nodded and frowned at the same time. Tanner hoped the nod meant agreement to more manpower while the frown was likely to be a concern for budgets and so on. Pearson sympathised with his boss and friend – budgets were the bane of all senior officers' lives, Tanner's included.

'OK,' was all Pearson said. 'What else have we got?'

'As I said, we should probably go through every line of the FO's information but I also wanted Handley working a couple of other angles. He's already been over to the Travers' place and collected whatever they could find in terms of fingerprints, hair and items that might still yield DNA. Looks like we've found some prints on an old paint can which is something. The rest is with forensics now, so we'll see what turns up. Also, I wanted him to work the Julia Metcalfe angle so I've sent him off to The Guardian and also got him checking as many sources as he can think of to try to track her down. We still figure they're together somewhere, so finding her may well lead to finding him.'

Again Pearson nodded. 'Yeah I think you might be right there.' He appeared to think a moment before saying, 'OK, tell you what. I can give you budget for two more bodies –

you can pick who you want to work with. That should give you enough to continue with the information from the FO and yet keep opening other lines of enquiry.'

Tanner raised his pint gratefully towards his boss and said a relieved thank you. Pearson raised his own glass in return.

'What are your thoughts on the Belgian angle?' Pearson asked after drinking nearly a quarter of his pint in one go.

'You've had my report on that Fran,' Tanner replied.

'Yeah I know, I picked it up the other day. I have to confess to only really skim-reading it – mind was elsewhere, I'm afraid. Besides, I prefer to hear what you actually have to say rather than what you've put in your report.'

'Ha, sure,' he said, knowing his boss' preference to hear what was going on rather than read it. 'Interesting, I would say. There are definite similarities, in MO and circumstance at least, so it's probable the murders were perpetrated by the same person – or a bloody copycat which would really screw things right fucking up. The Belgian killings would also explain why he went quiet in the UK. Anyway, the really interesting thing, the clincher, was that they spotted a pattern in some of the wounds on all five victims. I wouldn't have spotted it even if I knew what I was looking for but when Inspector Montreux pointed it out it's clearly deliberate. It's called the burning bush and is a symbol used by the Presbyterian church. So, I got our lab boys to see if they could spot anything similar on the UK murders we've attributed to the Charmer.'

Pearson looked pensive and interested in equal measure; he really wanted there to be a link, not just with Belgium but something that linked, conclusively, to the UK murders.

'And did they?' he asked, voice tightening slightly as he spoke.

Tanner took another draught before nodding and saying, 'Yep, on every single one, in the same place, they found the same pattern. He's got better at it as time goes on – practice, I suppose – but it's there, going all the way back to 2000 which is the earliest we have on file.'

Pearson let out a sigh of relief and triumph, he had been right all along. His conjecture – that they were dealing with the same killer, that it was a series – had always been based on the similarities in MO. Now he had concrete evidence that they were dealing with a serial killer. He was so caught up with his own satisfaction that he missed some of what Tanner was saying to him. 'Sorry, Malcolm, what was that?'

Tanner simply smiled and said, 'I was saying that I took the opportunity to share this information with every force. I've asked them to check any unsolveds not already attributed to The Charmer file, with particular focus on this burning bush mark. I figure this symbol holds some meaning for him and he is likely to have been carving that into his victims from the beginning. We may find some much earlier murders which could allow us to at least give him a locus for those ones. That's not necessarily useful to us now but it might narrow our search parameters and, more to the point, enable us to either keep Marcus Travers in the frame or eliminate him. If there was no way he was in the area at the time he's probably not our man. Either way we won't be using our resources on a blind alley.'

Pearson nodded. 'Good call Malcolm ... the earliest one I could attribute to the Charmer was 1999 and that was a bit tenuous, to be honest. So, I would suggest anything before that time. And maybe – if there are any that do match – he might have slipped up, made mistakes on those earlier outings and left some useable forensics, without any of the confusion we've faced since. I always suspected that the MO was too clean, too proficient, that there must have been others that were less well executed and messier. Serial killers need to hone their abilities just as much as anyone else.'

'My thinking exactly,' Tanner said. 'We might find some linking forensics, which would likely be our man. We still need to catch him first to prove that, of course.'

'Don't remind me,' Pearson said with a sigh. 'I know we're still swimming against the current but we need to gather as much as possible and hope we get a breakthrough and catch someone. Then we'll have something tangible to work with. My round.' Pearson stood to head for the bar.

While Pearson fetched two fresh pints, Tanner sat playing with his now empty glass, trying to determine what to do with the new resources at his disposal. He was still thinking when Pearson placed the beers on the table. He nodded his thanks – lips pursed and eyes looking into the middle distance.

Eventually he said, 'I reckon one direction worth looking into would be to see if we can't find exactly how far-ranging this guy is. I mean, we've got Belgium and the UK so logic would follow that he could travel further than that without raising too much suspicion. I could put Davey Roberts onto requesting information on similar murders in France, Germany, maybe Italy and Spain as well. Might just give us a bigger picture.'

'Yep, seems a sensible way to go,' Pearson replied. 'Might not tell us much but the more information the better I'd say.'

Tanner took a quick sip of his beer and cocked an eyebrow at his boss.

'Another thing. There won't be much of it – fewer cameras back then, plus poor image quality and tapes being re-used – but I think it might also be useful to go through all the old CCTV we've got for previous incidents.' Tanner said.

Before Pearson could reply Tanner waved him down. 'I know you went through every minute you had last time around, Fran, but you wanted fresh eyes on this and it'd be remiss of us not to revisit every angle. Besides, technology's improved a lot – if we can find a number of images where we think we're looking at the same guy we might be able to enhance the images and get a better look at him.'

'Yeah, again you're right, as always Malcolm. That should be high on the list,' Pearson said, smiling at Tanner's look of pride at the 'as always' part of his last statement.

'I've also been thinking that if there are any similar murders in other countries, we might be able to put a really accurate timeline together, essentially following him around,' Tanner continued. 'There might then be a chance we can spot him on ferries, flights, Eurostar or whatever. Also, we might get an idea of how long he stays in any given country. If there was a connected murder in France, for example, and then only a few days later another one in Germany, it's likely he only stops in one country for a short period of time. Again, we can test that against the FO's data, ruling Travers in or out.'

'That's a reasonable line of enquiry,' Pearson agreed, swallowing another quarter pint. Tanner wondered how his boss could drink so much beer and never put weight on – he was as slim today as 20 years ago.

'I have a concern,' Pearson muttered, staring into his beer. 'Is this whole Travers thing a total dead end? Don't get me wrong, there's clearly something going on there but is it anything to do with the Charmer? I mean, what do we have that really suggests it's him, or that he knows anything about the case at all? Do you think he's our man, Malcolm? Honest opinion please.'

Tanner considered this for a moment before replying. 'Well, Fran, without sounding defeatist he's about the only lead we've got and as such at least we're doing *something*. Having said that, my honest view is … I don't know, which I realise is a total cop-out. As I see it, we've got some reasonable circumstantial to suggest he's a 'probable' – right now I wouldn't even put him in the 'likely' category. We'll have a much better idea about it when forensics come back to us. If there's a match anywhere then he jumps to prime suspect. My gut tells me he's involved somehow but I can't tell you how.'

Pearson hmmed and nodded, still looking into his beer.

Tanner seemed to have another thought. 'I know we've checked the records for the periods of inactivity, in case our man was inside for something else – which, of course, got us nowhere. But we haven't checked those periods with Travers' movements and circumstances. I wonder, would it be worth going over those longer periods of inactivity with Mrs Travers? You know, in case there was something going on, family stuff maybe, that would explain the cessation? If there was a plausible reason for the killer to have stopped during that time it all adds up to more circumstantial evidence – again, it pins him or drops him.'

185

Again Pearson nodded his agreement. 'Yep, anything at all you can think of Malcolm. Like I say, the more we've got the better. I just wish it was substantial, real evidence – good, solid, physical stuff.' He prodded his finger on the table during these last four words, showing his annoyance and frustration at the whole affair.

'It's just like fucking last time,' he said, voicing a similar thought to the one Tanner had been having.

Tanner's phone began to ring. He fumbled in his inside jacket pocket trying to free it, mumbling curses as he went, eventually wresting it free.

'Tanner,' he said sharply on answering. 'Yes Tony, go ahead.'

He listened to Handley's report, nodding every once in a while. He finished the call with a quick 'Thank you, Tony, good work.'

Placing the phone back in his pocket, he sat back, face grim.

'Well?' said Pearson, eyebrows raised.

'Handley's found Julia,' Tanner replied.

'87

His thoughts wouldn't leave him alone. Every night and much of the day they were there – creeping, waiting to surface, then bursting into his consciousness, an explosion of images and feelings and desires. He found it almost impossible to push them back to the darker recesses of his mind. They were so strong, so powerful, that the urge to act almost overwhelmed him.

He would see *her* blood-soaked and pleading, and then *she* would morph into another woman, one he didn't know yet but felt he did. She – this other one – was his proxy, a mirror containing *her* reflection. She would be similar in so many ways: personality, looks and shape, with an unidentified something about her – something that at this time he couldn't quite pinpoint. And he knew she was out there, this perfect copy.

The images would swirl then – kaleidoscopic – into a rush of other faces, other bodies and over them all the burning bush would rise and flame and burn. This image, he knew, was for *them*. *They* who had made him stand and take the shame as *she* laughed. And he also knew this image would be carved into the flesh of every one of those other women. It would be there for all to see, but especially for *them* to see and then *they* would know.

He lay in the dark with eyes wide open, flicking his gaze around different points on the ceiling as though searching for something on the Artexed plaster above. And perhaps that was exactly what he was doing: the lumps, swirls, dips and peaks in the plaster seemed to move, forming shapes and pictures as they wove together and then separated, only to coalesce into something new – sometimes interesting, other times banal or plain ridiculous. But he wasn't looking for these shapes. They were just a consequence of his eye movements, and his eyes were moving as he searched for answers. Answers to questions he didn't want to ask with answers he didn't want to hear.

His fists and jaw clenched as these answers came to the forefront of his mind anyway, despite his best efforts. He didn't want to go down this path, he knew the consequences and the horror he would wreak on those he chose. He squeezed his eyes closed in an attempt to shut out the babble in his mind, but still the internal dialogue continued.

He could hear his parents in the bedroom next door, had heard them for the last hour or so. It had started with the occasional unintelligible mutter and had gradually grown into the unmistakable sound of sex, or whatever activity they considered to be sex. He hated hearing them, not because of the obvious embarrassment at being aware of your parents having sex, but because he envied them – envied the pleasure they clearly derived from their activities, a pleasure he knew he would never feel. He already knew that simple, straightforward sex would ultimately end in failure and rejection. The sex he wanted, needed in fact, was much, much darker – so dark most people would describe it as evil.

Turning his back to the wall that adjoined his parents' room, he tried to block out the noises. Closing his eyes again he gave in to the internal monologue, allowing the deep, dark thoughts to form and raise their questions and provide the images that sometimes haunted his dreams and other times aroused him so much he would ejaculate in his sleep. This would wake him and he would then lie there feeling sick at the act.

He felt the frustration of realising he couldn't even assuage these feelings by masturbating. Masturbation conjured feelings of self-loathing and disgust, of humiliation and hatred, another resentment to sit alongside the others in his psyche. It was a certainty – he would never masturbate again.

He knew he had been changed irrevocably on *that* day. When *she* had laughed. Until then his thoughts and fantasies about sex had, as far as he knew, been pretty normal. They had involved all the usual trappings of the desires of a young teenage boy: breasts, legs, the imagined feel of being inside a girl, the warmth and the excitement. They were all lost now. There would be no more fantasies so pure, so normal, so natural.

With his mind focused on sex and its consequences the images began anew – this time stronger, with more clarity and power. Penetration would now only ever occur with a knife. The act of plunging the sharp steel over and over into the soft flesh of *her* proxy would replace the mechanics of sex. This would be his sexual union with these women. This would be how he expunged the shame.

He would hunt for that one woman. The one that would be a perfect copy. The one that would make the desire, the urge to kill, stop. She would make the images disappear. And when he found her and delivered her to his rage, maybe then he could be normal and live the life he had imagined all those years ago. It would become his quest to find her.

Many others would die along the way, but they would simply be steps on the road to freedom, and each would bear the mark of the bush, burning on their flesh. Each would add to the guilt he would transfer to *them* and *her*.

They would know then, *they* would see publicly what *they* had done and feel his shame and his rage and his guilt.

As he explored these thoughts and found comfort in them, the urge to carry out his plans, to act on them and bring them to fruition grew in his mind. It became so strong that he knew he would no longer feel scared of capture or failure. The urge to achieve his goal would drive him on and sustain him for as long as it took.

He found sleep then with dreams of The One and The Quest to find her, with dreams of Delivering her and the others and behind it all The Urge raging, pushing him on.

As he slept soundly for the first time in months a small smile played across his lips.

Chapter Fourteen

Handley had spent most of the morning searching every public record he could think of for Julia Metcalfe. The problem he was having was that there were quite a lot of them in Greater London alone, never mind the rest of the country. With no image of her as yet and little other information he had very few ways to whittle down the list. Eventually, he gave up on his efforts and headed out to talk to one of the sub-editors at The Guardian, figuring he would get more luck there than on a computer.

Their offices were in Kings Place, a short walk from King's Cross St. Pancras station. Handley stepped out onto the St. Pancras concourse, relieved to be off the tube. He felt distinctly uncomfortable in the cramped spaces of the trains, especially during busy periods, where his already large frame seemed to grow larger as more people got on and he simply couldn't get out of the way.

He walked the 100 yards or so to Kings Place, trying to un-tense his shoulders and breathe a little more easily.

Whilst he was admiring the light and airy atrium of the building's foyer, the features editor he had arranged to meet approached and introduced himself. He was a trim, bustling man named Gary Cannon. They shook hands as Handley politely turned down the offer of a tour but gratefully accepted the offer of a coffee. Cannon led them to a café just across from where they stood.

Once the coffees where placed on the table between them, Handley outlined the information he wanted on Julia Metcalfe: address, phone number and NI number plus any other information HR or other offices might hold.

He finished his list by asking, 'Can you tell me anything about what Ms Metcalfe might have been working on in the last three months, Mr Cannon?'

'Not as such no,' Cannon began. 'She wasn't, as far as I know, thinking of submitting anything here during that time. But I did speak to her a few months back and she said she was working on a fairly major story – although I also remember her saying that it was all a bit vague and needed a lot more work.'

Handley noted this down and asked, 'Didn't she give any further detail as to what it was about?'

'No,' Cannon replied. 'As I said, she felt it wasn't very concrete at that point. She was obviously not ready to share whatever it was in any detail.'

'Can you recall exactly when you had this conversation with Ms Metcalfe?' Handley asked.

'Not exactly, but I would imagine it was about three or four months ago now,' Cannon answered.

'And have you spoken to her since then?' Handley asked whilst jotting down a note.

'No, can't say I have Detective Handley.' Cannon's brow had begun to crease.

Handley could see that Mr Cannon was starting to get curious about his line of questioning. About time your journalistic instincts kicked in, he thought, or have you spent so long looking at other people's stuff that you've lost your touch?

'And is that usual, would you say? Or would you normally have more regular contact?' Handley tried to keep the smile from his face as Cannon's features settled into an expression of clichéd curiosity.

'It is fairly unusual, yes,' Cannon replied, sitting forward and looking more intently at Handley. 'We would catch up relatively frequently, dependent on what work I had for her or what stories she had for me. So, I suppose we would speak about once a month, certainly once every six weeks or so.'

It was Handley's brow that now furrowed. 'Didn't you find it strange then that she hadn't been in touch at all during that period of time?' he asked.

'No,' Cannon said, stretching the word out with a rising tone that made it sound more like a question. 'As I said, she told me she was working on a big piece, so I assumed it was taking up all her time. And I've been pretty busy myself so I simply haven't got around to calling her recently. Look, what is your interest in Julia, DC Handley? Is she OK? Has something happened?'

About time, Handley thought, but said, 'We're not sure Mr Cannon. It's possible she's fine and just tucked away working on her story. But there is also a possibility she either knows the whereabouts of or is actually with the person we would like to talk to.'

'I take it, in that case, that you can find neither Julia nor this other individual?'

'That's correct, sir,' was all Handley would say.

There was silence for a while until Cannon spoke again. 'Tell you what, detective, why don't you finish your coffee and I'll pop upstairs and gather the information you're after – how does that sound?'

'That'd be great, sir. I appreciate your help with this.'

'Not at all,' Cannon said as he hurried off towards the lift.

Handley had just enough time to finish his coffee before Cannon reappeared with a brown folder under one arm.

'This is everything we could lay our hands on, detective,' he said handing over the folder. 'There's her profile photo in there and I also took the opportunity to dig out the last couple of articles Julia submitted here. I don't know if they'll prove useful but I thought they may be of some interest to you.'

'Thank you, Mr Cannon,' Handley replied, accepting the folder. 'Very thoughtful – and as you say they may well be useful.'

Handley rose from the table and held out a business card. 'Thanks for your time and assistance, Mr Cannon. If anything else occurs to you, please get in touch.'

'There was one more thing, detective, that may save you some time,' replied Cannon, taking the proffered card.

'Yes?' said Handley, wondering why people always drew stuff out, rather than simply telling you straightaway. Was it out of a sense of drama, he thought, or did he just not have the ability to obtain pertinent information with his questioning?

'I noticed,' Cannon said, 'from Julia's personal information, that her listed address is here in London, which to be fair is where she spent most of her time. Only she has a second place, you see? I don't have the exact address but I know it was out near Tiptree in Essex. It's not on the file, not that it would need to be of course, but I thought it would help you to know – you may not have come across it otherwise.'

'Indeed, thank you, sir. That is very useful and will have saved us quite a lot of time,' Handley said. 'Now I've disturbed your day enough, thanks again.'

'Not at all,' Cannon replied shaking Handley's hand.

As he exited the offices, Handley resisted the urge to pull open the file and call DCI Tanner immediately. He wanted a chance to work through what was there and follow up where he needed to. So, feigning a casual air, he

194

walked back to the tube station and began to make his way back to the office.

He decided to read the contents of the file on the tube. All the information he'd requested was there, including the address of her London home which was in Islington. Handley sat expressionless for a moment – in his mind his meaty hand had just delivered an almighty slap to his forehead. She lived in Islington. He was on the Piccadilly line heading south. Had he looked at the file before boarding he could have got on the Victoria line at St. Pancras and gone straight to Highbury & Islington from there. With a grunt of annoyance at his own lack of foresight he rose from his seat and waited for the train to stop at the next station so he could turn around and start all over again.

*

With mixed feelings of relief and wariness Handley pushed the key into the lock of Julia Metcalfe's flat. The block had been easily found a short walk from the tube station. During his walk there he had called the office to have a check run on the address.

On arriving, he'd knocked on her door twice to no answer and had tried her mobile phone twice, again to no answer and with no ringtone sounds coming from inside the flat. The office called back to say the flat was rented and so a second call to the letting agent had resulted in a young, skinny and nervous woman turning up with a spare set of keys.

The door swung open easily enough and Handley peered down a short hall with two doors off to the side and a third facing him at the far end. All were closed. He made to enter the flat then realised the young letting agent was shuffling about behind him, trying to see past him into the flat whilst at the same time trying to avoid actually entering.

'It's ok, you can wait outside. No reason for us both going in,' he said, to the girl's relief.

There were several letters and a pile of junk mail inside the door, testifying to the flat having been empty for some time. Moving these carefully to one side with the toe of his shoe, Handley entered the hall.

He tried the door to the left first, which led to a messy bedroom. Clothes were strewn around the floor, hung carelessly on a drier and draped over what looked like an old armchair – although it was hard to see what it was under the mass of jeans, jumpers and t-shirts. A dresser to one side was covered with make-up and jars of various creams. Its drawers were all slightly open – spilling socks, knickers and bras. The bed was a double and hadn't been made, duvet thrown to one side. Clearly it had been left like that the last time its occupier had got up.

It was hard to be sure but Handley felt the room had always looked this way and the mess had not been created by anyone other than Julia Metcalfe herself.

He turned his attention to the door across the hall. As he'd suspected it was the bathroom, except with no bath, just a shower. The room also showed a certain lack of care and attention; it wasn't dirty exactly, it just looked like its upkeep was very low on the occupant's priority list. Again, nothing particularly stood out as noteworthy or troubling.

Finally, he turned his attention to the door at the far end of the hall. He already knew it must be the living room and, he assumed, the kitchen.

As soon as the door was open, he knew that the mess in front of him was not the casual untidiness of a busy and non-house-proud individual. The room had been turned upside down: paper and folders were scattered across the floor, an armchair had been turned over, two filing cabinets were lying on their sides with drawers pulled out – their contents, presumably, the swathes of paper on the floor.

Handley took an involuntary step back – he was in a crime scene. For some reason he hadn't expected that to be the case. He had thought he would find the flat in an untouched condition but perhaps yielding a clue as to the last time Julia had been there or where she might be now. The place being done over like this hadn't crossed his mind and now that it was obvious he cursed himself for the second time that day. He would have to explain to SOCO that he had touched a number of objects and door handles without gloves. There would be much tutting and heavenward glances and much embarrassment for him. Malcolm Tanner's unamused, frowning visage came into his mind, shaking his bald head with deep disapproval. Handley shivered.

He turned and headed straight back out of the flat and called it into the station. Half an hour later, two uniforms, a team of three SOCOs and Handley's colleague DS Davey Roberts were on scene.

'Nice one Tone,' was all Roberts had said when he heard of Handley's blunder. They were standing outside the block of flats having made way for SOCO to do their thing and having sent the now visibly trembling letting agent back to her office.

'Someone was looking for something in there,' Roberts said once they were alone. 'That doesn't look like standard burglary to me. Door wasn't forced for a start and the telly's still there.'

Handley nodded. Davey Roberts was a decent sergeant and a good detective but had a propensity for stating the obvious and in a way that sounded like it was a revelation.

'How do we play this, Davey?' Handley asked. 'I couldn't track down DCI Tanner to fill him in and Julia's still missing. I think we need to concentrate on finding her now as the highest priority. Should we work together or spread the tasks between us?'

'Yeah, Tanner's in some management meeting or something, so I'm in charge this afternoon,' Roberts said with a grin. 'I'll bring him up to speed when he's out. I heard you found out about a second address for her, that right?'

Handley nodded. 'Yeah, I haven't got an exact address but it's out in Essex somewhere.'

'OK,' Roberts said, 'you head back to the office, see what you can find on this second address. I'll wait here and see what comes up, if anything, and let you know as soon as I do anything that seems pertinent.'

Relieved at the decision over their course of action being taken out of his hands, Handley headed back to the tube station.

The hour it took to get back to the office felt like an eternity to Handley. He was desperate to find the second address for Julia Metcalfe and more desperate still to find her. His gut feeling was that she was in real trouble – either she was with Marcus Travers and both were on the run from whoever had turned the flat over, or Marcus and her had not been bosom buddies after all and he was the one who had turned the flat over. In either case, the likely outcome for Julia was not looking great.

The office was quiet when he eventually got back in. Most of his colleagues were out and it appeared the management meeting was still going on as there was still no sign of DCI Tanner. Handley swiftly headed over to his desk and unlocked the computer. He knew that with the new information he had on Julia Metcalfe he should be able to track down her second address easily enough. The search took five minutes – her second property was a cottage and, as Gary Cannon had said, it was near Tiptree in Essex. After a further five minutes he had a landline phone number for the place. He tried this several times and was unsurprised when there was no answer. On the off-chance he tried her mobile number again. Nothing.

Handley sat for a minute, fingers drumming on the desk, wondering whether he should wait for DCI Tanner, call DS Roberts or head straight out to Essex and let them both know he was on his way there. It took him 10 seconds to come to the conclusion that he couldn't wait. Snatching his jacket off the back of his chair he made for the exit, dialling DS Roberts as he went.

*

As was usual for that part of the country, the drive took far longer than it should have. Traffic, roadworks and finally single-track country lanes conspired to slow his progress, with Handley becoming more and more agitated as time went on.

Eventually, he found the cottage. It was a typical picture-postcard country cottage: ivy growing up the walls on either side of the door, with what had probably been a neat and pretty garden out front. Handley noted it hadn't been tended for some time, but then thought of the state

199

of Julia's bedroom and decided it didn't necessarily mean anything. Surrounded by fields with a small woodland visible not too far away, the place was almost a cliché for the rural idyll. The nearest neighbours – he'd checked before leaving the office – were half a mile in one direction and a mile in the other.

Leaving his car unlocked, Handley made his way to the front door and knocked loudly. When there was no answer he began peering through the front windows. They both looked into what appeared to be a living room and it was in a complete state. The similarity with Julia's flat was striking in that there was paper and files everywhere and furniture turned over; the only difference in this case was that the TV had been knocked over and lay smashed on the floor.

Becoming increasingly worried and concerned, Handley rushed round towards the back of the cottage. He found a back door in the side wall, which was locked. Further along the same wall was a small window but it was too grimy to see anything through it. Moving to the rear of the cottage there were two further windows. The first looked into the kitchen. Shielding his eyes from the reflecting sunlight, Handley peered in.

At first sight there was nothing of note to see. It was just a kitchen – there was a cooker and a fridge, various utensils hanging from a stand and a spice rack on the worktop. About to move on after this cursory glance he then realised his brain had been screaming that he had missed something. He looked again, more carefully this time.

After a second of complete stillness, Handley stepped back, turned and ran towards his car.

This was his second crime scene of the day, but this one contained a lot more blood.

'89

This was it. He was finally ready to make his move. The Quest would begin here, tonight. His heart rate climbed another notch. The hairs on his arms rose and his skin tingled with the rush of fear and excitement. He tried unsuccessfully to calm his breathing which came in short, rapid pulses. He felt like a lion stalking its prey, inching nearer while muscles bunched, readying for the attack. Confidence, fear, worry, horror and elation filled his mind; this was the culmination of years of mental turmoil, months of suppressing the Urge and weeks of trials and practice.

He felt ready, knew deep within himself exactly how this would play out. He was already anticipating every move his target would make, every possible action and reaction. A thrill ran down his spine as she drew nearer to his intended capture site. Tonight, for the first time, he would Deliver a proxy. Tonight he would, at last, be able to penetrate *her* over and over, spilling this woman's blood for *her.*

He was only 10 yards behind now. Too close, he told himself. He needed to calm himself down – his carefully laid plans would disappear if he allowed himself to get over-excited and rush in. Besides, he wanted to remember tonight for some time, wanted to be able to savour his first time in every detail, to dream the events of tonight with perfect clarity: the knife rising and falling, the muffled screams and pleas from his victim, the carving of her flesh with the mark of their shame.

With a huge effort of will, he stopped and bent down to feign tying his shoelace, calming himself with deep breaths whilst continuing to watch his target closely. Through hooded eyes he judged the distance between them to be just the right balance between close enough to make his move and far enough back for her to feel safe.

He had spotted her in Edinburgh's Grassmarket, a square that sat below the looming, ancient castle that dominated the city. It was a popular nightspot for all sorts, from students and dealers to local hard men and tourists. It was Friday night and the area was predictably busy. He had visited a couple of the bars that occupied almost every other building and hung around watching, searching out an appropriate target. He'd been doing his best to blend in. He knew that a well-heeled, 20-something guy drinking alone would draw looks and attention he didn't want. So he had, over the last few months, become adept at placing himself on the fringes of groups of drinkers, giving the appearance of being part of the group whilst staying far enough back to avoid them feeling he was trying to eavesdrop or butt in. It was on leaving one of these bars that she had come to his attention.

She'd been walking alone towards King's Stables Road, that wound around the sheer sides of the mound on which the castle stood. She was of indeterminate age – younger than 30 but older than 20 – and by the way she was dressed he thought she had to be either a local 'schemie' or a prostitute or both. Either way, she was ideal. King's Stables Road ran past a number of isolated spots and if he could catch her near one of these, he would have a chance.

He had wasted no time in moving to follow her and felt the excitement grow immediately – thoughts of sating the Urge for the first time beginning to fill his mind.

The Urge had been building steadily over the two years since its inception. He had graduated with a first class degree during that time and walked straight into a job at the Scottish Office. He hadn't been home since then and had kept contact with his parents to a minimum. At first, he had used the Urge as nothing more than a comforting fantasy, one that prevented nightmares and allowed the semblance of normal sleep and life. But gradually, it had grown – becoming more and more powerful with each imagining. Eventually, he had been unable to resist acting on it. The problem was the dreams and images didn't show him how to go about the tricky business of obtaining a suitable proxy. That was something he would have to work out for himself.

He had initially thought that it should be relatively easy to identify a target in a quiet unpopulated spot, grab them, and then drag them into the bushes to carry out whatever he intended to do. In reality the city was busy and people, especially at night, could be found in every nook and cranny. Potential targets were not easy to follow and even harder to catch. Suitable places were few and far between and even when he found these they always felt like obvious spots for the police to patrol looking for nefarious types up to no good. Then there were the nerves and other elements that were out of his control. What if his target were to fight back much harder than expected? What if he were interrupted? And what if he were to lose his bottle? There was so much that couldn't be controlled and he hated not having complete control.

Eventually, he had determined to begin with following potential targets to see how far he could get. The first few attempts went badly – they had spotted him quickly and would keep looking round to see if he was still there and then quicken their pace or head into a pub or café. It frustrated him that he couldn't appear nonchalant enough to look as though he was simply following the same route and not interested in them or where they were going. There had to be something in his demeanour that alerted them to his intentions.

And so he had practised his technique for another three weeks, gaining some confidence and improving each time. He perfected a casual strolling gait that gave the impression he was just another person wandering their way home after a night out. He worked on observing his target from the other side of the road whilst never giving any hint he was looking at them or giving any attention to their movements. He would watch carefully as they neared junctions and learned to judge when they might turn or simply cross over and carry straight on. He got good enough on occasion to also be in front of them, listening to the sound of their shoes on the pavement to determine where they were and where they went.

After many practice runs, he had soon felt confident he could follow someone for quite some way without being detected. He still had no idea how he would catch hold of them and get them to an appropriate spot. This he pondered for another week or more whilst continuing to follow women around the city. He would look for potential spots where he could make his move and then abandon the chase to examine those places more carefully. He would move into their shadows and wait, seeing how many people passed and if there was anyone else using the area for other purposes – drug-taking, sex, sleeping. Slowly he began to recognise the right sort of places where he might have a chance.

This had still left the hardest element – catching them. Resuming his trailing exercises, he had begun to work on plausible ways he could move quickly up to his target and get close enough without frightening them. He tried simply upping his pace to see how close he could get but they immediately became wary and watched his approach carefully, their body language tense, ready for flight or fight. Gradually, however, a couple of techniques had begun to show some promise.

The first technique was to look around a lot whilst following them, painting the picture of a lost tourist or new arrival in the city. For this to work it was best to be on the opposite side of the road and keep pace with them, then move a little faster to get slightly ahead. As they approached a likely ambush point, he would look exasperated and whilst crossing the road call out to them with an innocent-sounding 'Excuse me, I wonder if you could help me?' Then he would simply ask for directions. The fact that he stood a little out of arm's reach and that he was asking them for help appeared to be sufficient to put them at their ease. His opportunity to pounce would come when they, inevitably, turned to point in the correct direction.

The second technique was even simpler and allowed him to jog towards them whilst offering a similarly innocent 'Excuse me.' He would make sure he had a fiver in his pocket and would then approach, waving the note, and state that he thought he had seen them drop it. Most people, it seemed, would drop their guard a little when confronted with a good deed and presented with money. He had two opportunities to act with this technique: when they looked down at the proffered note or when they reached to take it – either way they were distracted enough to stop paying attention to him.

During all those weeks of practice he had carried a large kitchen knife with him, one he had bought especially for

206

his forays out into the night. It served to remind him why he was doing this and helped concentrate his mind.

Now, as he followed the woman along King's Stables Road, he reached down and felt the handle through his jacket, checking it was secure in the pocket he had sewn into the lining specifically for carrying the blade. He had chosen the dropped fiver technique – she looked the sort who would readily accept some money, whether it was hers or not. As they approached a likely-looking area of grass and bushes right at the base of the castle mound, he quickened his pace and pulled the five-pound note from his pocket.

'Excuse me, dear!' he called as he jogged towards her.

She turned and eyed him warily, taking small backward steps as he made his approach.

'Aye, wha'?' she asked when he was still 8-10 feet away.

'I think you may have dropped this a moment ago,' he said with a smile, slowing his pace so that his approach appeared as unthreatening as possible.

She looked down at his waving hand and then at the note it contained. He watched as he saw the look of surprise cross her face, and smiled inwardly. He had been right to pick this technique – she probably needed the cash. He could have acted then but chose to wait, judging the distance and the timing to be slightly out.

'Aw, aye mebby ah did, thanks,' she said, visibly relaxing and extending her hand towards him to take the money. He advanced another couple of paces towards her.

His heart began to race and his mouth went dry. At last he was about to cross the threshold, the point of no return. The Urge would be sated for the first time in its existence. He could feel the tremor in his hands. She would succumb easily – he would overpower her and she would be his. The Urge felt like a caged, screaming beast in his mind, raging and spitting at him to take this chance.

He felt himself harden with the prospect of the knife plunging in and out of her body, the power he would wield over her filling his desires. Her face appeared ghosting over the face of the woman in front of him and he knew the Quest had started. This was it, this was where it would all begin.

Now! His mind shouted at him. This is your chance!

With snake-like speed he grabbed her arm with his left hand – the one that had held the note which now fluttered down towards the pavement – and reached inside his jacket with his right, all the while pulling her towards the dark area of grass.

But she was stronger than he had anticipated and resisted – screaming and shouting – slowing his attempts to drag her into the bushes. Eventually, with a great amount of hauling and pulling, he got her onto the grass where she slipped and so he could drag her more easily to where he wanted. All the noise she had been making un-nerved him. He held her down while looking anxiously as far as he could up and down the street. There was no one about. Clenching his jaw to steel himself for what was to come he turned his attention back to the struggling woman.

But that instant of inattention had been enough to allow her to squirm into a better position. Her legs were now free and she pulled both back then directed an almighty kick into his midriff. He was fit and well-muscled but he hadn't expected the blow and it forced the air from his lungs, making him double over and gasp. She took her opportunity and scrambled to her feet before placing another well-aimed kick towards his temple. It connected with a thud that rang through his head, the high heel of her shoe catching him just in front of his ear.

Dazed and confused he could do nothing to stop her running back down the street towards the Grassmarket.

'Bitch!' he screamed, as red-hot rage filled his entire being. Rage at the stupid cunt who reacted in all the wrong ways. Rage at himself for not committing himself, not anticipating events fully and not retaining control of the situation.

The Urge, too, raged and screamed and flailed around in his mind. It had been let out of its cage and now ran wild and free inside his head and body – unsated and hungry, furious at his inability to feed it the violence and death it needed so badly. It battered the inside of his skull with pent-up fury all the while spitting invective and insults at his shortcomings.

The anger quickly turned to fear. He was in real trouble and the fear of capture before he had even begun cut through all the pain and confusion in his mind. Rising a little groggily, he moved as quickly as he could out onto the street. He began to run in the opposite direction, knowing he could cut off this street and get into Princes Street Gardens and hopefully lose any pursuit in there. As he ran, he realised he couldn't feel the knife banging against his side from inside his pocket. It must have fallen out during the struggle and it was now too late to return for it. Similarly, the fiver had been left forgotten but hopefully that would just get blown away by the ever-present Edinburgh wind.

He made it back to his New Town flat without incident. His heart was racing and his face and stomach both throbbed horribly. The rest of that night was sleepless and restless. He had failed, and failed miserably, leaving evidence behind and on his face – when he looked in the mirror a large bruise was already forming. He cursed his lack of foresight and inability to properly control the situation.

At least he had the rest of the weekend to concoct a viable excuse to give work colleagues on Monday. He would most likely tell them he had been the victim of an attempted mugging and would practise an appropriate-sounding voice and demeanour to go with it.

The rest of the weekend was spent pacing the flat, trying to think.

On Monday morning there was a small piece in The Scotsman about the attack. It was relatively vague with a brief and unspecific description of the man the police were looking for. He read it with a mix of relief and shame. He could so easily have been caught on the night and could still be found if anyone named him as looking like the attacker or if a work colleague connected his bruising with the newspaper article's description of the attacker's likely injuries.

He spent the week under high anxiety, waiting for a knock on his flat door or to see a police officer head towards him at his work desk. But nothing happened. He began to assume he was in the clear.

As his fear relaxed the Urge began to return but now it was taunting him, gnawing at him every night. He had failed it and failed it at the first attempt. There was no going back to the techniques he had so carefully practised and worked through over the last two months. His plan had been a poor one and poorly executed. He would never fulfil the Urge that way, could not attempt that again.

210

But the Urge only grew stronger and more persistent. It needed to be satisfied and soon. He could resist it only for short periods of intense concentration, otherwise it would creep and slide to the front of his mind. Demanding. Screaming its desire. Decrying him as a fool and an incompetent. Filling and echoing around his head until he could take it no more.

The answer came to him one evening. He would pay for his lessons. He would pay for them like any other evening class student or learn-from-home language course. He needed to serve his apprenticeship and learn more each time. He needed to practise with professionals.

He would satisfy the Urge with patience and training, and with a clear plan of action. He would prepare himself with a mini-quest, one of learning and honing skills. He would perfect his art, readying himself to begin the Quest proper.

And then he would fully excise her from his thoughts.

That night he went in search of a prostitute. Prostitutes would be his practice and his tutors.

Two days later the news would be filled with the gruesome murder of an 18-year-old sex worker.

Chapter Fifteen

Handley had organised some backup from the local force and had yet another team from SOCO on site by the time he saw Malcolm Tanner's car pull up outside the cottage. His stomach turned a little as he noted DCS Pearson was in the passenger seat. Tanner made Handley feel nervous but Pearson virtually terrified him. He was relieved when they both lit cigarettes and Tanner waved over to say they would be a minute or two. That little extra time allowed him to run through what he'd done upon seeing the blood on the kitchen floor, mentally ticking off procedures and hoping he hadn't missed anything.

Handley, who had been resting against the bonnet of his car, pushed himself up as the two senior officers trod on their cigarette ends and headed over. They ducked under the police tape now stretched from the corners of the front garden to the far side of the road where they had been tied to traffic cones for the want of anything else to secure them to.

'You ok son?' Tanner asked, looking Handley over. 'You look a bit pale.'

'I'm fine sir,' replied Handley, who was genuinely surprised to find he did feel fine. 'Just tired, I think. And well, you can see there's been a lot to organise.'

Tanner simply nodded and grunted his response, turning to look at the cottage.

Fran Pearson continued to look at Handley for a little longer then also turned towards the cottage, saying in his trademark gruff voice, 'So is it definitely Julia Metcalfe?'

'Yes sir,' Handley replied, resisting the urge to stand to attention. Pearson had spoken to Handley on maybe four or five occasions, and on each occasion Handley had restricted his answers to those same two words – never venturing anything further for fear of making some horrendous slip or showing himself as the amateur he felt he was.

This time, however, Pearson wanted more detail and indicated as much by glancing over to Handley again and raising his eyebrows.

Handley took a breath … his mind kept harking back to his earlier mistake and he was now praying he hadn't made another stupid error here.

Managing to gain a modicum of control he said, 'I got a picture of her from The Guardian, it's definitely her sir.'

He then briefly outlined his day's endeavours to find Julia Metcalfe, ending with his arrival at the cottage and subsequent events.

*

When he had looked through the window a second time, the picture presented to Handley was very different to his first cursory glance. When he had shifted his weight over to move towards the second window a shaft of light from the lowering sun had caught the doors of the cupboards running below the worktop on the opposite wall. They were wooden or wooden-style veneer and so under his shadow they appeared unremarkably brown. But with the additional light now hitting them Handley could see smears and spatters over a number of the doors of something with a similar dark red-brown colour. The colour, the patterns and his instincts told Handley he was looking at dried blood.

The spatters criss-crossed over the width and height of the doors. Some were long and thin, running across more

213

than one door, others were shorter and fatter, ending in splatter marks. There were drips running down through the crosses and tiny spots could also be seen here and there. Finally, his eyes fell on a large smear running down one door – made, unmistakably, by a hand. He followed the smear down to the floor.

He could only see a very small area of flooring. The height and size of the window and edge of the worktop on his side of the kitchen obscured most of it from view. The part he could see had more splatters and blobs surrounding the trail of blood that continued out of view. Right on the edge of the frame of his view he was certain he could see the very tip of a finger, long-nailed and slender, almost out of sight and – presumably – attached to the rest of a body.

It was at this point that Handley had run for his car.

Breathlessly, Handley called dispatch and requested immediate backup from the local Essex force. He had been tempted to force one of the doors open and head straight into the property but had stopped himself. The blood was dry and old and what he could see of the hand was grey-blue and withered. He wasn't going to find whoever it was alive and anyone else in the cottage could easily leave through the other door, unseen by him.

The property, and therefore the evidence, was secure. The best course of action was to wait for backup, secure the area and only enter once SOCO had arrived.

A marked car with blue lights flashing had arrived soon after, bearing two uniforms, and between them they set up the cordon. The two officers from Essex wanted their local SOCO to handle the scene, citing the time savings to be had by getting a team there sooner. But Handley had insisted they wait for people from the team assigned to his office, pointing out that they had a linked scene in London and as such all evidence should go through one lab.

The argument had persisted until one of the Met's Scene of Crime vans pulled up behind the marked patrol car. Well done guys, Handley thought, pleased he had got his way – even if it was by default.

The front door had given way fairly easily under the ministrations of the male officer and his 'enforcer' battering ram. His female colleague had moved to the rear of the property soon after arriving, just in case someone was inside and ran for it. Handley – having donned a white coverall, over-shoes and mask, along with his forensic officers – entered first, shouting, 'Police!' before lifting the mask over his mouth and stepping inside.

The cloying, sickly-sweet smell of decay had penetrated his mask when he was less than two strides inside the door. It seemed to cling to the walls and carpet and Handley knew it would already have made its way onto his shirt and that it would need at least one soak in detergent and two washes to have any hope of getting it out.

The hall was small, with one door directly opposite the front door and a flight of steep stairs leading upward immediately to Handley's right. Beyond the stairs the hall terminated in another closed door. A couple of women's summer coats occupied two of the four coat hooks fixed to the wall between the two doors. There was nothing else to be seen.

Handley had assumed the door at the end led to the living room which he had already seen through the front windows. He hadn't looked into the second rear window earlier, but the PC now stationed at the rear of the cottage had checked and informed them it was a dining room. It followed that the door he was looking at would then open into that room.

With no sound of movement within, Handley had stood to one side and let go ahead of him. They moved past, awkwardly manoeuvring their large bags and pieces of equipment, the man taking the dining room door, the woman the living room. Handley followed the second SOCO into the living room.

Handley had been greeted with a different angle of the same picture he'd seen through the windows. The room was in chaos, furniture had been turned over and paper was strewn everywhere. Trying to take in the room, Handley realised he had no idea where to start so looked to the forensic scientist making her way carefully through the mess.

'This'll take some going through,' she said over her shoulder. 'Body and its immediate surroundings first though.'

Handley had nodded his assent and turned his attention to the open door leading to the kitchen. The tiled floor near the door looked clean and untouched but Handley knew from experience that might not be the case; there was every likelihood that under forensic examination tiny amounts of blood would show up, micro-droplets that would have sprayed the area like an aerosol out from the point where the assault took place. Again, he let SOCO take the lead.

She stepped carefully through the door and looked to her left.

'Christ,' was all she said as she put her bag down and stepped further into the kitchen.

Handley had stepped in a few paces behind her. Following the direction of her gaze his eyes immediately fell on the body – lying face down, head turned towards him in what would have been a large pool of blood, now dried and congealed. Even with the obvious signs of decay and the horrid rictus features of the long-dead, he knew it was Julia Metcalfe.

The other SOCO officer was already kneeling on the far side of the body, taking swabs from the copious amounts of blood surrounding it. He looked up as they entered.

'We're gonna need most of our markers just for in here,' he had said, indicating around the room with the cotton bud he was holding. 'No further than that please, DC Handley, we'll need to put plates down before you can move through here. Why don't you check out the rest of the place while we work in here?'

Looking around, Handley had taken in the blood that seemingly covered the whole kitchen. It was no less shocking for having dried. Glad that he didn't have to spend any more time in that charnel mess he nodded and retraced his steps back through the living room.

Moving back through the hall he had then glanced into the dining room. A table and chairs had stood in the centre of the room: the table had been pushed aside and was sitting at a skewed angle, three chairs had been knocked over and scattered across the floor, two stood incongruously upright and appearing to sit precisely where they should have done, the final chair had canted over and come to rest on two legs, back rest leaning against the sideboard that stood under the window. A smear of blood ran along the wooden floor and through the door into the kitchen, already marked with one of the yellow numbered markers used by SOCO.

With very little else to see, Handley had turned and headed up the stairs.

The first floor contained a bathroom, a bedroom – as messy as the London flat – and an office. With no sign that there had been any conflict up here Handley had turned his attention to the office. It was simply laid out: a desk and chair, a small filing cabinet and a set of deep drawers. There was a power lead and monitor on the desk but no laptop or PC. The drawers contained a myriad of hanging files, each with one or two document wallets inside. Each wallet was stuffed with papers, paperback books and newspaper cuttings. Handley shut the drawers with a sigh; the sheer quantity of paperwork that would have to be gone through between this office and downstairs was already daunting, then he remembered the piles back at Julia's London flat and the weight doubled.

The filing cabinet yielded yet more papers in hanging files. Each file had a title written on the label but no date. Handley pushed the last drawer shut with a muttered, 'Great.'

As he had turned to leave and head back downstairs his eye had caught a small photo frame sitting near the rear corner of the desk. It showed Julia smiling happily out at the camera, standing in between an older but equally happy couple – her parents, Handley presumed. He realised, sadly, that he had yet to trace any of Julia's family and that now this would have to be a priority. He had been hoping to find them to gain information as to her whereabouts but now would have to track them down only to deliver tragic, heartbreaking news.

Returning downstairs, he had called to the SOCO team in the kitchen that he would be outside, walked out the open front door, pulled down his mask, slumped against the bonnet of his car and called Detective Chief Inspector Tanner.

*

Pearson had absently nodded his way through Handley's account of the last three hours. He had spent much of the time with his eyes fixed on the upper windows of the cottage and had only turned his gaze back towards Handley to ask about the position of the body and the circumstances in which it had been found. Handley had the impression that his mind was somewhere else entirely.

'So, what's your initial thoughts Tony?' Handley took a moment to realise it was Tanner who had asked the question. He had been watching DCS Pearson so intently that he had been ignoring his immediate superior.

As if reading from an internal script Handley replied, 'It's Julia Metcalfe, no question, and she was murdered – stabbed multiple times, front and back. She's been there a while – SOCO are unwilling to say how long but hopefully the pathologist will be able to give something of an answer. She's on her way, by the way. Place has been turned over, there's papers and the like everywhere...'

Handley paused and thought for a moment. 'Interestingly, there's no sign of that upstairs. Whoever it was seemed to think they would find what they wanted downstairs. Or she interrupted them and they left immediately after killing her, which doesn't really make sense. After all, if she was dead they could have spent a month going through this place undiscovered.'

'True,' Tanner said. 'From what you've seen do you reckon SOCO are gonna turn up some physical? Fingerprints, shoe prints, fibre?'

'Yes sir,' Handley replied, 'almost certainly. They've found hundreds of traces – we've got to sort them of course but it's unlikely they are all Julia's.'

219

'And who else do you think we'll find here, Tony?' Tanner asked, voice low.

'I think we both know that, sir,' Handley replied.

'93

It had been a problem for some time, one he knew would only become more complex and harder to explain as time went on. It had become a topic of note in the office, one that generated mild ribbing or, in the case of some of the older women, sympathy. His closer friends commented from time to time and offered words of advice or encouragement but their enthusiasm would likely wane over time. It was a sticky subject for him to negotiate.

He had never had a girlfriend, nor shown any inclination towards having one.

He obviously couldn't explain why this was the case to his well-meaning friends. He could hardly say that the idea of 'normal' sex left him cold and angry. There was no way he could tell them that his real desires lay in the killing and marking of women with the symbol of his hate, that the *only* sexual interaction he wanted with women entailed a knife and blood and death.

The few female 'friends' he had — no more than colleagues in reality — would try to persuade him to meet with their single friends or come out with a crowd of them in order to 'take his pick'. But he knew from past experience that even if there was a girl he liked the look of and found he got on with, *her* face would creep into his mind. And before long all he would see was the girl he was talking to lying on the floor with blood spilling from hundreds of stab wounds and the burning bush carved into her thigh. He would then have to make his excuses and slip away.

He was smart enough to know that he couldn't risk any obvious association with anyone who could become a proxy. He would soon be discovered if a close associate were killed and then connected to the prostitute murders – as yet unsolved – that were being reported in and around central Scotland. The similarities in method would soon become apparent and he could find himself on the list of suspects. There was no way he would risk the Quest over such an obvious mistake.

He had come to realise, however, that the lack of romance in his life was drawing too much attention. That it could, perhaps, lead to friends and colleagues starting to wonder, should a news report or police statement use the word 'loner' or 'unattached'.

Besides, society generally expected a well-heeled young man to have his pick from any number of willing and attractive women. And at 28 years old, he knew it was starting to appear odd to his friends and colleagues.

And the one thing he knew he had to be was unremarkable, he had to blend into the crowd. He needed good camouflage to be able to maintain the Quest. If he could give every indication that he was a normal man with normal tastes then he could operate more freely, become more picky about his proxies, and therefore fulfil the Urge with greater ease.

There were, of course, rumours going around the office that he was secretly gay and trying to hide it. Perhaps they thought he worried that his career prospects might be harmed if his sexuality became common knowledge. He knew that would not be the case – several of his colleagues were openly gay and had had no trouble climbing the career ladder within the Scottish Office. He toyed with the idea of keeping that rumour alive or even proclaiming himself to be gay. It would stop the gossip, at least. But the thought repelled him and there was no way he would be able to keep that particular illusion up for long.

222

The only course of action, then, was to join the dating scene – to court eligible young women with apparently nothing more than relationships and sex on his mind. He might even find a suitable partner who he could stay with, maybe even marry, to completely dispel the myths and rumours. They would have to be a pretty understanding sort, he thought, in order to abide a relationship that would ultimately prove to be loveless and sterile. But, he might just strike lucky and find such an accommodating woman. The more he thought on this scenario the more he came to think that it could be the ideal solution. A married man would attract far less attention than a bachelor.

And so he embarked on a sustained assault on dating columns and night clubs, known pick-up bars, and anywhere he could think of where he might meet women who would be interested in him. He read every piece of literature he could find on the secrets to successful dating and 'how to find the love of your life' type manuals. He employed all the suggestions from these books and articles and went to all the types of places they suggested. He even attended Latin dance classes, badminton, tennis clubs and a myriad of other tedious social-type groups.

Over time he found he became quite good at it all, realising he appeared quite attractive to women and that he had developed an easy charm that they seemed to fall for on more occasions than not. He worked hard at obtaining knowledge of a wide range of subjects such that he could have long and apparently interesting conversations on just about any topic they would express an interest in. Eventually he realised – he had become quite the ladies' man.

The final hurdle was sex. Normal, heterosexual, basic sex.

It wasn't that he was a virgin exactly. He had experienced sex once and it had not gone particularly well. He had bumped into a girl he knew from university one evening a few months ago, a girl who had attempted to entice him to bed when they were there. The issue of sex had already begun to play on his mind by that time and so he had allowed himself to succumb to her advances and go back to her place.

It had gone OK for most of the rest of the evening until they reached the actual penetrative sex. It wasn't that he couldn't function. He knew it all worked but once he was inside her he found that any pleasurable sensation had gone. That, in reality, this was a poor and unsatisfactory substitute for *his* sex. After half an hour of grunting and sweating he had simply given up and rolled off the girl, leaving her confused and frustrated.

Now with his sexual performance with women beginning to improve he needed to find a way to give every appearance of being able to actually enjoy sex. He needed to be able to finish the job. He turned back to his old teachers, the prostitutes he would hunt and prey upon. This time, however, he used them to practise in a more regular way.

With each encounter he would close his eyes and try to clear his mind, allowing his body to carry on with its more animal instincts. He failed more often than not.

After a time a number of the working girls came to recognise him and would know that this was the guy who couldn't come. There was one girl who eventually took pity on him and tried to help him overcome what she saw as his 'affliction'. He even became a regular of hers and stopped going to any others. After several unsuccessful sessions, she suggested that rather than trying to blank his

224

mind he should allow it to wander and slowly focus on what he found sexy and exciting. She told him that he didn't have to share what that was with her, and that it didn't matter how bizarre – or even illegal – his desires were, if put into action. The important thing was that they aroused him and so would allow him to climax.

The next time he visited her he tried her suggestion. He nearly lost his erection entirely when the first image to come into his mind was *her*. But then he allowed his imagination to follow that image and create its own scenario. He saw *her* lying down and holding her arms out to him; he fell into her embrace and they kissed passionately. But then, to his horror, *she* laughed, that mocking laugh that had haunted him for all those years. In his mind his anger grew and the knife came to mind – he imagined stabbing and thrusting that blade into her chest and stomach. He slashed her breasts and face, cutting chunks of flesh from her arms and shoulders. He saw the knife pierce her thighs and belly. The thrusts of the knife became closer and closer together, faster and harder each time, with the blade sinking deeper and deeper. In his mind he had reached the height of his frenzy. He could see the blood spraying out and over his face, and feel its warm, slick presence on his skin.

At that moment his face contorted into a snarling grimace and he felt the overpowering, unstoppable, thrilling wave of pleasure and release from his groin. It was a sensation he hadn't experienced since he was a young teenager. Through the haze of blood and gore in his mind he heard the girl below him grunt and make a strange high-pitched noise. Opening his eyes he saw that he was holding her tightly by the wrists and she had a strange look on her face, one of satisfaction mixed with discomfort, with a hint of horror in her eyes. When he rolled off her she told him that he should never, ever let her know what he had been thinking about, and that the look on his face had been vicious and terrifying. He had also gripped her so tightly that there were already bruises beginning to appear around her wrists.

He left her with a feeling of elation – not the warm and happy feelings of post-coital success but the inspiring, uplifting joy of having accomplished another goal towards his Quest.

That evening he mulled over what he had managed to achieve. He could now associate with and have relations with women with all the pretence of normality. He could, he was sure, learn to control the more violent aspects of his fantasy such that he didn't hurt them during the act.

His thoughts now turned to his increasing dissatisfaction at using prostitutes as his proxies. He had found he was gaining less and less from each one he Delivered. He knew he wouldn't find the One among their kind, had known this for some time, but had until now had no means of moving on to better, more likely candidates.

Now he had the requisite skill. The missing piece to the jigsaw. He would now be able to approach women, women he didn't know or have any connection to. He could entice them to offer to take him back to their place and there, in safety and privacy, he could Deliver them fully. He could work with less rush and more precision. He would, finally, be able to leave the mark that *they* would recognise, and finally rid himself of *her*.

He would become the very epitome of a charming man.

He smiled at the new direction the Quest would now take and began whistling quietly along to the tune playing on the radio.

Chapter Sixteen

Charlotte awoke, surprised to find she had no hangover. There was the mild feeling that she had slept poorly and her mouth appeared to believe she hadn't drunk any water for a month, but aside from that she felt surprisingly fine — certainly nothing a couple of cups of tea wouldn't cure.

Rising from bed, her mind wandered back to the previous night. Had Agatha really called Marcus a twat? And had Sir Frederick made some sort of pass at her? Or was that a terrible misinterpretation of his attempt to show he cared? And what was she to make of the police's new-found interest in Marcus?

As she slowly came around, her mind took her back to her own thoughts and considerations of the previous night. Marcus had been, at best, untruthful and, at worst, up to something that the police were now taking an interest in. She knew now that her husband of 12 years was not the man she'd thought he was and that he had been callous and deceitful enough to hide it from her all that time. She knew if she looked hard enough she would find proof of this: receipts and mileage returns, diary dates, emails and texts would likely all support her belief. But what would she do if she did find all this? What would any of it prove? It would prove she wasn't entirely stupid and that she hadn't lived blindly following a fantasy world of her own invention. It might just help find him and solve all the conundrums she still faced. It might, as Agatha had so eloquently pointed out, also let her get her due and move on.

In the end it took three cups of tea and a shower before she felt able to face the world. Picking up the phone she dialled DC Handley.

When he answered, Handley sounded as though it was he who had spent the evening drinking whiskey. Charlotte told him as much.

'Well, I'm glad you had a chance to let your hair down Mrs Travers,' he replied, his voice quiet and lacking energy. 'And yes, it was a long night and a very long day, yesterday, for that matter. I'm glad you've called however. It's saved me a job.'

Charlotte remained silent for a while. Handley sounded very subdued, which could have been the rigours of a long night, but it sounded to her like he had bad news for her. Had he found Marcus? In what state? Why, though, did he sound so matter-of-fact? There was little – if any – sympathy in his voice. Whatever the job was that she had just saved him from, it was likely not going to be good news for her.

'What job was that, Detective Handley?' she asked, keeping her voice even and calm. Handley's tone worried her but she had learned enough over the last few months to hide what she could of her feelings from her voice, as long as she needed to.

'I need you to come into the station Mrs Travers,' Handley said, flatly. 'There have been a number of developments regarding your husband.'

'Have you found him?' Charlotte rapped straight back. She was really beginning to hate the police's tendency to be opaque in their communications. They would never simply tell her what to expect or what they wanted, relying instead on inviting her to the station for some obscure, as yet to be disclosed, reason.

'No, Mrs Travers, we haven't found him,' Handley said, voice still lifeless. 'But I need you to come down as soon as possible. I can send a car if that would help? Shall we say half an hour?'

His insistence gave his voice some of its old character and Charlotte knew that she would get no further information from him unless she went. She also knew there was no way a police car was pulling up outside the house again – there had been several since she reported Marcus missing and she was fed up of the sight of them.

'No, no, I'll make my own way,' she replied firmly.

She had left the house within a minute of putting the phone down.

*

She had the sensation of déjà vu as she sat opposite DC Handley in the same tiny office they had occupied three weeks previously. Two plastic beakers of coffee were sitting on the desk between them, positioned – it seemed to her – in exactly the same places as before. The only noticeable difference was the size of the file Handley had in front of him.

He looked grim and dog-tired with large dark bags below his bloodshot eyes and a distinct stubble on his chin. His suit was rumpled and his shirt was creased. Charlotte sat, hands clasped in her lap, and waited silently for him to begin.

He flipped through the file in front of him for a while then looked up at her, his expression a disconcerting mix of sympathetic half-smile and harsh, hard stare.

'Mrs Travers,' he began, 'I need to show you some items – please tell me if you recognise them.'

Charlotte felt a deep sense of foreboding in her stomach. If the police suspected these items were Marcus' then they must believe they had found him, and since they were asking her to identify them then he was clearly in no position to identify them himself.

'Are they Marcus'?' she asked, knowing it was an obvious question with an obvious answer.

Handley duly supplied the obvious answer: 'They may be, we don't know, which is why I need you to see if you recognise them.'

He then took a series of pictures from the file and placed them on the desk, facing Charlotte. At first, she simply glanced over them, apparently not really taking them in and more intent on getting some answers from DC Handley.

'You think you've found him? Is he alive? Where do you think he is?' she asked. She had a long list of another 15 or so questions queueing up behind these ones.

'No Mrs Handley, we haven't found him, so I still can't say for certain whether he is alive or not.' Charlotte made to interrupt but Handley forestalled her with a raised hand. 'We are assuming he is still alive at this time, and I need to inform you that due to certain developments since we last spoke our efforts to find your husband have now taken on a more urgent nature. Since last night it has become imperative that we find him.'

Charlotte remembered the previous night and Agatha's warning that she felt the police were interested in Marcus for reasons other than simply finding him. She had also picked up on DC Handley's tone and demeanour. Something very serious was going on, she realised.

She continued looking at Handley, deliberately not looking down at the photographs, and took a moment to compose her thoughts. After a few seconds she spoke: 'DC Handley, I need you to explain to me exactly what is happening. You say you haven't found Marcus and yet believe you have some of his belongings. You say it is now imperative that you find him from which I can only infer that you now believe he is involved in something serious.'

She paused, then continued, speaking slowly and quietly but with real authority in her voice: 'Tell me everything that you think is happening and what you think Marcus' involvement is or I will refuse to help you.'

Handley held her gaze without flinching but Charlotte didn't relent and it was he who dropped his eyes first. A small but hollow victory, she thought. But she needed Handley to be open with her, not to feel guarded and under threat. Noticing she had tensed and was sitting forward in her seat, elbows on the table, she made herself relax and then dropped her gaze slightly. As she sat back, she morphed the confrontational aggression on her face into a more bewildered, confused expression. Handley visibly responded – she saw his shoulders relax a little and some tension leave his face. He believed he was in control of the situation again, she thought, smiling inwardly. So easily managed, DC Handley, she thought, and you don't even know I'm doing it.

Handley rubbed his huge hands over the stubble on his cheeks, looked down at the file on the desk and then up at the junction of wall and ceiling above Charlotte's head, one hand coming to rest on his chin. He stayed that way for nearly a minute, during which Charlotte neither spoke nor moved.

He eventually appeared to come to some sort of conclusion and turned his gaze back to Charlotte.

'Ok, Mrs Travers,' he began, his voice emphasising his obvious exhaustion. 'I will take you through everything I can, in as much detail as I can. But –' he stabbed at the photos once with an audible thump as his finger hit the desk – 'you must first look at these images and tell me if any of the objects in them belong to Marcus.'

'Yes, they do,' Charlotte replied without looking down.

Handley looked at her for a second and blinked. 'Mrs Travers, you haven't looked at them – please, I need you to be sure.'

'I don't need to look at them again, DC Handley. I saw enough earlier. The watch is definitely Marcus', the small nick in the strap is enough to tell me that. The wallet has a small blob of blue paint in the corner there, you see?' She pointed to a tiny spot on the wallet in the picture. 'It's a splash of paint that Melissa got on it one day when they were painting together. Marcus refused to wash it off. A little reminder of his little monkey, he called it. Surely if you found the wallet you must have found cards or a driver's licence, DC Handley? You wouldn't need me to identify it. And, finally, although I couldn't say for sure it's his, I think that's the tie Marcus was wearing the day he disappeared.'

A tear had escaped and rolled down her cheek as she described the small details – and the memories associated with them – that told her that these were her husband's belongings.

'The wallet was empty,' Handley said after clearing his throat, demonstrating his inability to deal with her emotions. 'That was quite a remarkable piece of observation, Mrs Travers.'

Charlotte wiped the tear from her cheek, nodded her response and then looked directly into Handley's eyes. 'Now,' she said, the earlier steel back in her voice. 'For the second time of asking, what the fuck is going on, DC Handley?'

To Charlotte's satisfaction, Handley visibly caved; there would be no need to 'manage' the information out of him now. She would get the full story.

'This is not going to be easy to hear, Mrs Travers, and I can think of no way to put this that would soften the blow. Your husband is now our prime suspect for the murder of Julia Metcalfe, and we would like to talk to him regarding up to 15 other murders dating back over 10 years now – some in the UK, others in Belgium.'

A profound silence and stillness pervaded the small room where they sat. Charlotte felt as though she had suddenly become totally deaf. The silence seemed to spill out of the room and encompass the larger open-plan office outside. She found she could no longer hear the sounds of phones ringing and people talking – all of which had been very obvious, but ignored, before and were now gone as if a switch had been thrown and turned the world to mute. She stared at DC Handley, mouth agape, head shaking slightly, brow creased, finding she couldn't form a single word never mind a coherent sentence.

'This must be a huge shock, Mrs Travers. I realise it's not something you ever expected to hear but I am afraid it is the fact of the matter at this time.'

To Charlotte it sounded as though Handley were under water or speaking through thick glass. Eventually his words sunk in and she formed an appropriate response.

'Julia Metcalfe?' she asked, her voice flat and emotionless. 'I take it that is the Julia from the notes?'

'Yes,' Handley said. 'I found her last night at a property in Essex. She had been dead for some time, certainly a number of weeks. She was murdered and the only other person we can find evidence of at the property where she was found is your husband.'

'What – his watch and wallet?' Charlotte asked, a little more life now entering her voice with her incredulity. 'You once suspected they had run off together. That could still be the case. Maybe they were robbed or attacked or whatever. He could be somewhere nearby, hurt or...or...' She couldn't finish the sentence.

'No, Mrs Travers, we don't believe so.' Handley was deliberately keeping his voice low and quiet. 'There is no evidence that your husband was attacked at the property, only Julia Metcalfe. What we did find were the items in front of you and fingerprints all over the property that match those of your husband that we took the other day. We are still waiting on results from some other samples taken from there, but we are confident they will also match your husband's.'

'So, what do you think happened?' Charlotte asked, still clearly not taking in the enormity of Handley's accusations.

'Again, we don't really know exactly,' Handley replied. 'It would seem that there was a fight, as such, and Ms Metcalfe was stabbed – we presume, by your husband. Beyond that ... only he can tell us. Which is why it is extremely important that we find him. Mrs Travers, is there anywhere you can think of that your husband would have headed for? Anywhere he might feel safe or able to hide?'

'God no, if I did you would've known by now. Detective Handley, I can't quite take all this in. You think Marcus killed Julia?' Handley nodded and Charlotte continued, 'But why? And... and... you mentioned, what, 15 other murders? This is just insane. Where on Earth has that come from? It's like you've just conjured the most insane nightmare and landed it on my door. You can't seriously believe any of this is true, can you? I mean, Marcus? You're trying to tell me he's some sort of serial killer? This is... is... it's just...'

Disbelief and terror combined to raise Charlotte's voice to almost hysterical levels. She drew deep, wracking, breaths as she gripped the table. Nothing made sense and she had nothing else she could say to Handley. Instead she tried to calm her breathing and wait for him to respond. Maybe if she could calm herself, she thought, she could make sense of all of this.

Handley realised that unless he got through the rest of it they were going to go nowhere. He needed to tell her as much as he could without her interrupting; she needed the story and the evidence as they saw it for her to be of any use to them. And most importantly, she needed to be calm.

Requesting that she not interrupt him, he outlined the developments in The Charmer case, the Belgian connection and the fact that Marcus was potentially connected to these crimes.

When he had finished, Charlotte looked even more incredulous.

Giving a short bark of a laugh, she said, 'This is ridiculous. As before, Detective Handley, where is your evidence? I'm no lawyer but I'm pretty sure you can't arrest somebody for being near a crime scene, whilst they are at work!'

'Look, Mrs Travers,' Handley said firmly. 'I needed you in here to identify the possessions we found at the scene of a murder. You've confirmed that they belong to your husband. Whilst that does not necessarily mean he is the murderer, it does mean that unless we find evidence that someone else was at that property, he is most definitely a suspect for the murder of Julia Metcalfe. As to the other murders, well, we'll cross that bridge when we come to it. But it is now vital that we find him. I have told you all of this out of courtesy, you understand? I am forewarning you of what is to come.'

Charlotte's earlier indignation subsided – it did sound likely that Marcus was involved in a murder in some way, but she couldn't quite bring herself to believe it of the man. She needed time to let this sink in, needed to give herself the opportunity to decide what it all actually meant – and more to the point, whether she could believe that Marcus was indeed a killer.

'I don't know what to say, Detective Handley, this is one hell of a shock,' she said, her voice expressing her confusion and concern.

'I realise that, Mrs Travers, and sincerely you have my sympathy. I would not want to have that news delivered to me about a loved one. All I would ask is that you continue to think and try and remember any further details, no matter how small, that might allow us to locate your husband.'

'I will, DC Handley,' Charlotte said quietly, 'although I've told you all I can already, I'm afraid.'

She rose to leave. There was nothing more to say and feeling numb, dazed and confused she allowed DC Handley to escort her back down the now familiar route to the exit.

Handley paused for a moment, watching her retreating back through the main door of the police station.

'Poor cow,' he muttered, as he turned and headed back to his desk.

'07

It was over. The Charmer case files would be boxed and stored in the archive warehouse. The case would be reviewed periodically but as of that afternoon it would be listed as 'unsolved'.

DCI Fran Pearson had felt sick when he received the news from his Super, news couched in a number of platitudes and praise for his work and dedication.

'Look Fran,' his boss had said. 'You've done all you can on this. No one's doubting your effort or your methods – they've both been sound as ever – but there is only so much resource and money that can be spared. The case will be reviewed again, I promise. But until then, it's off your books, ok?'

Pearson had accepted it with a mute nod and immediately left the station, heading straight for the nearest bar. This was London and so within less than 10 minutes he was sitting with a pint and a whisky chaser, staring down at the table and trying, unsuccessfully, not to grind his teeth. He had smoked a cigarette on the way there but already wanted another one. Downing the whisky, he headed outside.

As he dragged viciously on his cigarette, he tried to decide what he felt – anger, certainly, with regret, hopelessness and sorrow all shuffling around vying for attention and space in his mind. He was angry at his superiors for pulling the case but couldn't blame them really. He was furious with himself for not making any progress. He knew he was being brutal with himself, though. He had made some progress, just nowhere near enough. He felt hopeless faced with the lack of clear evidence or even any idea as to a motive for the killings.

He had engaged one of the top criminal psychologists in the country and although he had been helpful his findings amounted to the lump sum of zero in terms of the investigation. And then there was the sorrow he felt for the victims and their families. There would still be no justice for them. And, finally, the regrets were too numerous to mention with the one obvious one being his inability to catch the killer.

Stubbing out his cigarette, he rejoined his drink inside, ordering another whisky before taking his seat. Looking into the dark surface of the beer he tried to run every last detail of the investigation through his mind, trying to spot the one piece of information that would unlock the whole case. But it had been three years and while every major detail remained etched in his mind, many of the small and so often significant details were lost to him now. Three years, he thought, Christ I should have got him!

He knew, deep down, that with what they had there was little chance they would catch the killer. For the last year they had been relying on luck rather than judgement. As every line of enquiry had proved to be a dead end and the list of potential leads had continued to grow rather than shrink, it was clear that what they needed was for the killer to slip up and get himself arrested for something else. They needed, in other words, a lucky break … but it hadn't come. Still he pushed on, arguing his case at every review meeting and pushing for more men and more resources, while continuing to assert that they were close and if only…

If only what? If only they had a crystal ball? If only the killer had seen the film Seven and decided to walk into the station and announce himself? The thoughts ground bitterly round the inside of his skull. If only they had *any* clue as to the identity of this man or where to start looking or who to concentrate on. But they didn't, they had nothing. He had failed and he now had no arguments left, nothing more to give his superiors to make them change their mind.

He ordered another round and as he drank, he felt his mood shift from anger and disappointment into a maudlin depression. The faces of the victims – all 15 of them – ran across his vision. He now knew many of them so well that it felt like he had known them when they were alive – rather than merely reading about their doings and business, and ultimately their fates, in file reports. All of them were young women with much to live for. It was the loss of their futures he felt the most: their potential to go far or the children they would never have and see grow – all of that lost on the crazy whim of a sick bastard with a grudge.

There was nothing more to be done, he thought sadly, but that didn't mean he would do nothing. He would not forget this case – he would hold it in his head every day he was at work and if anything ever seemed relevant or looked remotely like it might be connected he would demand the case be reviewed and re-opened. He would not forget those women or their families. He would bring them the head of the man responsible for the wrecking of their lives.

He left the bar then with a new-found resolve. This was one baton he wouldn't be passing on. If anyone was going to catch this bastard it would be him. It might take the rest of his career, but he *would* be the officer that put the Charmer in a cell.

'One day,' he said quietly as he left the bar behind.

Chapter Seventeen

The following morning, Handley knocked nervously on DCS Pearson's office door. He had never been in the Super's office, had never been to these heady heights of the station. He felt like a cat, secure in his own back garden domain, suddenly being thrown into a tiger's enclosure.

Stop being stupid, he thought, you've got all the information you need to be able to hold your own – just get on with it. Pearson called for him to enter and with that final thought in his head he swiftly turned the handle and entered the office.

DCI Tanner was already inside, sitting in one of the two seats in front of Pearson's desk. Handley placed the file he was carrying on the desk and took the remaining seat, having nodded greetings to his senior colleagues.

'So, Tony,' Pearson began. 'Have we finally made some form of a breakthrough?'

Pearson's voice, though still deep and gravelly, was softer in the office and Handley relaxed into 'detail and reporting' mode – the *lingua franca* of coppers everywhere.

'Yes sir,' he replied. 'We now have fingerprints, DNA from blood, blood type and some hairs and fibres we are pretty certain belong to Marcus Travers. All were found at the scene. Mrs Travers has also identified certain items as belonging to Mr Travers, also found at the scene. The DNA can only be confirmed once we have him in custody, of course, but we already had his fingerprints and hair samples from his home and they both match. Medical records confirm a blood type match. We also have the murder weapon, we believe, but there are no prints on it so it's as yet unclear whether Marcus Travers was actually the killer. At the moment all we can do is place him at the scene. But since there were no traces of anyone else having been in the cottage, we can safely assume that it was him.'

'Good,' Pearson stated. 'So we have Marcus Travers as our primary suspect for the murder of Julia Metcalfe. We need to immediately circulate his picture and his description to all other forces, and have these circulated to all officers – both here and in the other locations. I think it's time we got the media team on it, with a general public appeal for information on his whereabouts and any sightings. Malcolm, can you get on that? Be sure to also include a warning that he should not be approached.'

Tanner, who had sat impassively silent throughout this exchange, nodded and said, 'Will do, sir. We've got him for this one, but what about The Charmer murders? You must have lab results in by now, Tony?'

'Yes sir, I was about to turn to that,' Handley replied, pleased he was fully prepared for this meeting.

'The results were longer in coming as the lab had to cross-reference against a lot of evidence from the old Charmer files. This is still ongoing but we have already got a match. Hair found at the scene of one of the cases attributed to The Charmer, that of Suzanne Hill murdered in Leicester in 2003, matches that of Marcus Travers. Again, this only puts him potentially at the scene because there were, as with many of the other murder scenes, other hair samples found that were from different individuals.'

'Not very conclusive then?' Pearson asked.

'Not on its own, sir, no. But I just got another lab report in as I was coming up and they've found a second match.'

Both Pearson and Tanner sat forward a little as Handley said this.

'This one's from 2005,' Handley continued, 'in Bristol, the victim was a Geraldine Barton. Again, it's a hair match with Travers. But, there was another hair sample found that didn't match. What's interesting here was that Travers' hair had no follicle whereas the other hair did. The lab report says that Travers' hair was shed – not cut – and the other was either plucked or pulled from the other party. Now, that could mean one of two contradictory things: either Marcus Travers' hair was shed at the scene and he deliberately placed the other one there, or Travers' hair was deliberately placed at the scene and the other one was pulled out by the victim during the attack. So either party could be implicated by the presence of their hair samples. The lab is cross-checking the other hair for matches across the series. They can extract DNA from the hair with the follicle, so we can be quite definitive about this other party.'

Tanner grunted and shook his head. 'So although we've got matches, they only *potentially* put Marcus Travers at two of the scenes – we can't say for certain that he was there. And maybe this other hair sample is actually our man.'

'Correct, sir,' Handley replied. 'However, we've also completed most of our checks on the dates and times Travers was out of the Foreign Office against the murders in the files. There are a number of matches that I've already pointed out to DCI Tanner.'

Tanner nodded and indicated with a short wave of his hand that this had already been passed along to Pearson.

'Well … we have more,' Handley continued. 'Travers was in Belgium, officially, on at least three of the dates

242

correlating to the murders over there. And, on two further occasions he was reportedly off sick at the same time there were murders here in the UK. In the Belgian cases, and in those where he was away on business in the UK, he was within two hours' drive of the murder scenes. Now, again, whilst it's not conclusive – and bear in mind that he wasn't the only one attending these meetings – we do now have nine murders where Marcus Travers was in the vicinity at the exact same time. Coupled with the small amount of forensic evidence, I think the weight of probability now lies on Marcus Travers' side.'

'Ok, good,' said Pearson. 'There may still be some unanswered questions here, but in my eyes, what we've got is still enough to make Marcus Travers our prime suspect. Definitely for Julia Metcalfe and now a distinct probability for The Charmer too.'

'One thing that bothers me, sir ...' Tanner began. 'If we assume for a moment that Travers is The Charmer, then we have to assume that Julia Metcalfe knew this. Why else would she state in her note to him that she would go to the police? And if she did know, why would she want to meet him?'

'Well,' Handley replied, 'it could be that she wasn't sure he was The Charmer. She may have wanted to see him in order to verify her theory; maybe she thought she could ask oblique enough questions that it wouldn't make him suspect she knew. Or she had picked up on the Foreign Office angle from somewhere and was simply using Marcus to fill in the blanks. Eventually he began to suspect that she knew more than she was letting on and killed her?'

'All reasonable arguments, Tony,' Tanner replied, 'but like many things in this fucking case it's conjecture and nothing more.'

Handley felt a little envious that his immediate superior could swear so readily in front of his boss, something Handley would never consider doing with Tanner.

He conceded Tanner's point with a nod before replying, 'Yes sir, I know that. But then we still have no idea whether they were even discussing The Charmer case. I think we might get some answers when we've finished going through the paperwork found at Julia Metcalfe's flat and cottage. There's loads of it so it'll take some time, but initially we're ignoring anything that doesn't at first glance appear to be directly about The Charmer. That's the quickest route to discovering if there is anything of value in there. If we don't find anything – and so far we haven't – we can assume that this wasn't what they were meeting for and start looking for what they might have been discussing.'

'Good work Tony,' Pearson said, 'and well thought through. Right, looks to me like we're making progress, slow progress, but progress nonetheless. Anything else you have for me, gents?'

Tanner shook his head.

Handley made an 'ooh' shape with his mouth. 'Ah yes, sir, sorry I meant to say, we've had the Belgian lab results over and our guys have found some matching samples from their cases. None match Marcus Travers' but they go towards confirming that all the cases are related.'

'Right, good stuff, that could be useful. We need to keep the lab boys working every angle they can and we need to move faster on the Julia Metcalfe paperwork. Ok, let's get cracking. Tony, keep on with what you're doing and inform DCI Tanner the moment you have anything. Malcolm, you get onto the press – you're the one running the show so I think you should be in front of the camera with the press liaison officer.'

Tanner groaned and looked mournfully at Pearson who smiled wickedly, saying 'Oh you love it really Malcolm, you big poser.'

Tanner simply shook his head.

Tanner set a brisk pace as he and Handley headed back downstairs towards the Press Liaison Office and the CID room respectively. Although taller than his boss, Handley had to lengthen his stride to keep up.

'Good work in there Tony,' Tanner said as they started to descend the stairs.

'Thank you, sir,' Handley replied, pleased with the praise. 'I just wish we could move things on further. I mean we do appear to be getting somewhere but there are still so many loose ends. We're ploughing through Julia Metcalfe's notes as quickly as we can but it doesn't feel quick enough. Then there's all the cross-referencing between current evidence, old cases and Belgium – that's taking forever. And we're still no closer to finding Marcus Travers.'

'Patience son,' Tanner said quietly. 'You know by now that the main attribute a good detective needs is patience – that and bloody hard graft, followed by luck. I understand your frustration but we have to work through these things. Dot the i's, cross the t's and hope that it all comes good. You'll get there.'

Tanner gave Handley an out-of-character reassuring tap on the arm.

'Besides,' he continued, 'my bloody TV appearance might just give us something on Travers. It fucking better had. I'm not doing it more than once.'

Handley gave a small laugh. 'DCS Pearson seemed to think you're a natural, sir.'

'Don't push it, Tony,' Tanner replied gruffly.

Handley quit while the going was good and they parted ways at the bottom of the stairs.

The office was eerily quiet as Handley entered. All his colleagues were either working heads down through Julia Metcalfe's paperwork or talking quietly on the phone. They all had the same aim: the sifting of information, the tying together of loose ends, and the painstaking cross-referencing of new to old case notes. Handley began to weave through the desks heading for his own.

Halfway there, he bumped into DS Roberts who was standing with a piece of paper in his hand and a quizzical look on his face.

'You alright Davey?' Handley asked, trying to see what was on the paper Roberts was holding.

'Hmm? Ah Tony,' Roberts said as he looked up, 'didn't see you coming there.' He looked back down at the paper with a scowl creasing his forehead.

'What's up?' Handley asked, trying to sound nonchalant but feeling curious. Roberts had clearly found something.

'Not sure, Tony,' he replied. 'Is the Chief about?'

'Press Office,' Handley stated. 'Have you got something then?'

Getting information out of Davey Roberts involved the proverbial bloody stone. He could only be described as old-school; in a day and age where information sharing was key to police work Roberts liked to keep things to himself. He was a hoarder of information, only releasing it when it

246

would do him the most good. Handley liked the man but hated his methods.

He watched as Roberts weighed up his two options – telling Handley what he had, knowing Handley was meant to co-ordinate in Tanner's absence, and the small personal victory of revealing something important to Tanner himself. Eventually, Handley won simply by looming over Roberts and making himself impossible to ignore or fob off.

'Well ...' Roberts began eventually. 'I've been going through Julia Metcalfe's contacts and address books that were found at her flat.'

Again, Roberts ground to a halt but Handley knew to remain patient and to let him spill the information in his own time.

'It's probably nothing but there's an entry here with no name against it, just an address, see?' Roberts pointed to the relevant entry on the piece of paper.

'Yeah, I see, and...?' Handley prompted this time.

'Well it's up in the north of Scotland. I checked the postcode, it comes out somewhere near Aberdeen,' Roberts said looking up at Handley with raised eyebrows.

'So?' was all Handley could think of to say.

'Well, doesn't Marcus Travers come from Scotland?' Roberts shrugged as if to indicate that that piece of knowledge was widely known and that this was probably just a coincidence.

Handley looked at the paper again and then blankly back at Roberts for several seconds.

'There are no other addresses associated with Marcus Travers – I checked months ago – nothing on the land registry, and no bills or the like associated with a second property,' Handley said in a voice that sounded both distant and robotic.

Roberts shrugged and began to turn away with a quiet, 'hmph'.

Suddenly, Handley's eyes widened. 'Shit!' he exclaimed and grabbed the piece of paper from Roberts' hand.

'Oi! What the fuck Tony?' Roberts complained loudly, but Handley was already past him and on his way to his own desk.

'Parents!' Handley muttered as he sat down. He had just recalled his conversation with Charlotte from over a fortnight before; they'd been looking at an old photo of Marcus standing with his father, the two looking less than comfortable together. She had said at the time that Marcus and his parents weren't very close and that both were now dead.

Although Handley had already checked and found no additional properties in Marcus Travers' name, he hadn't considered that there might be a property that had belonged to his parents that had perhaps been willed to someone else after their death or simply sold off. Either way it was a potential address that hadn't come onto Handley's radar to check. If this was his parents' old address, Travers would have grown up there and would likely know the surrounding area like the back of his hand – it could be an ideal place to hide away in.

Pulling up the appropriate programmes on his screen, Handley re-read the address. There was a house name – 'Fàilte Teine' – Handley had no idea what that meant or even what language it was in. He reasoned it would be Gaelic but couldn't be sure. Thankfully the rest of the address was in English.

Checking Google maps, he could see the property was in a very rural setting – isolated was the word that occurred to Handley. Again, the thought crossed his mind

248

that this might be an ideal area to hide out in. Closing that window, he turned his attention to discovering the current and past owners.

The land registry search came back with the owner's name almost immediately and it stopped Handley in his tracks. He simply couldn't decide what to make of it, couldn't see how this fitted with anything else they knew.

He looked again at the details. There was no mistake – the current owner was Sir Frederick Alasdair McDougal Derringham.

Why did Julia have an address for a property belonging to Sir Frederick Derringham? And how did that fit in with her and Marcus Travers?

Handley picked up the phone, there was only one way to find out. Dialling the Foreign Office, he hoped Derringham was there and not out on business or finished for the day.

Agatha, Derringham's secretary, answered: 'Sir Frederick's office, how can I help you?'

'Ah, er, Agatha isn't it?' Handley asked but didn't wait for an answer. 'I need to speak to Sir Frederick, please. It's quite urgent.'

Agatha's voice was as cool and calm as ever, as she responded: 'I am afraid Sir Frederick has left for the day. Who's calling please? Can I take a message?'

Handley cursed himself for rushing in to his request to speak to Sir Frederick and not introducing himself at the outset.

'It's DC Handley,' he replied. 'It is quite important that I speak with Sir Frederick.'

'Ah yes, Detective Constable Handley, I thought I recognised your voice. As I say Sir Frederick is out of the office. I can try to put you through to his mobile but I can't promise he'll be available.'

'Yes, please try that – thank you.' Handley waited while there was a series of beeps on the line.

'I can put you through now, DC Handley,' Agatha said.

The background noise changed to the sound of a car moving at a reasonable speed. The sounds of other traffic could also be heard.

'DC Handley,' Derringham's unmistakable voice rang through the receiver. 'What can I do for you that's so urgent?'

'Are you driving, Sir Frederick?' Handley asked, ever the policeman.

'Being driven old boy,' Sir Frederick replied with a chuckle. 'One of the perks of being a knight of the realm.' Another short laugh followed.

'Right, that's fine, sir,' Handley mumbled. Different worlds, he thought – not for the first time when talking to Sir Frederick. 'You won't be aware, Sir Frederick, but Julia Metcalfe has been murdered.'

There was a short pause and then Sir Frederick spoke in a much lower and less jovial tone. 'Good Lord, really? I read of a murder in Essex the other day, was that her? Hadn't you connected her to Marcus somehow? Is he all right? Have you found him?'

'Yes it was her and yes there was a connection between her and Marcus Travers. But, Sir Frederick, what I want to ask you is you said when we met last time that you didn't know her at all, is that correct?'

'Yes DC Handley, that is correct. As I told you I have never met the woman. I only came across the name when I had Agatha check the visitor logs against Marcus' name.'

'Right,' said Handley. 'It's just that I have an address book here, found in Julia Metcalfe's flat, with an address in it that is listed as belonging to you – the one in Scotland, with the unpronounceable name? How could she have that information, Sir Frederick? And why?'

There was another long pause before Derringham spoke again. 'I have no idea, DC Handley. I would imagine she gained the information the same way you did, she was an investigative journalist after all. But as to why she would have it I really can't tell you. Bit creepy though, I must say.'

'Yes, she could probably have got the information as easily as I did,' Handley continued, 'but I can't see why she would want it. Did Marcus know about the property? Might she have got the address from him?'

'I take it, Detective, that you haven't found Marcus as yet?' Sir Frederick asked.

'No, we haven't. Did he know about this place, Sir Frederick?' Handley repeated, unwilling to be dragged off subject.

'Yes, he did,' Derringham replied. 'I took him up there a few times. Hunting, shooting, fishing trips, you know? That sort of thing. So yes, I suppose she could have got the address from Marcus.'

'How long have you owned the property, Sir Frederick?' Handley asked.

'Oh years,' Derringham answered. 'I can't say I can recall exactly how long but at least 15 maybe as long as 20 years. Bought the place when I was relocated to London and the Foreign Office after the Scottish Office was all but closed. The new parliament up there and all that. So that would have been 1999, so I think I would have bought the place around 2000. I knew I'd miss Scotland – at least

251

certain aspects of it – and wanted somewhere to retreat to when I could.'

Handley thought for a moment and then asked, 'When was the last time Marcus Travers visited the house?'

Derringham was quiet for a moment, then replied, raising his voice, 'Look Handley, why all these questions about my home in Scotland? I don't really remember the last time Marcus was there. What is it you are trying to find out, Detective Constable?'

Handley noted the dropping of his rank at the beginning of Derringham's outburst – what was he getting so riled about? – he wondered.

'Sir Frederick,' he said, keeping his voice even and controlled. 'I very much need to find Marcus Travers in connection with the murder of Julia Metcalfe, and your home in Scotland appears to be about the only new lead I have as to his whereabouts. Please just answer my questions for now. If I have a chance and I'm able to I will give you further details at a later date. Now, when did Marcus last visit the house and would it be possible for him to gain access to the property should he have gone there alone?'

'Good Lord,' Sir Frederick breathed. 'Marcus, a murderer?'

'I haven't said that sir,' Handley corrected. 'At this stage I just need to speak to him – he could be a vital witness as much as a suspect at this stage.'

'Right, yes, of course DC Handley,' Derringham's voice reverted to his normal tones. 'I think it would have been about 18 months or so back. We stopped by after a G8 meeting at Gleneagles. And yes, he could have gained access. I showed him where I hide the emergency key.'

'Right,' Handley said decisively. 'Thank you, Sir Frederick.'

Without waiting for the reply, he put the phone down and began to rise from his seat. He got about halfway up when DC Sonia Mallen arrived at his desk.

'I take it you are collating information in DCI Tanner's absence?' she asked.

Handley sighed – he was beginning to see why his boss wore a permanent frown. He sat back down and nodded.

'Right,' she said, placing a file on Handley's desk. 'PM report on Julia Metcalfe, more cross-referenced lab results and DC White has something on CCTV apparently.'

Handley lifted the file, then frowned. 'Who the hell is DC White?'

'Tanner brought her in, apparently a bit of a genius with technology. She's over in the other corner,' Mallen replied, pointing out a desk on the far side of the office.

'OK, thanks,' Handley said, looking nervously between the report, DC Mallen and the desk she had indicated that held DC White.

Mallen left Handley to it with a slight smirk on her face; she knew he had trouble with prioritising and a fear of making wrong calls in the absence of the boss.

With three pieces of information all needing to be dealt with, Handley was feeling the weight of the decisions he would have to make and was annoyed at his lack of decisiveness. Mallen's smirk only served to add to his chagrin. He tried to clear his mind by counting to 10 and thinking of nothing during that time. It didn't really do the job he wanted but it allowed him enough headspace to come to the conclusion that it didn't matter what order anything was done, as long as it was done and delivered wholesale to DCI Tanner.

Using the eeny-meeny method he chose to go over to DC White's desk first.

DC White was a petite, attractive woman in her late 30s to early 40s. Handley had to mentally stop himself checking her out as he approached; it was something he rarely if ever did, and it always made him feel uncomfortable when he caught himself doing it.

'DC White,' he said, almost stammering over her name as he held out his hand in greeting. 'I'm DC Handley, you've got something for me on the CCTV footage?'

'Yes, it's not great,' DC White replied, ignoring the proffered hand, 'but it might just give you a glimpse of your man. Pull up a pew and I'll run you through what I've done.'

The only chair Handley could see was several desks away so he opted for crouching beside the desk instead.

'Right, so the first thing I did was run everything we had through various image-enhancing routines,' White explained. 'This cleaned up some of the newer stuff reasonably well but has only mildly improved the older material.'

Handley nodded, hoping she wouldn't get too technical on him. He was no luddite but if she went into more detail he would be lost and likely lose the point of the exercise.

'Then once I had everything as clear as I could make it,' she continued, 'I ran facial recognition software on it to see if it picked up any facial patterns or other features that might indicate the same person in each piece of film.'

So far, so good, Handley thought. 'And did it?' he asked.

'Kind of,' White replied, hedging her bets.

'Kind of?' asked Handley. 'What do you mean "kind of"?'

'Well,' she replied, 'there's more than one match for a start.'

She pulled up two different sets of images on the screen, containing somewhat grainy, indistinct images of two different men. The first set of three images showed a man that could have been anywhere between 35 and 50, with fair hair that was receding at the temples. He was wearing a suit in two of the images and casual clothes in the third. If he squinted Handley could just about see that there was at least a passing similarity between each of these images. He didn't recognise the man.

'This guy only appears in the older footage,' White said, indicating the top three images.

The second set contained four images and they immediately drew Handley's attention. He leaned closer and peered intently at the screen.

'Jeeesus,' he hissed.

'I thought you might be more interested in this set,' White said, then pointed out the first two of the set of four. 'These are from the older material – that one is from a bar in Manchester and this one is outside a restaurant in Brighton.'

Indicating the second two images she continued, 'These two are more recent, one is from Belgium – from Anderlecht – and the other is Manchester.'

Handley nodded absently as he continued to stare at the images.

'Are these really all the same person?' he asked.

'That's hard to say. This is based solely on what the facial recognition software could come up with. But I agree that it's pretty hard to say conclusively that it's one person – it could potentially be four different people.'

The images all showed a man of above-average height with a strong, athletic-looking build, but in one image he was distinctly blonde, in another he had longer hair, and in the other two his hair was dark. The man's clothes in each of the four images were all different, ranging from high-end casual wear to an expensive-looking suit, to jeans and T-shirt. Handley honed in on the two of the dark-haired man. These two had drawn his attention immediately. Again, he had to squint slightly at the images but when he looked closely, he was sure they could both be taken for Marcus Travers.

'Can you print these two?' he asked.

'Already have,' was White's reply as she handed over four glossy printouts. 'So, you're not interested in contestant number one then?'

'I don't know,' replied Handley distractedly as he looked at the images he now held in his hand. 'He's not in any of the recent images and it could just be an anomaly of the software, you know, picking up a typically northern face-type and throwing these three images up. But *this* guy –' he held up the two images of the dark-haired man – '*this* guy looks quite like the man we're looking for.'

He paused then, still looking at the printouts. 'Thing is …' he said eventually, 'I hadn't realised how alike they were. I could see either of them in these pictures…'

'Either of who?' White asked with a puzzled expression.

'Hmmmm?' was all Handley uttered as he rose from his crouch and wandered back to his desk, still staring at the images.

'18

Recollections

She remembered that their first storming row had come some time shortly after their wedding. She had been seething and it was nearly all over right there and then. It was funny, she reflected, how back then the reason for the row had seemed so important, so make-or-break, but now it seemed trivial and immature in light of everything that had happened since.

It had started, as so many arguments do, with a little niggle. Marcus had come home late on three occasions one week and twice the following week. He hadn't called or said before he had left for work that this would be happening; he had simply strolled in around midnight. It wasn't that she felt she was his keeper and as such should be informed of his whereabouts, or that she didn't understand he had a demanding job which meant he sometimes had to put in long hours. It was the lack of communication that had riled her. What would it have cost him to make a quick call? She had prepared dinner and then sat waiting and waiting, expecting him home at any moment, only for him to appear several hours later.

After the fifth time she had raised the subject. And for whatever reason – tiredness, stress or simple misunderstanding – the conversation had quickly escalated into a blazing row. She demanded that he tell her where he had been and why he hadn't called, while he demanded that she respect his decisions, adding that it was all 'unavoidable' and besides which – when had he been required to check in every five minutes?

It had gone on for over two hours, eventually boiling down to the realisation that they clearly had contradictory views on personal freedoms and responsibilities within a marriage. She had finally stormed out, vowing to stay away until he had reconsidered and changed his ways. He had just thrown his hands in the air and spat 'fine!' as the door had slammed shut.

Too embarrassed to go to her mother's – knowing the lecture she would get on only just being married and that it takes time to adjust and so on – she escaped to her friend's place. It took Marcus two days to call and apologise. She had packed and gone straight back home as soon as the call had ended.

She smiled, now, at how much he had changed almost overnight. From that point on he had always called to tell her if he was going to be late home or had let her know ahead of time when he expected to be kept late at the office. That habit had remained right up to the day he disappeared. That was why she had known there was something wrong as that long, dreadful evening had worn on and there was no sign of him.

It felt a little odd to her now that she was able to recall that argument so clearly. She was also a little puzzled by Marcus' sudden change of heart – seemingly switching from a vehement believer in complete personal freedom to a man who would call his wife if there were a longer-than-normal queue at the fish and chip shop. What had motivated such a change? With all that had happened she now wondered if it hadn't been a calculated move. Had he simply realised it would be easier and less suspicious if he just called her and let her know where he was and what he was doing? Thought about in that way, it certainly would have given him a great deal of personal freedom. If he *had* simply manipulated the situation in this way then he could have got his excuses in early and then have had however many hours – or in some cases, days – to do as he pleased.

It distressed and angered her to think he might have manipulated her in such a way. But with the benefit of hindsight and the damning evidence from the police, it was hard to see it any other way. She felt the anger rise as she realised all the ways he could have used the 'loving husband and father' routine to hide anything he wanted from her and the world in general – to feign any number of reasons for his absences and lateness and then use that time to slaughter women. The thought made her sick to her stomach.

She tried to recall now all those calls home – had any of them ever sounded suspicious or false? She couldn't remember ever thinking so. But then, if the police were to be believed, this was a man who could persuade any woman he chose to believe whatever he wanted or needed them to. Why should she be any different?

She didn't want to have these thoughts of Marcus; she wanted to remember him as the loving husband and father she had believed him to be all those years. She still loved him, she knew, but now that love was slowly being eroded into something resembling hatred. Her husband of 12 years was turning out to be a callous, manipulative and depraved man, a man she had never known.

There would be no forgiving him this time if all this turned out to be true. There would be no going back for them.

There would be no call to apologise and no happy reunion.

All she hoped for now was that they would catch him and put him far away from her and the children for the rest of his life.

Chapter Eighteen

After the devastating news from DC Handley, Charlotte spent the rest of the day in a numbed haze. Most of the time was spent just sitting in the lounge staring at the photos of Marcus and her and the children. She simply couldn't reconcile the events of the last three to four months with the happy family portraits that hung on the walls. She only moved and got up when it was time to collect the children from school.

After seeing to the children and eventually putting them to bed, she retreated to the small room they had called the office. There she sat, toying with the few things that lay on the desk and idly flicking through files on the computer – mostly old letters, photos and videos – paying little attention to any one of them before moving on to the next.

One video held her attention a little longer than the others. It showed a garden party in what looked like the grounds of a stately home or a millionaire's mansion – likely one of Sir Frederick's acquaintances, she decided. There were a lot of long shots of the gathering guests as they emerged from the large, elaborate rear doors of the house and spilled out onto the patio and lawn. Generally looking radiant, the guests appeared to be laughing and chatting, with cocktails or champagne glasses in hand.

She recognised the place and realised it was one of Sir Frederick's 'little gatherings' as he called them. She couldn't remember who owned the property but did remember it as a stunning late 18th century mansion: 14 bedrooms, an enormous dining room and one of the most elegantly decorated sitting rooms she had ever seen.

It had been a glorious summer's evening and she recalled that both she and Marcus had thoroughly enjoyed the event. She smiled as she watched some younger guests arrive, less assured of themselves in their fine evening wear, staying in close groups as though to protect themselves from the marauding hordes of managers and old duffers.

Then she saw herself enter the garden. She took a modicum of pleasure in how good she had looked in her bright and airy summer frock. She was a little surprised, though, that she wasn't on Marcus' arm. He would always make sure he was close by at any Foreign Office do they attended together. Then a few seconds later he appeared alongside Sir Frederick; they appeared to be talking quite animatedly.

The camera moved in closer and centred on the doors from which people were still spilling and where Sir Frederick and Marcus were standing, the new guests washing around them like a stream around a large boulder. The camera wasn't close enough to pick up any one person's voice but she now had a clearer view of Marcus and Sir Frederick. As she watched she realised that they seemed to be having something of an argument, gauging by the looks on both faces. This, to her, was unusual in itself – she couldn't recall Marcus ever telling her that he and Sir Frederick had had a disagreement – but to appear to be having such a public argument was out of character in the extreme, for both of them.

The video timer showed it had half an hour left to run as the camera moved away from Marcus and Sir Frederick and started catching close-ups of various guests around the gardens and the house. Charlotte was intrigued by the apparent argument and rewound the footage to watch again, but there was no further clue as to the subject of their conversation. On her second viewing she caught the briefest view of Marcus moving away, presumably towards her. He hadn't, as far as she could recall now, mentioned anything to her either that night or at a later time. It was a puzzle, but probably of little consequence, she decided.

She scanned quickly through the rest of the video to see if there was any more footage of her and Marcus. But aside from a few very brief moments there was little else. Right at the end, the camera had been moved to the front gates and was filming the guests leaving in their varying cars: an odd mix of family estates, sports cars and what appeared to be old bangers. As the last car drove past the camera turned to follow it. On the far side of the road, opposite the gates, it showed a single house and the hedge that surrounded its garden. It would have been considered quite a large place had it not stood looking out on the grounds of the behemoth at the other end of the drive. Something about it made Charlotte think of a vicarage, although she couldn't recall if there was a church nearby or not.

The thought of a vicarage reminded her of something Sir Frederick had said to her in the St. Martins' Lounge the previous evening. He had been talking about Marcus' relationship with his parents and how it was similar to his own. But she now recalled he had mentioned something about a house and how Marcus' parents had left theirs to the church. She had never visited the place and had no idea where it was but the idea boomed in her mind. Could that be where Marcus had gone? If it was church property now, he may well have been able to gain access and hide out there.

She rushed downstairs to where she had left her phone, lying on the arm of a settee. Making to dial DC Handley she realised it was 11 in the evening and he would likely have left for the day. She scrabbled through her purse and bag, sure she had a business card of his somewhere in there. Eventually, she found it and dialled his mobile number.

It rang for some time but eventually a very tired and groggy-sounding Handley answered.

'Detective Handley, it's Charlotte Travers,' Charlotte said with a note of urgency in her voice. 'I may have some information for you regarding Marcus' whereabouts.'

Handley made a noise she couldn't decipher although she imagined he was shifting in his bed in order to better take the call.

'What is it you have, Mrs Travers?' he said, suddenly sounding more awake. 'We already have one good lead on where he might be but another would be very helpful.'

'Oh, you have a lead?' Charlotte asked. 'Well, it may be the same one. Anyway, I was reminded just now of something Sir Frederick Derringham said to me the other night – we met by chance while I was out – and I thought it a very likely place Marcus might go.'

'OK,' was all Handley said.

'His parents had a house up in Scotland, quite far north I believe. Anyway, they didn't leave it to Marcus when they died – they left it to the church, apparently. Sir Frederick said it didn't appear to cause Marcus too much grief but I thought it might be somewhere he would go if he wanted to hide.'

'That's very interesting, Mrs Travers,' Handley said. 'That's two properties in Scotland we can search now. Do you have any further details?'

'I'm afraid not, no,' Charlotte replied. 'All I can give you is his parents' names – Gregor and Elspeth Travers. I don't really know much about them and even less about their house. Would you be able to trace it with just their names?'

'Yes that may well be possible, Mrs Travers. Thank you, I'll get straight onto it and let you know what I can when I can. Good night.'

Charlotte hung up the call and slumped onto the settee. She was suddenly exhausted and drifted into sleep with a feeling of satisfaction that she might at last have come up with something that would lead her and the police to Marcus.

Two properties? – she thought, just before she dropped into the obliviousness of sleep.

*

The alarm woke Handley at five in the morning. He groaned and turned over, readying to slam a hand onto the snooze button. Then he recalled that he, Pearson and Tanner were meant to be heading to Scotland and he was driving. And now he had to tell them of a second property that needed checking before they left – one that they had no address for at this time. The two could be next door to each other or 400 miles apart!

Still groaning and grumbling, he climbed out of bed and headed for the coffee jar.

While the kettle boiled, he put a call into the station knowing he'd catch whoever was still on from the night shift. It was Mallen who answered.

'Sonia, it's Tony,' Handley said, cutting her off as she was giving her name. 'I need you to find the address of a property for me. All I know is it's in Scotland and at some point it was owned by a Gregor and Elspeth Travers, and was subsequently bequeathed to the church.'

'You're not asking much, are you Tony?' Mallen replied dryly. 'And a "good morning" would have been nice. A "how was your shift?" even better.'

'Sorry, Sonia,' Handley said, trying to sound contrite but only getting as far as slightly bothered. 'I've got to drive up there today with Tanner and Pearson so I'm pretty edgy right now. And it's five in the morning. I could do with the info before we leave which is in two hours, so I can plan our route.'

'You forget I've been here all night, Tony, so I know it's five in the morning,' Sonia replied without too much rancour. 'OK leave it with me, do you want me to call or text you the address? *If* I find it.'

'Cheers, Sonia, text it me please.'

Call made, Handley dressed and packed a small overnight bag. He had enough time for another coffee before he had to collect DCI Tanner and DCS Pearson, so settled down at the kitchen table. God, he thought, nine hours or more of driving all the way to bloody Scotland! He couldn't see why they couldn't request the local force go check the property out but DCS Pearson had been adamant that they go in person.

'Look,' Pearson had said the afternoon before, 'we've got more than enough for the murder of Julia Metcalfe and a decent amount on him for The Charmer murders too – we *have* to bring him in. And yes, I know the local force could do it but if he is The Charmer, *I* want to be the one who brings him in.'

Neither Handley nor Tanner could find an argument to counter him.

That previous afternoon had been something of a blur, after Handley had returned from Pearson's office. The lab report Mallen had brought over to Handley had confirmed that the DNA found in the second hair sample from the scene in Bristol didn't match with any DNA found at any of the other scenes, ruling out the other individual as a suspect and therefore keeping Travers as top of the list.

With the CCTV images still bothering him, Handley had headed back out the office to find Tanner and Pearson and bring them up to speed. He found them exactly where he expected – out the back of the station, cigarettes at full steam.

'We have an address and something further on the CCTV,' Handley had said, trying to keep downwind of the smoke.

'Great, where is the address and what have you got?' Pearson had asked, taking a last drag and stubbing his cigarette.

'Address is in Scotland and the CCTV could – and I have to say only *could* – show Marcus Travers at four places where victims were also seen on the same nights they were killed.' Handley was still unsure whether to raise what bothered him about the images so had chosen to keep quiet.

'Excellent,' Tanner had said, clapping his hands together, 'let's go inside and look at what we've got and decide how we play it from there.'

Less than 10 minutes later they were all back around Pearson's desk, looking at the CCTV images. Pearson and Tanner had listened to Handley explain the recent lab results and his discoveries around the mysterious address Julia Metcalfe had had in her address book..

'I'll get on to Scotland as soon as we're done,' Pearson had said. He looked back down at the images on his desk and then back up at Handley. 'You seem a bit reticent about these, Tony? Don't you think there's enough of a likeness?'

'It's partly that, sir,' Handley had replied cautiously. He didn't want to say anything that might get scoffed at by the two senior officers in the room. 'I mean, there are some really obvious differences between the four images – hair colour, dress, and even in the case of the third one here a potential difference in height, if you compare them all. And yes, I can see the similarity with Marcus Travers but equally I can see that it could actually be someone else.'

'Anyone in particular Tony?' Tanner had asked.

'I can't be totally sure, sir. But this could equally be Sir Frederick Derringham,' Handley had replied, keeping the note of caution in his voice.

'Could it?' Tanner responded. 'I've never met him so I couldn't say. But so what? Lots of people look alike and why on earth would you think it's him? There's been nothing to make us look at him in connection to this. In fact, you interviewed him to try and find Travers and you didn't raise any doubts then. So why now?'

'I suppose I hadn't really noticed a likeness before and now the address we have happens to belong to Sir Frederick, which might just have made me wonder,' Handley had said, beginning to feel a little foolish.

'Look,' Pearson had said firmly, 'all the evidence we have points to Travers being responsible for the murder of Julia Metcalfe. That's what we're after him for right now. Anything to do with The Charmer will be looked at once we have him in custody. There is nothing we have that points to Sir Frederick Derringham at all. And I have met him too and yes, it does look a little like him but it also looks a lot like Marcus Travers to me. So, we're going for Travers — let's not start muddying the waters again, ok?'

Handley and Tanner nodded in unison. Pearson had made himself perfectly clear and there would be no arguing from that point on.

Pearson had called Police Scotland while they were still in the office and surprised both Handley and Tanner by requesting they just drive past the property to see if there was any sign of life but not approach.

They were even more surprised when he had said, 'My colleagues and I will be driving up tomorrow to investigate further so please have the local station ready to meet us when we get there.'

'We're going up there?' Tanner had asked — then remembering it was not just him and Pearson in the room, added, 'Er, *sir*?'

It was at that point that Pearson had made it clear that they were going because if anyone was going to collar The Charmer — whoever that turned out to be — it would be him.

*

The drive north proved to be more interminable than even Handley's most pessimistic forecast — nearly 500 miles, over 10 hours of driving with Pearson in the passenger seat and Tanner in the back. There were long periods of silence over the journey, with Handley still wondering about the likeness between Derringham and Travers, and Pearson flicking through files and brooding over The Charmer cases, past and present. Tanner was just brooding.

As they pulled into Knutsford services on the M6 Handley's phone chimed. It was the expected text from DC Mallen with the address of the property once owned by Travers' parents. The message ended with the line, 'This took fucking ages Handley you owe me seriously big time!' Checking the time, Handley realised just how much time Mallen must have spent on it after her shift had finished and made a mental note to make sure Tanner knew about it.

The new address was searched for over coffee and sandwiches and turned out to be a little under 20 miles north of Derringham's cottage. It was agreed they would continue as planned to Derringham's place first and then have the local officer accompany them to the Travers' old house, should they need to. With that, it was back to more mind-numbing driving.

As they crossed the border Tanner piped up from the back seat, 'My dad was a Scot, you know?'

'Really?' said Pearson, turning in his seat to look back at Tanner. 'You never told me that before, Malcolm.'

'Didn't really come up before, Fran. He was from Greenock, the miserable old sod. Mind you, I visited the place once and it all made sense. No wonder the old bugger never cracked a smile.'

Pearson and Tanner shared a chuckle. Handley found it strange and a little disconcerting to hear his senior officers chatting in such a casual manner but attempted a light-hearted chuckle. I'm going to have a headache before we get to Glasgow, he thought.

Eventually, and to Handley's marked relief, they made it to the police station in Aberdeen – where Pearson had been told to collect their local officer from. With moans about aching backs and cramped legs the three of them

270

entered the station. It was now nearly six in the evening and they were an hour later than Pearson had promised. Fortunately, they had phoned ahead with progress reports and the officer they were to meet had agreed to stay on and wait for them.

Sergeant Donald Monaghan arrived in the reception area five minutes later. He was of average height and build with a square, strong face and hands far larger than his frame would suggest. The only one who appeared to hold his own during the handshakes was Handley and that was because he had witnessed the bone-crushing grips applied to Pearson and Tanner. With the introductions over they headed back out to the car.

'It's not too long a drive out, you'll be pleased to know DC Handley,' Monaghan stated as they climbed in the car.

Handley noted the similarity between Monaghan and Sir Frederick Derringham's accents, although Derringham's sounded slightly more anglicised. Handley wondered if that was a result of years in England mixing with well-spoken types on a daily basis or whether Derringham had always sounded that way. He also wondered if this was how Marcus Travers sounded. It seemed odd to Handley that he felt he knew Marcus Travers inside and out by now but that he had never heard the man speak.

Monaghan explained they were heading towards a place called Kintore, with the property they were after just outside that small town.

'I drove past it twice yesterday after you phoned, Detective Chief Superintendent Pearson. In the afternoon and at seven after I clocked off. And again this morning, early,' Monaghan said, the lilt in his voice giving it a sing-song quality.

'Good man,' Pearson replied, 'did you see anything?'

'No, not really,' Monaghan answered. 'There were no lights on at any of the times I went past and I couldn't see any sign of damage from the road – no windows broken or anything obvious like that.'

'OK, well thanks for keeping an eye. He might not be here but we have a second address that we want to check out.' Pearson gave Monaghan the details.

'Aye, I know where that is. It's a wee way from where we're heading, mind.'

'Still, I'd like to go there tonight if he's not at this one. Hope we're not keeping you from anything important, Sergeant Monaghan?'

'Nah, only Mrs Monaghan and the soaps, sir.'

'Glad to hear it.'

The cottage was a large well-kept property situated down a one-track road about two miles outside Kintore. The area, whilst very attractive, was a lot flatter than Handley had imagined. There were no heather-clad mountains to be seen, no great glens or impressive rivers. But, he conceded, he could see why Sir Frederick Derringham would want to have a retreat out here – it was incredibly peaceful and tranquil.

They parked the car across the front gates – blocking a potential escape route as much as possible – and walked up to the front door, Pearson leading the way. As they were making their way along the short path Tanner laid his hand on Handley's arm, turning him slightly. Handley looked at his boss who, without speaking, nodded towards Pearson and then lifted his finger to his eye before pointing it back at the senior officer. Handley nodded, message understood.

Handley had noticed slight but tell-tale signs that Pearson had been getting more and more tense as they neared the cottage. He reasoned that his boss was readying himself for an arrest but also that the years of stress and tension from his failure to capture The Charmer were now weighing heavily on him. Handley could see, and it appeared so could Tanner, that Pearson was too uptight, too tense and too ready for action. And, that if Marcus Travers did decide to cause trouble, this might prove to be an unhealthy state of mind for a policeman to be in at the time of an arrest.

Pearson was no longer young and lacked the fitness and muscle Handley and Tanner could supply – if Travers kicked off Pearson could get hurt. On the other hand, in his wound-up state, Pearson could go in with a little too much force and Travers could get hurt, and that could jeopardise the whole operation and subsequent case.

As Pearson strode up to and knocked on the front door, Handley manoeuvred himself so that he would be the first through should it be answered. It wasn't.

A second, longer, more persistent and louder knock also proved fruitless. Pearson looked round and indicated that Tanner should go around the property one way and Monaghan the other – both obliged silently. Handley moved to the window at the front of the house, to the left of the door, with a disturbing sense of déjà vu. Not again, he thought.

But the room he could see through the window was a neat and tidy office, and as far as Handley could tell – untouched and free of any bodies.

Tanner and Monaghan appeared back round the front at much the same time.

'Place seems empty, sir,' Tanner said as he rounded the corner. 'No lights on, no sign in any of the rooms I could

273

see that anyone's recently been in them. There's no cups or dishes in the kitchen. In fact, everything looks pristine.'

Pearson grunted.

'Right,' he said gruffly, 'let's go in. Handley, you know where Sir Frederick keeps the spare key?'

'Yes, sir,' Handley replied and moved to the right of the door. The doorway had a ledge built in above it – Handley reached up and felt along the top edge, eventually locating the key that was stuck there with blu-tack.

'We have got permission to enter, haven't we Tony?' Pearson asked as Handley was about to insert the key in the lock.

'Yes sir, I called Sir Frederick back and he was happy to oblige,' Handley replied, recalling Derringham's protestations and final grudging acquiescence.

The four of them entered the house and split up to check each of the rooms. Within five minutes it was clear to all of them that Marcus Travers wasn't there. Pearson still wanted the place thoroughly checked over before they left. There might still be signs that Marcus Travers had been there.

Tanner and Pearson took the downstairs rooms whilst Handley and Monaghan took the first floor. There were three bedrooms and a bathroom upstairs and all three rooms looked undisturbed.

It seemed reasonably clear to all of them that nobody had been in the cottage any time recently – including Marcus Travers. Just before they went to leave Handley thought to check the large free-standing wardrobe he'd seen in the last of the three bedrooms he'd looked in.

'Jesus, Handley,' Tanner grumbled, 'why didn't you check it before?'

Handley mumbled an excuse and headed back upstairs.

274

The bedroom was larger than the other two and Handley surmised this would be Sir Frederick's room. Previously, he had only given it a cursory look from the door; this time as he entered the room he gave it more attention. The room was large enough to accommodate the king-size bed with accompanying bedside cabinets, two large chests of drawers and the wardrobe. There was a full-length mirror attached to the wall between the drawers. Sir Frederick's impeccable dress sense clearly applied to his days off too, thought Handley, surveying the mirror.

Out of curiosity Handley opened the top drawer of one of the chests. It contained a large number of jerseys in neatly folded piles. Handley closed the drawer and, on a whim, bent and opened the bottom one. This contained two low racks of shoes, and between the two racks was a scrap of paper, presumably dropped there by accident. Handley picked it up. It had torn perforations at the top which looked like those from a page torn from a reporter's style notebook. There were only four words written on it: Jane, Doncaster, 4th April.

Handley put the note back with a shrug and a half-smile – a note to remind Sir Frederick of an assignation most likely, he thought, and turned his attention to the wardrobe.

The wardrobe was large, made of oak and looked very expensive. Handley pulled the double doors open and peered inside. It was crammed with clothes hanging from two rails: suits, shirts, polo shirts, t-shirts and jeans were all hung neatly from clothes hangers. Underneath these were about a dozen shoe boxes stacked on top of each other and a briefcase propped against the side.

To Handley there seemed to be a lot of clothes here for a holiday home. But then he thought that he didn't really know how many clothes the average wealthy, single man might have. The briefcase seemed a little incongruous in the wardrobe – there was an office downstairs, wouldn't it be kept there? He reached down and picked it up. It had combination locks so he couldn't open it but it felt light and was probably empty or contained only a few bits of paperwork. Handley figured that it probably had a few personal papers in it and placed it back where it had been.

Finally, he picked up one of the shoe boxes. It wasn't heavy enough to contain shoes but there was enough weight to it to indicate it contained something. As he began to lift the lid, Tanner's head appeared round the door.

'Fuck sake, Tony,' he spat, 'he's not going to be in the fucking shoe box is he? Now come on!'

'14

A glass of whisky was in order, he felt. Time to relax and reflect. It had been a good day all round and now – at some time after one in the morning – he could unwind.

Sipping his drink, he thought back over the last 20 years – had it really been that long? All those years searching, working and improving. All those years living with the Urge and the Quest. All those years living a wholly successful double life and becoming an expert at both.

He thought of all those who had given their lives in aid of his Quest. He couldn't recall how many there had been now. There were the prostitutes, in the early days, that he had slain so casually – and messily, he had to admit. Then there were the untold mistakes he had made that could easily have led to his capture and the end of the Quest. Then came the refining, the perfecting of his methods – the art of seduction being primary among them, allowing him to move on to those women with far more potential.

He thought of the boys and men who had died to fulfil a more prosaic need. They were of little consequence to the Quest per se but a vital part of his ability to carry on. He was proud of his ability to work around all the forensic and scientific advances as they had emerged. He was especially proud of his use of others' hair, blood and semen – those 'foreign bodies' placed so thoughtfully on and around the women he Delivered. Many of these men would never be found or even missed. He could kill them with impunity, he knew, and took pleasure in the fact that he had become so adept and professional in his dealings with these people.

Then there were those the police would say had been framed – the men, and women, who had yielded their traces without him needing to kill them. The casual brushing of a hair from a jacket, the careful swabbing of a glass – out of their sight, naturally – after they had had a drink. There had been so many ways to obtain the material he needed to throw the scent off himself.

He smiled at the thought of the police, still baffled and chasing shadows after all these years, no nearer to a suspect now than at the outset. He knew that there was little chance of capture – they would have had him by now. He had become impossible to catch and so could carry on the Quest at his leisure. Still careful and astute, and always looking for ways to improve and refine his methods, he felt he had become a mythical creature that could strike at will and disappear into the night, unseen and untouchable.

He took most pride in his own development – the setting and achieving of goals in order to develop what he saw as his primary career. The other pathetic, inconsequential one in the 'real' world always took second place. It was his ability to set his own targets for improvement, understanding his weaknesses and vulnerabilities and turning them into strengths and points of success. Each move, each progression had brought him to this point of freedom, the zenith of his powers. He could act, now, on the Urge virtually whenever he wanted. He was delighted that the outside world saw him as one of them; the outward appearance of decency and normality so hard won over the years had been a cloak making him invisible to any prying investigation. He was above reproach and therefore consideration.

And, of course, there were the women he had treasured – all those women he had so expertly seduced and finally Delivered. Married, single or otherwise attached, it hadn't mattered. If he felt they would fit the profile of The One then he would have them in his power.

278

They all fell into his arms willingly and easily. They had all come to realise true bliss and the eternal nature of the love he had given them.

A note of melancholy now impinged on his reverie. It was something of a regret that The One hadn't yet materialised. His search was still unfulfilled and the perfect model of *her* still eluded him. He wondered then if he hadn't already found her but let her slip out of his grasp – she who had been right under his nose for six years or more. But the association prevented him from acting. He couldn't now Deliver her without all suspicion falling onto him. He was pretty sure that she was as close as he had ever got but she was beyond even his prodigious abilities to ensnare. But he would keep searching; she was out there somewhere, he was sure, and he would find her.

He replenished his glass and turned his thoughts to the Quest once more. He had Delivered another one tonight and she, like all the others, had fallen short in some way. He knew he could only continue for maybe another 10 years, 15 at the most. He knew he would begin to lose his strength and with it his ability to control any given situation. The chances of someone close to him discovering his secret life, by accident or design, had also been increasing over the years which would of course curtail his longevity. He would have to consider carefully when and how to stop – an exit strategy, as it were. He would need to be more selective and cultivate future proxies, targeting them more thoroughly and therefore raising his chances of success.

The thought of stopping filled him with a strange mix of emotions. He would be elated at completing the Quest, at finding The One. But it would feel very strange indeed to leave behind the life he had made for himself. Could he stop? Would he stop? He didn't know the answer to those questions.

Did he want to stop?

That was a different question all together and the answer was straightforward – no. If he thought hard enough on it, he knew he would never want to stop; he felt deep down that he would never find the perfect One and so would carry on, year after year, until he either died or got so old and sloppy that they caught him.

The thought of carrying on ad infinitum comforted him – there was a pattern to his life and he was happy and safe within it. He would simply become smarter as he got older, as that detestable slogan went – 'work smarter, not harder'. He was safe, untouchable and could do as he pleased with no interference. The Quest would continue and while it did, so would he.

With that pleasing thought he drained his glass, poured a refill and turned on the radio. Sitting back in his armchair he began to whistle quietly along to the tune.

Chapter Nineteen

They trooped out of the cottage, all four of them feeling a little disappointed at having found nothing. Pearson seemed the most down of all of them, reverting back to the brooding state Handley had seen during the drive up.

'Never mind, sir,' Handley ventured, 'there's still the next address to check.'

'Yes, I know Tony, just feels like we're chasing shadows – again!'

With that they all got back in the car and started the short trip to the Travers' old house. On the way, Handley explained what little they knew about the property.

'We think, well – Sonia actually thinks that they bought the place to retire to. It was purchased in 1996 so they would have been well into their sixties by then. All we know beyond that is that it was willed to the church on their death. Charlotte Travers told me some time ago that Marcus rarely if ever spoke about his parents so she knew next to nothing about them and very little about his family background. But Marcus certainly knew about the house and given its remoteness it would seem a logical hiding place.'

'If it was willed to the church,' Tanner put in, 'surely they would have occupied it – or would be using it for something? He would stand out a bit just showing up, don't you think?'

'Yes, true sir,' Handley replied, 'but it's the only other lead we have and has to be worth following up.'

'The kirk doesn't always put its property to good use,' Monaghan said from the back seat, 'so there is a chance it's sitting empty.'

They drove the rest of the way in silence.

The Travers' old place was a far cry from the cottage they had just left. It was old and worn-looking with a small but completely overgrown front garden. There was a low dry stone wall along the front with a rusty-looking gate standing higher than the wall. On the gate hung a sign: 'Property of the Free Church of Scotland'.

'Ah, the Wee Frees,' Monaghan said knowingly.

'What are they when they're at home?' Tanner asked.

'They are a branch of the Church o' Scotland. Formed a couple of hundred years ago – I must confess I know very little else other than the nickname and that in some eyes they're seen as a bit more –' Monaghan paused, looking up at the sky – 'um, radical?'

'Radical?' Handley asked. 'As in fundamentalist?'

'They could be called that, but probably not in the way you're thinking,' said Monaghan. 'The Church of Scotland is based on Calvinist ideas – Calvin was a radical Protestant – and as I understand it the Wee Frees adhere to those ideas as fundamental to their whole belief. So yes, fundamentalists but definitely not terrorists.'

'Yeah, well all very enlightening I'm sure,' Pearson put in, 'but we're here to look for Marcus Travers not talk bloody religious doctrine. So, shall we?' He extended a hand towards the gate.

Handley went through first, carrying the jemmy he'd brought from the car, followed by Tanner and then the other two. There was a short path leading to the front door; the concrete was broken and uneven with weeds encroaching through every crack.

'Think you're right Sergeant,' Handley said over his shoulder, 'this place doesn't look like it's been used for quite some time.'

'Aye,' was all Monaghan said in reply.

The front door had obviously once been a shade of dark blue but was now faded, the paint cracked and peeling. There was an old and creaky-looking knocker attached about two thirds up the door. As Handley moved to raise the handle of the knocker, Tanner forestalled him — gesturing that they should have a look around the outside first.

As they had at Derringham's cottage, Handley went one way and Tanner the other, circling the house.

'Well?' asked Pearson on their return.

'Place is pretty run down,' Tanner answered. 'You can't see through the windows except one at the back that's broken. There was no furniture in the room I could see into. No signs of life.'

'OK,' Pearson replied, 'let's get in then. Let's not knock this time, eh?'

Handley nodded and lifted the jemmy, forcing it between the door and the jamb. As he hauled on the end there was a crack and a chunk of rotten wood fell away. Tanner sighed and shook his head. Handley tried again, feeling that he should be able to perform this operation with a little more ease and professionalism.

This time the door gave in — in a shower of splinters and a wave of musty, damp-smelling air. All four officers waited a few seconds, listening for signs of movement from within. There was nothing.

As they entered the hallway, the smell of ruin became much stronger: a mixture of dust, damp and rotting wood ... there was also a tang of something else in the air, something more metallic, with an organic undertone.

With more than a little trepidation Handley entered first followed again by Tanner. Tanner gestured for

Handley to head towards the back of the house while he checked the door immediately to his right.

'Fuck!' Tanner exclaimed loudly.

Handley, who had only gone a few paces, turned swiftly back towards his boss. Tanner was already entering the room, his mouth twisted into a grimace of distaste. Pearson and Monaghan were only a pace or two behind him.

Monaghan looked through the doorway, let out a hiss and immediately turned away. Pearson hesitated and then strode into the room, his expression unreadable.

Nervously, Handley followed the DCS through the door.

Pearson had stopped a few paces into the room so Handley had to look over his shoulder to see in. Tanner was stood in the centre of the room with the same grimace on his face, shaking his head. Handley followed his gaze and promptly wished he hadn't.

The only furniture in the room was a single ancient-looking armchair. It was occupied by a male corpse, arms hanging slackly over the chair arms, legs splayed out. More than half his face was missing, so all that could be seen was a gaping chasm full of gore and broken teeth. There was no nose left and the remaining eye hung loose from its socket. The wall behind the chair was splattered with blood and what Handley could only assume was brains.

He gagged.

Pearson moved slowly further into the room to stand next to Tanner.

'Marcus Travers, I presume,' he muttered quietly, turning to Handley for confirmation.

Handley forced himself to look more closely at the mess of the man's face, trying to pick out any details whilst mentally trying to add in the parts that were missing. He gagged again.

Taking a deep breath, he nodded towards his boss. 'Could be,' he managed to say. 'Hard to tell really, but yes – what's left of his face looks like Travers.'

Pearson nodded in return and looked at Tanner. 'Suicide?' he asked.

Tanner surveyed the room. 'I reckon so,' he said eventually. 'Shotgun's there, look.' He was pointing at a double-barrelled shotgun lying on the floor several feet away from the body.

'But the gun's nowhere near him,' Handley said. 'Surely if he'd killed himself the gun would be right next to him or still in his hand?'

'You've never seen a shotgun suicide, have you son?' Tanner asked. Handley shook his head.

'See the thing is people expect the gun to be next to the body but these things have an almighty kick – if you blow your head off then all the muscles relax instantly and the recoil throws the gun across the floor. Which makes me think this is a genuine suicide as not many murderers would think of that little detail.'

Pearson turned away from the ruined corpse. 'Right,' he said with authority, 'we need SOCO in here pronto. Let's get moving boys. Monaghan!' He called through the door as he began exiting the room. Tanner followed, giving a very green-looking Handley a pat on the shoulder.

Handley took a last look around the room. There was no carpeting, and the bare floorboards looked every bit as aged as the rest of the house. The only piece of decoration was an ancient single-barrelled shotgun attached to the far wall; Handley gave it a cursory glance before turning back to the man sprawled in the chair.

285

If he ignored the mess of a head he looked every inch like a man who – exhausted from a long day's toil – had slumped into his favourite chair and dozed off. He forced himself to look at the face again. He had never had to attend a shotgun suicide and the red gaping mess it left in the face and head continued to unnerve him. Steeling himself, he moved round to look at the back of the head. Most of it was gone – he could almost see back through to the other side. Shattered fragments of skull clung to the inside of the wound and protruded outward, flower-like in its pattern.

The blood and blue-grey blobs of organic tissue that were glued within it all looked relatively fresh, certainly no more than a day or two old.

He closed his eyes and shook his head. So Marcus Travers, he thought, this is how I find you? After all this time he had still believed he would find Marcus alive. He hadn't known under what circumstances he would find him in but he would be alive. He had always envisaged being able to tell Charlotte Travers that her husband was alive and well and that she would be able to see him again. If only you'd hung on another couple of days, he thought. It saddened him that he had to find Marcus destroyed so horribly and, perhaps, with his name forever linked to the brutal killing of so many women.

He turned his gaze away and down at the floor, still shaking his head. As he did so his eye caught a scrap of paper lying under the chair clearly dropped by the limp, lifeless hand that dangled just above it. He bent and collected it.

It only had a few words scrawled across it at an incongruous angle. It read:

It's all my fault. I couldn't stop it.

There was no signature to show this had been written by Marcus Travers but Handley suspected it would turn out to be his handwriting and indeed the last communication Marcus Travers made to the world.

He turned and left the room.

He exited the house, seeing the other three all on their phones and radios. Monaghan was requesting immediate assistance from his colleagues at his station. Tanner was some way off on his mobile – Handley couldn't make out what he was saying. Pearson stood nearby, also on his phone.

'Identity will have to be obtained forensically,' he was saying as Handley approached. 'No one is going to be able to ID him by sight.'

As he was finishing, Pearson turned and looked at Handley who mutely handed over the note. Pearson read it quickly and then said into his phone: 'Almost certainly suicide, I've a note here that seems to say he's guilty of it all, whatever "it all" is.' With that he hung up.

'Well sir, what do you think?' Handley asked.

'I think we got the bastard, Handley. And I think we'll now have more than enough to say he killed Julia Metcalfe and link him to plenty more Charmer murders too. After all these years I think we have him. And just as he knew we were closing in he goes and tops himself, fucking coward.'

Handley simply nodded and moved past his boss, walking up the path and out the gate to stand on the verge of the road, looking out across the surrounding countryside.

He still felt nauseated by the sight inside the house and saddened for Charlotte Travers and the news he would have to bring to her. But he also felt a swelling of pride and satisfaction at his part in this whole investigation. He had played a major role in capturing one of the most prolific serial killers in British history. He had not just been a cog in the investigative wheel but he had been instrumental in the tracing of Marcus Travers and linking him to the Charmer crimes. For the first time since he had joined the force he felt pivotal.

He had made it onto the 'one to watch' list.

'81

Ailsa was coming over! After several months of lukewarm relations with her and no more visits to the Manse, she was finally coming again. Her family had been invited by his parents to a prayer meeting with several church elders. They would be along within half an hour. He felt his excitement grow at the prospect of seeing her outside of school again. He would have a chance to renew her interest in him away from all the other competition. They would have a chance to reignite and strengthen the bond that he knew they had. He could rekindle her love for him — a love he knew for certain she held deep inside. This was his chance to kick-start his dreams of love and romance.

There was an old armchair in his room that he could relax in and so he sat there trying his best to ease the nerves that fluttered in the pit of his stomach. He lay back a little and slowed his breathing, closing his eyes as he tried to imagine how the afternoon would go. They would be sitting next to each other and he would make her laugh with wry comments on his father's diatribe. And when in prayer, with eyes closed, she would reach out her hand and lightly brush his arm or, even better, his thigh.

His mind focused on that single, imagined act — her hand softly and lightly running up his thigh, continuing further and further up, risking a brush against his penis and testicles. He started to become aroused at the thought, rubbing his own hands up and down his inner thighs and enacting the daydream that played, clear as a movie, inside his head.

Suddenly, they were alone in the room. All the others had simply melted away. They turned to each other and kissed — a long, deep kiss. He held her close to him and let his hands roam over her perfect body. She responded with small shifts in her position and small, low sighs as his hands continued touching. Moving further up her torso he risked cupping one breast. She inhaled sharply but didn't object.

He was fully hard now. Opening his eyes, he listened carefully for any noises upstairs – all was quiet. Feeling safe and free from the danger of being caught, he undid his trouser button and slid the zip down. Closing his eyes again, he relaxed back into the world of his fantasy.

They were half-undressed now, he in boxer shorts and she in bra and knickers. He could feel her warm, smooth skin against his body. The soft material of her bra was now stretched taut against her nipples which brushed against his chest as they continued to kiss and move together. Each touch of her nipple against his own sent tingles of pure pleasure down his spine. He could wait no longer. Reaching round he unclasped her bra effortlessly – no fumbling, clumsy fighting with the catches – as though he had done it a million times before. Her breasts, when freed, were small, pert and perfectly formed – it took his breath away just to look at them. His hands moved to run over her silken skin and already erect and receptive nipples. Her breathing became sharper and more rapid as he began to play his hands over them.

He opened his eyes, checking again for sounds of nearby movement – still safe. He slid his hand into the opening in the front of his shorts and freed himself. He stroked gently along the shaft, not wanting to rush but instead savouring his dream as long as possible. His penis was so hard by now that it almost hurt.

Eyes closed again – they were fully naked now and the sight of her made him inhale sharply, both in his dream and in reality. He slid his hands along the inside of her smooth, firm thighs, then reached between her legs to feel the moist warmth there. Slowly at first and then with more and more vigour he explored with his fingers, making her gasp and moan. Occasionally she would let out a high-pitched squeak of a sound as his fingers delved deeper inside her.

He could contain himself no longer. His hand moved over his erection, gripping tighter and tighter, his legs involuntarily stiffening and lifting his feet off the floor as his strokes increased in tempo.

He was inside her now and their bodies were moving more and more rapidly – both feeling they had become one body, one soul, joined forever.

He could feel the climax rising from the base of his penis, beginning to warm the shaft, the head becoming more swollen and sensitive to his touch.

The door opened then and slammed against the wall. He ejaculated instantly with the shock.

His father roared incomprehensibly as he strode across the room towards him. He was desperately trying to pull up his trousers and cover himself but his father reached him before he could get very far. His arm was grabbed in a brutally strong grip and he was hauled to his feet.

'You bloody filthy little wretch,' his father screamed in his face. He felt spittle hit his eyes and cheeks.

With his trousers still undone, he was hauled roughly out of the room, all the while fighting to hold them up and not trip as the legs got caught up under his feet.

The stairs were even more perilous and he nearly fell twice on the way down, but his father's vice of a grip held firm as he half-dragged, half-carried him the rest of the way. As they reached the hallway he realised with a growing sense of horror that he was being hauled to the front room – the room in which they received their guests.

His father had ranted and raved the whole way down and now his voice rose in pitch and volume. He couldn't make out a word of the venomous tirade.

He struggled harder to get his trousers securely back on and to free himself from the painful, unrelenting grip on his arm. But his father held firm, his strength and resolve proving too much to resist.

His father flung open the door to the front room and dragged him inside. His growing sense of dread doubled as he was pushed inside the room.

They were all there already. The three elders were sitting on one couch and Ailsa, her father and mother on the other. His mother was sitting in one of the two armchairs. All seven of them turned and stared open-mouthed at the commotion – all of them staring at him.

And there, over the fire guard, hung the pulpit tabard from the kirk, its needlework image of the burning bush now blazing in his eyes. He tried to focus on that, desperate not to make eye contact with those in the room. But the image burned and glowed unnaturally, as accusing and disgusted as the people in the room.

He turned his eyes away from the image.

'This filthy wretch of a boy was in his room committing a disgusting act of self-gratification with heathen abandon,' his father shouted to the whole room. 'Self-abusing in *this* house with you all here. I am ashamed to call him my son and sickened by his actions. It was a vile sight to behold and a vile act to commit at any time – but today, now, he chooses to defile my house. A house of God!'

The others in the room continued to stare with shocked, slack-jawed bewilderment and wide-eyed incredulity, their expressions turning to disgust and loathing as it dawned on them what his father was talking about.

He struggled again, feebly this time, knowing it would do him no good.

His father was screaming now. 'Driven by his own lusts and perverted desires – heedless to our meeting here and its purpose – he has sullied his own hand with this….'

Before he could do anything his father moved his grip and grabbed his wrist, pulling away the hand that clutched, white-knuckled, to the top of his trousers. With his free hand his father grabbed his trousers and underwear and hauled them down so that they crumpled around his ankles.

He died inside.

He felt sick with embarrassment and shame. He was powerless and exposed and humiliated.

The room gasped collectively, with several of the women holding their hands over their mouths. His mother was sobbing with her face in her hands. But his focus was on Ailsa. She was sitting directly opposite him, staring – red-faced, mouth agape – directly at his groin.

He nearly collapsed when he looked down and saw his penis had shrivelled – with the adrenalin and shame – to a small pathetic stump, barely protruding through his pubic hair. Another wave of nausea struck him as he saw that there was semen clinging wetly to the hairs and around the tip of his penis. He knew without looking that there would be some on the hand his father was now holding up for all to see.

At that moment, like a sickening parody of his daydream, the room seemed to shrink, leaving only Ailsa and him standing alone.

She continued to stare, mouth still open, with an unreadable expression on her face and a spark of light in her eyes. Was that contempt? Pity? Or something else he saw there? He had no idea and no inclination to find out. He just wanted to run and keep running as far from there as possible. The crazed thought crossed his mind – if he ran far enough and fast enough, maybe he could undo this whole incident. Maybe he could simply make it disappear from existence and then return to find that all was well.

He couldn't speak, could hardly breathe and couldn't drag his eyes away from hers.

And then she laughed.

It started as a blurted 'Ha', and then turned into a babbling, hissing giggle that appeared to him to go on and on. He couldn't tell if she were laughing through embarrassment, humour or disgust. But to his mind, she was laughing at his pitiable penis. And through his now near-insanity he convinced himself that she had somehow seen the images he had been fantasising about, and was laughing at his pathetic attempt at love-making and the woeful inadequacy of his manhood.

It was too much. His mind broke.

He finally ripped his arm from his father's grip, pulling his trousers up as he ran from the room and the house. Blindly, he ran – terrified and shamed to his very core.

He knew what was to come. This was a small town and no one hesitated to gossip to anyone who would listen. It would be everywhere within hours and all over the school when he returned on Monday. He couldn't face that –

there was no force on Earth that would convince him to go back to school and stand the torment facing him there.

But he was powerless against his father's will and knew he would have no choice. His father would drag him there personally if necessary and wouldn't care about humiliating him further.

As he ran, the image of the burning bush glowed red-hot in his mind. The very symbol of wrath and disgust and humiliation, it seared a scar in his psyche – one he knew would burn there forever.

But even that paled in significance next to the one thing that echoed again and again in his mind.

Her laughter.

She had laughed.

And she would continue to laugh for the rest of his life.

Chapter 20

Handley stood in the now empty and clean Travers' house, staring around the room where they had found Marcus Travers a week before. He had taken three days off, and early on the first morning of his leave had travelled back up to Scotland. He wasn't entirely sure what he was doing there but something had been nagging at him since Marcus Travers had been officially declared as the Charmer and the case had been closed.

He had trusted his instincts; he had been right to keep plugging away at Travers' disappearance – after all, look where that had finally led. And now, standing in the echoing house where it had all come to a gruesome end, he knew something was amiss.

The past week had gone quickly. Samples taken at the scene and during the autopsy confirmed that Marcus Travers' DNA did match the only sample found at Julia Metcalfe's cottage. And matches were also found with two further Charmer murders. Detective Chief Superintendent Pearson had been ecstatic – they had finally found the man he had been chasing for over 10 years. The general consensus was that Julia Metcalfe's murder could be filed in the Charmer case notes – as the final victim of a brutal murderer desperately trying to cover his tracks. They had never found anything among her notes to give a direct link to Marcus Travers but it seemed obvious that he had killed her to silence her.

The physical evidence and the grainy CCTV images were all Pearson seemed to need, and Marcus Travers' suicide note was the final nail in his coffin. He had called an immediate press conference and proudly told the assembled media that they had found the killer of Julia

Metcalfe and linked the man responsible to The Charmer murders. Case closed. It had been drinks all round and applause for Handley from Pearson, Tanner and the rest of the office. He had indeed made the 'one to watch' list and at the time felt on top of the world. Mission accomplished in every sense.

But as the week wore on, and Handley found himself with two muggings and an assault on his desk, his mind had wandered back to the last month or more. What was it that bothered him about The Charmer case? Why did he feel there was something more to it? Had something perhaps gone awry in the investigation? Or was he making mountains out of molehills?

The evidence had seemed to be fairly incontrovertible. They could link Travers to several Charmer murders and definitely to the murder of Julia Metcalfe. But Handley had been wondering – surely, they would have found *more* evidence matching Travers with The Charmer killings? But then, as DCI Tanner had said, it was clear that Travers was very forensically aware and clever in the way he apparently distorted and manipulated the evidence. Tanner also speculated that Travers had eventually begun wearing a fully-protective suit and gloves, which would explain the lack of physical evidence in the later cases.

All of this was very likely true. And yet Handley still had a nagging doubt. The CCTV images still bothered him. And then, five days after the case was closed, it occurred to him that they had found no trace of Travers having used any dating sites, or other dating services, to connect with his intended victims. The theory for some time had been that at least some of the victims had met the killer via online dating – or other equivalent services, for the older 'pre-internet' murders. And yet there was no evidence on

Travers' computer, or the laptop recovered at the scene of his death, that he had been anywhere near those types of sites. There was evidence from some of the later victims that they had indeed met someone on the night they were murdered, but the dating profiles of the men – or man – had been set up with a fake name and address, and later deleted. Handley had conceded that perhaps there was another computer they simply hadn't found.

Then there was the suicide note. Only those few words to sum up over a decade of slaughter? This was one of the questions now running through his mind. And to Handley, the wording didn't strike him as much of a confession. It seemed to him that a man about to blow half his face off with a shotgun might have made a more definite statement of guilt. But then both Tanner and Pearson seemed to be happy to accept it at face value.

But still it worried him and that niggling itching at the back of his mind would not go away. So, before the end of the week he had asked Tanner if he could take a few days off – citing exhaustion after the hunt for Marcus Travers as his reason. And because he was the golden boy, Tanner had had no problem sanctioning the leave.

And so he now stood in the musty semi-darkness of the living room in the Travers' old house. He had no idea what he was looking for but kept looking anyway. He examined the chair Marcus had been sitting in when they found him and the surrounding rug. He looked carefully along the wall where the shotgun had been found. Nothing.

With a sigh he began to concede defeat. He was giving the room one last look-over when his eyes fell on an old-fashioned-looking shotgun hanging on the wall. He recalled seeing it when he was last here but their focus had been on the weapon on the ground, and no one – including

SOCO it seemed – had given it much attention. He moved back across the room towards the gun with a curious look on his face. He wasn't sure what it was but something told him to take a closer look.

The gun was a very old single-barrelled shotgun – the sort that was seen in old photographs of gamekeepers and the like. It was long and very sturdy-looking, with scratches on the wooden stock and metal barrel. The gun was mounted to the wall by two brackets that looked purpose-made. He had no idea whether it was an old Travers heirloom, left behind after they died, or had been mounted there sometime after. Either way it didn't really matter, he thought.

As he got nearer, he saw what had been bothering him. The gun wasn't mounted properly on one of the brackets, with the barrel sitting a little proud of the niche it should have been slotted into. There was also a distinct lack of dust at the end of the barrel, whereas the rest of it had a fine but visible coating.

Lifting the gun clear he examined it carefully. There were marks in the wood of the stock where it had been slotted into the bracket and equivalent marks on the barrel. So it would seem that the gun *had* been sitting fully in the brackets at some point in the past, Handley thought. Aside from the marks and the lack of dust on the barrel there didn't appear to be much else to see.

With a shrug and a 'tsk' he began lifting the gun back into its proper place. I've wasted my time, he thought, annoyed at himself for driving all this way when he could have been chilling at home. He remounted the barrel and turned slightly to look along the length of the gun to check it was now fully back in its brackets. As he was checking, something caught his eye on the inside of the barrel.

Quickly taking the shotgun back down he peered down into the dark tube. There was definitely something in there and it looked like a piece of paper. It had been carefully rolled and pushed a little way down. Placing the stock on the floor, Handley fished out a pen from his inside pocket and began teasing the paper out, eventually working it out enough to be able to pull it clear with his finger.

Breathing slightly faster now and with a concentrated frown, he unrolled the paper which revealed itself to be, in fact, two pieces rolled together. He read the handwritten notes, lifted his gaze to the ceiling and closed his eyes.

'Shit,' he muttered quietly to himself.

*

Charlotte was sitting on her sofa, staring at the wall opposite – her eyes fixed on the family photo that hung there. She fixated on the image of Marcus, standing proudly next to her, his arm around her shoulder, and with the two kids beaming away in front of them. She couldn't pinpoint her feelings towards the man in the picture. She still loved him, in many ways, and felt his loss more deeply than any time before. She also hated him. She hated him for putting them through the torment of his disappearance but more so for being the killer of countless women over the entire time of their marriage and for years before. She hated herself for having not seen anything earlier. She castigated herself for being so blind, so stupid.

'There was no way you could have known, Charlotte.'

Sir Frederick Derringham was sitting on the other couch, holding a cup and saucer in one hand and stroking down his tie – a little nervously, it seemed to Charlotte –

with the other. He had appeared to read her mind; she had said nothing to him about how she was feeling.

'Maybe you're right, Frederick,' she said at last, 'but it doesn't feel that way. I *should* have spotted something, should have realised something wasn't right. I really should have been able to spot that my own husband was a bloody murderer!' Her voice rose as she spoke, showing her anger and frustration.

'Look,' Sir Frederick said, 'there have been many cases over the years where a killer has gone undetected by their wives. I'm sure they felt as guilty as you, my dear, but they — like you — can't change the fact that the men they lived with were clever, devious and determined. Look at the lengths Marcus went to — to cover his tracks with the police.'

Charlotte nodded silently. Many of the details of the evidence against Marcus had come out in the press after his body had been found. Detective Constable Handley had filled her in on the rest. It seemed pretty clear that Marcus was guilty and that he *had* been as duplicitous as she'd feared. Frederick was right — he was clearly very smart and an adept liar. She still couldn't fathom how he managed to hide the clothes he'd worn or dispose of other forms of evidence, but then neither could the police.

'My dear,' Sir Frederick said after a long silence. 'This will sound trite and hollow now, but in time you will feel better. This will fade into the background and you will be able to rebuild your life.'

Charlotte nodded dumbly. She looked over to him and eventually shook her head. 'I very much doubt it, Frederick. But thanks for trying to make me feel better anyway,' she said in a quiet voice.

'You know, I've known Marcus longer than you and I didn't spot anything either. It just shows that maybe you never get to know someone properly, not deep down. Lord knows, I've enough skeletons in my closets,' Derringham said, giving a small laugh.

Charlotte laughed – just a small chuff of a sound – and nodded again.

'I had best go,' Sir Frederick announced, standing up.

'Thank you for coming over and for your words of comfort, Frederick. Please drop by again when you can,' Charlotte said, her voice still barely above a whisper.

'Of course, my dear, I'm only sorry I couldn't offer more in the way of comforting words. I've said before, Charlotte, that I think you are very special. You are certainly very dear to me.'

Sir Derringham hesitated a moment, then smiled at Charlotte. 'At another time, perhaps you could have been the one for me,' he added, before turning to go.

Charlotte showed him to the door and watched as he left.

He walked down the drive, straightening his tie and whistling quietly to himself.

Coming soon from Colin A. Millar

Two Weeks in the Sun

Oh I do like to be beside the seaside....oh I do like to be beside the sea...da de dum de da de dum....

Da de dum da de dum....beside the seaside....beside the sea.

The first one I offed was more 'n twenty years ago now. Right smelly old tramp he was. Did him with the garrotte, up close and personal like. God, he stank to high heaven. But it was good, you know, to see the garrotte work proper for the first time. I'd looked it up on the internet, see, you gotta get the knots in the right place, crush the larynx and some of the main veins and arteries. Subdues 'em quicker. Worked a treat. The old cunt was out for the count in less than a minute – mind, he was off 'is tits on bog cleaner or whatever. But they're not dead then, see, so then I held for another three minutes, you know like it said – the internet that is – and Bob's your fanny fuckin' Aunt he was gone. Checked 'is pulse and stuff to make sure, but the smell of shit gave it away – well 'e stank of shit anyway but it got worse, y'know what I mean?

Then I did the prozzie. Knifed her. Now, was she on the same holiday? Or was that the next one? No, no, she was the next one. I remember now, she was in Liverpool – the old fucker was in Oxford. I remember now 'cos I got a PB carp when I was down Oxford. Got bugger all up Liverpool way. Cor, that was a bewt, nearly thirty pounds it was. Lovely spot too – gravel pit, like – but they done the lanscapin' lovely. All trees and bushes an' nice grass an' that. Anyway, I spodded out a big bed of hemp and then got the old spod full of, like, crushed boilies an' nuts and pulses, you know the sort of thing? Then a little splash of the old vanilla essence – carp love the sweet stuff they do. Anyway, I'd barely got me indicator set and the bloody

304

thing roared off. Bloody screamed away it did. Took me near half an hour to get that fucker in, lovely it was though. Twenty-eight pound common – beautiful scales.

So yeah, the old tramp 'e was Oxford and then the prozzie was Liverpool.

'Course I wasn't staying in Oxford – well not the city, like – I was out in the sticks, near the fishin'. Smart enough to have me phone on me all day then left it at the B&B before I went looking for me first victim, as it were. Found him quick enough. See though, the thing with him was it was all a bit too easy, you know? Not that much of a thrill. Well, I say that, but it was good, you know, being the first one and all that. I got a big rush at the time – fuckin' marvellous it was – almost creamed me pants! Thing was though, I was all excited after but then I had to remember to pick everything up, leave no trace an' all that. Think I got everything though. I knew that from watchin' them crime documentaries on Sky. You know the kinda thing? With whatsisname? Fred someone. You know, they tell all what the coppers did and what the stupid mistakes the psycho made an' all that kind of thing. 'E used to be on telly a lot, you know, like, years ago an' then he just seemed to disappear. Made me think a bit about what I was doing first, you know? Oh what was 'is name? Nah it's gone.

Lovely city Oxford, all them colleges and places of learning. Wasn't that Inspector Morse from Oxford? Sure it was there. Thought I saw a couple of bits there that had been on the telly. Nicer than Liverpool that's for sure.

It was all right, I went round the Tate and The Cavern an' all that kinda fing, but not the same as Oxford. Well I say that, but I liked the Tate – that was sort of interesting. All that modern art an' stuff. Stayed not far from there, actually, nice place, lovely breakfast. Then I went further out, you know edge of town, so's I'd be further away from me phone an' me car. Got buses and stuff, you know? So yeah, I found 'er up this manky-looking street – proper red-light district stuff. Anyway, that's me getting ahead of meself again – that was the second holiday, not the first.

See, the first one was alright, but I was just learning then. More into house-breaking an' car theft an' that sort of thing…..

What was that bloke's name? My fucking memory, I tell ya.

So, car-breaking and house stuff – that's what I did first off, like. Just a bit o' fun really. Used to pop out of whatever B&B I was in and test meself with different locks and types of car, you know? Never took nothin' – it's all just for a bit of excitement. Got the old ticker going, you know?

Anyway, most of that's pretty irrelevant now. All things considered. Funny combo though innit? Fishin' and killin'. Funny as well 'cos I've never killed a fish in me life – just people. Funny how it is. Care deeply about fish. Couldn't give a fuck about people.

Don't get me wrong – I don't mean everyone. Your mum don't count o'course – or you or your sister. You lot are alright. Well, more than that I suppose, you know what I mean don't ya? But the rest? Well – fair game in my opinion.

See the thing is most people are just twats – not a brain cell among 'em in my view. Did the world a favour I reckon. Mind, that's not totally true, did for a few more select types, like. There was this businessman-type I remember – can't think where that was just now – but he was all pinstripes and bowler hat an' that. Weird in this day and age to see that kind o' fing. Oh, what a bloody mess he made. Blood an' guts an' stuff everywhere. Squealed like a little girl as well. The great nonce. Proper effete – if you know what that means? Funny the words you pick up when you're out and about in't it?

God, way ahead of meself again. Proper muddle I'm getting in. Stick to the subject Charlie you old git – your mother was forever sayin' that to me. 'Stop bloody wandering about all over the place – always the bloody same, start talking about one thing and before you know it it's off on somin' else.' God she went on.

So in her memory I'll tell you some more about Oxford....

DINENAGE, that's the bugger, Fred Dinenage. Oh, I liked 'is programmes on the old Sky Crime channel. Brilliant they were. Used to make me think about this stuff. Long before I did anything about it.

Printed in Great Britain
by Amazon